FL

Flood Tide

Carol Anderson

First published in 1998
by HEADLINE BOOK PUBLISHING

A HEADLINE LIAISON paperback

10 9 8 7 6 5 4 3 2 1

ISBN 0 7472 5826 0

Typeset by CBS, Felixstowe, Suffolk

Printed and bound in Great Britain by
Mackays of Chatham plc, Chatham, Kent

HEADLINE BOOK PUBLISHING
A division of Hodder Headline PLC
338 Euston Road
London NW1 3BH

Sex is as important as eating or drinking and we ought to allow the one appetite to be satisfied with as little restraint or false modesty as the other.

Marquis de Sade (1740–1814), from L'Histoire de Juliette, ou les Prospérités du Vice, pt. 1 (1797).

Chapter 1

On the rising tide a fishing boat made its way back to harbour after a starlit night on the eastern fishing grounds. Sailing slowly through the maze of salt marshes, the little boat passed under the shadow of Albion House, a sure sign that they were no more than a mile or so from home.

Within Albion's sheltered gardens, Rachel Ingram picked her way across the uneven grass, stopping for a few seconds to watch the boat's progress, but finding her attention drawn instead to where Daniel Grey was working. Once she had spotted him it was impossible to take her eyes off him. His torso was magnificent, glowing in the sunlight as if it had been oiled. Tiny diamonds of sweat glistened between the boy's muscular shoulder blades as he moved amongst the trees and shrubs. He looked like a sleek cat.

Watching him from between the contorted pines, Rachel was horrified to find her mouth watering. She blushed, surprised that her desire bubbled so close to the surface. Part of her ached to take Daniel in her arms and run her tongue over that glistening skin. She swallowed hard and, regaining her composure, called his name.

The boy turned and swung the scythe again in a hypnotic arc. Seeing her approach, he lifted a hand in greeting. She held the tray of drinks higher. He grinned and propped the scythe against a bush, picking up his shirt and pulling

1

it on as he walked towards her.

'Morning, Mrs Ingram. It's so hot out here today. It's starting to look better though, don't you think?' He held up a hand to shade his eyes and survey the garden before running his fingers back through his long, sun bleached hair. 'It's a wonderful view you've got.'

Rachel smiled and set the tray down on the stone wall that divided the garden from the marram grass and dunes beyond. 'I thought you would like some lemonade.'

He nodded his thanks.

As she moved closer she could smell him, a hot subtle musk that made her shiver. She was so close she could pick out individual beads of sweat where they rose in the pit of his throat. His tanned skin offered a startling contrast to the faded cotton work shirt. Looking away quickly she followed his gaze out past the dunes and boat house towards the sea.

'There really is no need for you to slave on in this heat, Daniel.' Her voice faltered over his name, her rogue imagination creating a delicious alternative to work that startled her. 'Why don't you come back later in the day? It should be cooler by then.'

The boy shook his head. 'My step-father's got another job for me tonight. I'd like to get this piece finished if I can.' As he spoke he scooped up a glass from the tray, then looked across at the broad swathe he'd cut through the garden. 'There's still a lot of work to get done. It'll be autumn before you know it.'

He downed the lemonade in one long, cool swallow. The closeness and heat of his body made Rachel dizzy. She avoided his eyes and glanced instead at his muscular torso. His shirt clung to every curve, framing curls of fine blonde hair in the V of its open neck. His waist and hips narrowed dramatically, emphasising the breadth of his shoulders. Moleskin breeches accentuated the length of his legs.

Rachel, feeling something uncannily like hunger, clambered up onto the wall beside him, enjoying the wild, dramatic view out over the dunes, but also the chance to move closer to Daniel. She was trying to delay the moment when she'd have to go back to the house, back into her studio, back to the painting she had begun that morning – a new canvas of a glorious sun-kissed boy.

She stared across into the windswept, sandy wilderness, blushing with the intensity of her desire. It created a strange mixture of emotions. Part of her hoped Daniel wouldn't notice, whilst the other part ached for him to sense the mounting need in the pit of her belly. A warm summer wind tugged playfully at her hair, ruffling her composure even further.

'Have you thought any more about teaching in the autumn?' she said, steering her mind away from the lust glowing inside her. 'I'm sure you'd have no problem getting a position. I would be happy to write you a reference if you think it would help.'

Daniel shook his head. 'Thank you, Mrs Ingram, but Ted, my step-father is dead set against it. It was my mother who wanted me to be bookish. I told you she paid for me to go to Comptons School?' He grinned, wiping his hands on a rag tucked in his belt. 'He begrudged every penny. I should think I must have paid him back double if not treble by now. It would have broken my mother's heart to know Ted's got me doing gardening for the gentry.' He paused and coloured slightly. 'No offence meant.'

Rachel waved his comment away. 'None taken. It just seems such a terrible waste.'

'Maybe in time,' he said with a hint of regret and then leant casually against the wall beside her, barely more than a breath away. The smell of his body made the hairs on the back of her neck prickle. She fought to retain some sense of balance.

Finally she stammered. 'As it's so hot, why don't you leave the rest of the mowing until Monday? A few more days really isn't going to hurt.' She glanced across at him and he grinned.

'Are you sure you don't mind?' As he spoke he leant closer.

For a split second she thought he was going to kiss her and felt every nerve-ending flash, white-hot. The shock made her gasp. Instead, he stood the empty glass back on the tray.

Rachel shook her head, fearing her voice might betray her. 'No, really, that will be fine,' she said, sliding down from the wall.

'If you say so, Mrs Ingram. I'll clear up then, if you're certain you don't mind me finishing early?' There was still an element of doubt in his voice.

'I've got your wages up at the house.'

There was something else she had intended to ask, something she longed to suggest – a tantalising idea that fluttered at the back of her mind.

Heading back cross the garden, Daniel was already swinging the scythe up onto his shoulder, knees bent, muscles taut. She took a deep breath and picked her way between the eddies of weeds and grass, aware that her knuckles were white where they gripped the tray. Above her the summer sky was hypnotically and stunningly blue.

At the house the telephone was ringing. Rachel cursed and hurried to pick up the phone in the hall.

'Hello, Carfax-Staithe one-oh-three.'

'Hello, darling, It's me. I'm just checking to see that it's still all right for me to visit this weekend.'

'Can I ring you back, Anthea?' Rachel said quickly.

'You sound fraught.' There was a pause and then a giggle from the other end of the line. 'Oh no, not the gardener, Rachel? Not that darling little boy of yours?'

Rachel snorted and cursed herself for ever mentioning Daniel to her friend Anthea. She glanced down the hall into the cool inviting shadows – Albion was still and quiet.

'No, not yet and maybe not at all if you don't hang up.' She paused, wondering who might be listening in at the local telephone exchange.

'Oh, come on, do tell me . . .' Anthea began.

'Not now,' snapped Rachel, hearing the soft snick of the

back door opening. She slammed the phone down onto its cradle, picked up a bundle of towels, and hurried towards the kitchen before her courage failed her.

Daniel had just stepped inside the kitchen. The room was cool and dark after the heat of the garden. Amongst the shadows his heat and youth seemed to surround him like a soft, diffused halo. Rachel couldn't take her eyes off his stunning body and experienced the most intense wave of tenderness and desire. Smiling, she picked up an envelope from the table.

'Here we are,' she said, stepping towards him. 'It's all there.'

Daniel frowned as he read the front.'

'You've paid me for this afternoon, but I'm leaving early.'

Rachel shrugged. 'I know, don't worry, you can do an hour or two extra next week to make up the time.'

He nodded and thrust the envelope casually into the back pocket of his trousers.

Rachel hesitated for an instant, aware of the pulse in her throat. The moments of hesitation let all sorts of doubts and fears take hold. If she left it much longer Daniel Grey would turn and leave.

What are you doing? whispered a dark little voice in the back of her head.

She closed her eyes for a split second, pushing the doubts aside and said lightly. 'If you'd like to have a wash before you go. I've brought some clean towels through and there's hot water on the stove.'

Daniel stared at her as she pulled a bowl out from under the sink. 'You said yourself it was hot work in the garden. Here,' she indicated the towels and jug standing side by side on the scrub-top table.

The boy looked apprehensive. After all, they both knew Rachel was mistress of the house not some skivvy meant to run around after the hired hands. 'Are you sure you don't mind?'

'Not at all.'

She turned and hurried back into the main house. In the hall she felt a tiny ripple of anxiety in the pit of her belly and along with it a tiny, glistening, silvery plume of triumph.

After a few seconds Rachel peered back through the open door, watching the boy slip off his shirt. He moved gracefully around the cool kitchen, pouring hot water into the enamel bowl, refilling the jug from the kettle, adding cold so it was the right temperature. She waited until he was about to begin washing and then pulled a bar of soap from her pocket. Taking a deep breath she stepped back into the kitchen and smiled with a confidence she didn't feel.

'I forgot to give you this,' she said unsteadily. Daniel blushed and snatched up a towel to cover his bare chest.

As she spoke, she extended her hand. Daniel stepped close. For an instant their fingers touched. She moaned without thinking. This was the touch she had imagined in her fantasies, this was the body her mind desired in its dreams. The heat from the boy's body captivated her and without thinking she ran her hand across the flat plain of his chest.

Daniel glanced at her, his breathing shallow, eyes suddenly wide and nervous. She smiled at him reassuringly and lifted her hand to his face. It seemed as if her fingers had a will of their own. A deep throaty sigh rose in his throat and he leaned into her caress. She stroked gently along the line of his jaw and to her delight he rubbed against her, catching hold of her hand and holding it tight against him.

Rachel swallowed hard, every nerve ending alight. Deep inside she could feel the insistent rhythm of her pulse and was aware of every breath rising in her chest. She looked up into Daniel's clear blue eyes. His face was pale, despite his tan, and his expression held a bright, haunted look. Their bodies were just a heartbeat apart. Glancing down, Rachel could make out the hard press of his cock pushing against his faded trousers. She looked back up at him and smiled.

'I'm so sorry, Mrs Ingram,' he stammered, his pallor suddenly replaced by a dramatic red flush. Nervously he

6

stepped away from her, looking left and right. 'Maybe I ought to go after all, I'm sorry.'

'It's all right,' she whispered and caught hold of his arm. 'Whatever you do, please don't apologise, Daniel.' Her fingers tightened. 'This is what I want.' She took a deep breath, steadying the words before she spoke them. 'I want you.'

She was almost as surprised by her admission as Daniel was, but knew that she had to stay in control, afraid that if she didn't Daniel might turn and run. She had crossed the line and there was no going back. She moved closer to him, sensing the mixture of fear and desire mingled and, standing on tiptoe, she brushed her lips against his. Her kiss was barely more than a breath – the most tentative of caresses. Daniel shivered. She lifted her hand to stroke his chest again. Beneath her fingertips she could feel the excited beat of his heart; the wild smell of his skin made her ache.

'It's all right,' she repeated. His eyes were as wide and dark as the ocean. She began to trace the generous, almost feminine, outline of his lips. They opened under her touch, the tip of his tongue brushing her finger. She moaned and closed her eyes. Suddenly he surged forward. She felt the intense heat of his body through her thin blouse, felt him towering above her and for an instant her fingers were trapped between their lips, as, eagerly, he pressed his mouth to hers.

His power surprised her as his tongue teased her lips apart, his kisses an unnerving mix of delicate caresses and eager, impatient thrusts. She whimpered and opened her lips to him, letting his tongue explore her mouth. Her senses were alive with the sweet taste of his kisses. He smelt of the sun and the sea and she realised, her head spinning, that she wanted to make love to him more than anything on earth.

She did not resist as he pushed his hands up under the thin fabric of her blouse. She felt her skin tingling beneath his touch, aware of every callous, every whorl of his fingertips against her flesh. Trying to control her own desire, she gently pushed him away.

7

'We've got plenty of time, Daniel, there's no need to rush,' she said breathlessly. 'My housekeeper and Molly have finished for the day, there is no one in the house but you and I.' Her voice was barely more than a whisper.

He frowned, his expression betraying his uncertainty, though his eyes were dark, their pupils dilated into deep glittering jewels. She glanced down at the bowl on the table. He followed her gaze.

'Why don't you let me wash you?' she whispered and dipped the soap she was clutching into the water.

'If that's what you want,' he purred.

He dropped the towel alongside the bowl and stood waiting for her to move. Rachel, trembling slightly, worked the soap into a lather and began to soap his chest, fingers working into the taut muscles. Touching Daniel was like heaven. She could smell his sweat and feel the excitement shimmering just beneath his skin. He moaned as her hands worked lower, circling his nipples, caressing the blonde down on his belly.

'Oh, my God,' he murmured, voice thick with emotion as he moved instinctively under her touch. She shivered. The unspoken threat of his desire added a *frisson* of danger she had not anticipated in all her fantasies.

'Would you like to touch me, Daniel?' she whispered.

He hesitated, reluctant to take his eyes off her.

'It's all right. I'm not going to run away,' she said softly. Dropping the soap into the water she began to unbutton her blouse, pushing it off her shoulders to reveal her slim frame. She saw with pleasure that he swallowed hard, licking his lips. His eyes moved instinctively to the heavy swell of her full breasts and taut dark nipples. She saw him shiver and could detect the low, earthy vibration of his excitement. She let her blouse drop to the cool tiled floor. Neither watched it fall.

She stepped in front of him and, catching hold of his wrists, guided his hands onto her body. He caressed her nipples which hardened like cherry pips under his fingers.

'Mrs Ingram?' There was hint of fear in his voice.

8

'Rachel,' she corrected him gently. Then she hesitated. 'Are you sure you want to do this, Daniel?'

For an instant his composure crumbled. The young man was momentarily replaced by an uncertain and nervous boy.

'You're not going to make me ask, are you?' he said, deep voice unsteady, fingers still toying with her breasts.

She swallowed and then shook her head, her hand on the thick leather belt round his waist. 'No, I won't make you ask,' she whispered. 'But I don't want to take anything you aren't prepared to give. I want you to be certain that this is what you want.'

The boy's eyes flared as she slid the silver buckle undone, her fingers working at the button of his flies.

'Oh, I'm certain,' he whispered and arched back his head, surrendering to her.

She could see the pulse hammering in his throat and stretched up to run her tongue along the pit at the base of his neck. The taste of his skin was everything she had imagined. the saltiness of it made her quiver and, as her breasts brushed against his wet, sun-kissed body, she whimpered. The buttons of his trousers gave easily under her insistent fingers. Smiling, she pressed her lips to his throat again, letting the tip of her tongue trace the knot of muscle. Lifting her hands to his hips, she pushed his breaches down over his taut buttocks. As she moved, her nipples brushed the light covering of hair on his torso. The sensation was electrifying.

Freed by her insistent fingers, his cock sprang forward, unleashed and eager, pressing against her belly, desperate for her touch. She broke off from her kisses and looked up at Daniel. His complexion was flushed and for a split second he looked embarrassed. She smiled and let one finger trace around the throbbing head of his erection.

'You are quite, quite beautiful,' she whispered.

He sighed and thrust forward into her caress. His foreskin felt like spun silk, slick and delicate under her fingertips.

'Get undressed,' she murmured, 'let me wash all of you.'

9

Turning slightly, Rachel slipped off the rest of her clothes, letting them drop in a whisper onto the tiled floor.

Daniel watched her, dark eyes glittering. She thought he looked incredibly vulnerable and young. She lifted the bowl down from the table and stood it alongside him on the floor. Wordlessly, he slipped off his boots and trousers and stepped into the basin.

Closing her eyes for an instant, she picked up the soap and began to work her hands up over the boy's muscular calves and thighs. He shivered as her hands moved to soap his cock. His delight echoed hers. She knew she was wet, her anticipation and excitement building with every passing second. Beneath her fingertips Daniel's shaft throbbed as if it had a life of its own.

Her hands moved back and forth along his cock. The soapy water made his flesh glisten like ice. Her thoughts felt muddled but even so she could sense that Daniel was rapidly reaching the point of no return. She stopped, stood up, and pouring more water from the jug, let the flood course down over him. Turning to refill the jug from the kettle she sensed him behind her and then felt his strong muscular frame against her back, the brush of his belly and the insistent press of his erection against her buttocks. For an instant he felt hot, almost feverish – then the cool air drove his heat away. She thought she heard him whimper.

The next few moments were breathtaking, a devastating cocktail of sensations. His hands worked across her back and shoulders and then stealthily round to cup her breasts. She pushed back against him, grinding her buttocks against his rampant, throbbing sex. Opening her mind and her body to his caresses, she moved slightly so that he could slip his hands between her legs. She bent forward a little more, moving so that her hands joined his. He gasped as her fingers found his cock and folded tight around it. She stroked him, guiding him into her.

The tightness of her sex closing around him seemed to

wake Daniel from a dream. His hands began to work furiously, cupping and circling the outline of her breasts, a finger tracing the tight puckered skin round her nipples, nipping and teasing at the charged flesh. She let out a soft, throaty groan and leant back against him, letting him continue the exploration of her body. His caresses made her feel drunk. Why she had waited so long for this moment?

Daniel began to move rhythmically, pressing his cock deep into her throbbing quim. She could feel her own excitement growing, echoed in the hot, fragrant wetness that threatened to drown them both. She closed her eyes and concentrated on the ripples of pleasure as they formed and reformed in her belly. Head thrown back, she cried out in ecstasy as Daniel's fingers moved down, down over her narrow waist, circling the soft swell of her stomach, heading lower towards the white hot bud of her clitoris. He was already close to the point of release and she knew she wanted everything he could give her. At the very last moment, as she felt the dam about to burst, Rachel wriggled away from him and turned around in Daniel's arms.

For an instant the boy's face registered shock and then disbelief. She smiled, glancing down at the proud arc of his cock and took a deep breath before encircling it again with her fingers. He groaned as she slid his foreskin back slowly, revealing the engorged, scarlet head, while her other hand slipped between his legs to cup the heavy distended bulk of his balls. He shuddered but didn't resist as she pulled him closer to her. Slowly, she sank to her knees and took his cock into her mouth. Above her the boy gasped in astonishment.

Her lips tightened around the swollen crown, sucking and teasing, while her fingers circled, moving along the length of his shaft, echoing the tracery of her lips. She worked back and forth, knowing as she did so that it wouldn't be long before he lost control. He started to move again, his movements growing more and more instinctive as he thrust against her lips. She could taste the first salty prelude to his orgasm and then suddenly he bucked fiercely towards her.

Grabbing the base of his shaft, she slipped the end of his cock from her lips so the hot arc of his seed hit her chest and spurted down over the rounded orbs of her breasts.

The moments passed and for a few seconds they both seemed to freeze. Daniel pulled her up towards him, breaking the stillness and opened his eyes slowly as if waking from a deep sleep. His expression was a mixture of intense emotions. She looked reassuringly at him and took his hand.

'There's more, so much more,' she said softly, wiping away the silvery seeds of his desire. 'Come with me, we've got plenty of time before you have to leave.' Still holding his hand she picked up the two thick towels from the table. Between her legs she could feel a hot, silky trickle of wetness. She longed to show Daniel just how much more there could be . . .

'. . . My God, and then what happened?' asked Anthea Leven eagerly. Rachel's oldest friend leant forward to light her cigarette from the candelabra, which stood amongst bowls of summer flowers on the centre of the dining-room table.

Rachel pushed her chair back and rolled her wine glass between her fingers. The crystal facets broke the candlelight into a rainbow of diamond reflections. She turned towards Anthea and smiled easily.

'For someone who says my desire for my gardener is disgusting and borders on melodrama, you're showing a remarkable amount of interest. Or is this just your morbid curiosity?'

Anthea snorted and then exhaled deeply; the air around her rolled with silvery billows of tobacco smoke.

'I'm *supposed* to say it's terrible, darling. That's the sort of thing sensible friends are meant to tell you. That and, "It'll all end in tears, there's no future in it," and all those other awful truisms. However, I'm reserving judgement for the time being.' She grinned. 'Meanwhile, it's a damned good story. Are you going to tell me how you spent the rest of the afternoon?'

Rachel shrugged and lifted the glass to her lips, the deep ruby wine reflecting the golden candlelight. She thought about the new canvas she was working on upstairs in the studio, a life-sized study of Daniel. Even if Anthea didn't approve, she didn't care. She turned her attention back to her friend.

'Do you *really* believe the things you said?' Rachel said softly.

Anthea nodded. 'I'm afraid I do. It's not that I don't wish you well. I really do want you to be happy, darling. I suppose a part of me even envies you, but this love affair spells total disaster, Rachel. Really truly, darling, cross my heart and hope to die. You should try and make proper friends of your own class round here. Find someone civilised.' She hesitated. 'There have to be some nice people in Carfax-Staithe. People like you. You're just not making the effort to meet them. You ought to get out more.'

'Daniel is very beautiful,' Rachel said flatly.

Anthea snorted. 'Oh, I don't doubt it, but what are his people going to say? His friends, or other people when they find out? It hardly bears thinking about. You'll be ruined if it becomes common knowledge.'

Rachel pulled a face. 'I wasn't planning on rushing over to the village and telling everyone.'

Anthea pulled a face. 'Don't be so naive, Rachel. People inevitably find these things out, it's always the same. And he's barely more than a boy—'

'He's twenty for God's sake. He's not a child,' snapped Rachel defensively.

Anthea pulled a face and picked up her glass. 'And you're thirty-four, Rachel. That's a big gap. Look, why don't you let me set you up with someone more your own age, not to mention your own class? It's all right for the chaps to go around seducing their housemaids but bedding your handyman is really not the done thing.'

Rachel's expression hardened. 'So some dull middle-aged man is going to be better for me, is he? I don't think so, Anthea.'

Anthea grimaced and ground her cigarette viciously into

13

the ashtray. 'Since you inherited this damned house you think you're in some sort of world apart. You're becoming a hermit.'

Rachel laughed and helped herself to more wine. 'Really, Anthea! It's you who uses Albion as a bolt-hole from reality. This is the third weekend in a row you've invited yourself down here. Besides it's not true. Country people just take more time to accept strangers, that's all.'

'It won't happen at all if you go around seducing the hired help.'

Rachel sighed. 'I'll be careful. Besides, people are beginning to get used to me being here. Last week I had a letter from one of my neighbours introducing himself.'

Anthea's eyes lit up. 'Now, that's more like it. Is he single? What did he want? Was it an invitation to have supper?'

Rachel giggled. 'For goodness sake, no. He wants to know if I would consider renting him the jetty for his pleasure boat.'

Anthea rolled her eyes heavenwards. 'It hardly counts as a social coup, does it? You ought to arrange a dinner party or—' she saw the expression of reluctance on Rachel's face and stopped. 'But I suppose it's a start. What have you told him?'

'He's going to come and see me next week.'

Anthea smiled. 'All right, so you're starting to settle in. But, and this is a big, big, but, you need to make some real plans for a real life. Hiding out here in the sticks isn't healthy.'

Rachel laughed and took another sip of wine. 'Says who? I've just inherited a house I truly love, and André left me enough money to keep me for life. And . . .' she hesitated, staring back into her glass.

Anthea smiled gently. 'And you're finally getting over losing him?'

Rachel grimaced and looked Anthea straight in the eye. 'I didn't lose him, Anthea, he died. Inheriting Albion has been the only bright star in a very, very, dark sky.'

Anthea nodded. 'But why come here? Surely the London house would be better for you – or if you want a real change what about André's estate in Kenya? You could easily afford to buy somewhere you really like. Good God, woman you're spoilt for choice. I certainly wouldn't have picked this little backwater to live out my days.'

Rachel said nothing. She couldn't find the words to explain why it was important that she had something of her own, something that was finally hers and not some shadow of the marriage she had had with André Ingram.

Anthea sighed. 'All right, what about this boy, Daniel?'

'Daniel? Daniel is a glorious indulgence, and you're right, it's one I'm probably foolish to allow myself. But I want him, Anthea. Why can't you understand that? Until now I've never taken something I want, purely and simply because I wanted it.'

Anthea walked across the dining room. Outside, against the gold of the evening sky, the dunes seemed black and crisp along the horizon. Here and there in the colourful canopy the first stars twinkled. Through the open windows the sound of the sea caressing the distant beach echoed on the warm breeze. Anthea sighed. How blissful Albion seemed. Tonight the dining room was lit with table lamps and scented candles and, despite the heat of the day, Rachel had lit a driftwood fire in the hearth.

'You don't want Daniel, Rachel,' said Anthea slowly. 'What you need is a real man. Someone like you. Creative, witty . . .'

'What you mean is a potential husband.'

'Not necessarily.'

'Don't lie to me, Anthea. You're not fooling anybody. All my life I've done the right thing. Now, for once, I'm going to do what I want. I married André because my parents insisted.' She paused. 'I was so lonely with him all those years, Anthea, you've really got no idea. This time I'm going to have what I want.'

'Don't you think that's selfish?'

'No, I don't. I'm not planning to hurt anyone.'

'What about your pretty little Daniel?'

'Him least of all. The only person likely to get hurt here is

15

me. I mean, how long is he going to want an old woman in bed with him?'

'You're not old,' Anthea snapped.

'No, not to a man of forty I'm not, but can you remember being twenty? Anyone over twenty-five was practically senile. I was twenty when I married André and he was nearly fifty – it seems obscene now. No, the one likely to crawl away broken-hearted from this liaison is me. Me and my silly foolish heart. Shall I ring for coffee or would you like another glass of wine?'

Anthea sighed and turned around slowly. 'Coffee, darling, but promise me you'll let me introduce you to this super man I met at Pippa Holliday's dinner party last week. He's staying in town next week on business. I promise you he's absolutely gorgeous, much more your type. Trust me, Rachel. Why don't you come up to London with me and spend a few days back in civilised society? We all miss you dreadfully. Everyone is busily planning the house-party circuit for the summer.' She pouted provocatively. 'Please say yes, darling, I do so adore match-making.'

Rachel couldn't help but laugh at Anthea as the housekeeper came in with their coffee. 'If you're so keen why don't you get yourself a man?'

Anthea clutched her chest and groaned in mock horror. 'What? Settle for one when I can have them all? No, poppet, marriage isn't for me. I'm really not the marrying kind.'

On Sunday afternoon Rachel and Anthea travelled back to London leaving Rachel's new car at the station. On Monday evening Rachel was introduced to Anthea's idea of her ideal man at a cramped and smoky night club. Rachel's heart sank as he introduced himself and guided Anthea and herself towards the bar. Anthea retired discreetly after a single drink, winking conspiratorially as she made her goodbyes. Her parting words were, 'I won't wait up.'

When the waiter came to tell them their table was ready,

Rachel sighed and followed her companion into the dimly lit dining-room.

'So, Mrs Ingram, Rachel – may I call you Rachel? Anthea tells me you're an artist.'

Rachel smiled and picked at an indifferent supper while her ideal man plunged into a blow by blow account of his complete medical history. Ruefully, she wondered why she'd allowed herself to be persuaded by Anthea yet again.

Later, her dinner date smiled and moved a little closer. Even in the subdued light of the dining room she could see that his toupee didn't quite match the original colour of his hair.

She made her excuses, just as the waiter brought them the bill, and a little before her companion could reasonably suggest a night-cap at the hotel where he was staying. Instead, she wished him goodnight, made plausible excuses about a long journey home, took a taxi to the station and caught the last train back to Norfolk.

Anthea had offered to let her stay the night, but Rachel, though dog tired, longed for the familiar surroundings of her bedroom at Albion and to be woken by the gentle sounds of the sea.

The train arrived well after midnight. With the lights of London far behind her, Rachel hurried across the station yard, cranked her car into life and set off home. The lonely coastal road twisted like silver ribbon beneath the cat-black sky. It was the early hours of the morning when Rachel finally guided her little car along the narrow lane towards Albion. All the way home she had fantasised that perhaps Daniel might be waiting for her and images of his beautiful sun-tanned body helped pass the hours on the road.

She had managed to keep Anthea in suspense about the remains of the afternoon she'd spent with Daniel. Now, as she drove towards the house, in the sensual darkness of the ocean night, she let the memories guide her home . . .

★ ★ ★

17

. . . From the kitchen she'd led Daniel up into the master bedroom at the very top of the house. It was a huge, sunlit room. On the ceiling the reflection of sea shimmered and glittered like spun silk. To one wall French windows opened onto a balcony with a view out over the sea. She'd left them open to let the cool breeze blow through and great swathes of butter muslin billowed like full sails at the bedroom windows. The centre of the room was dominated by a canopied bed, the linen as white and pure as virgin snow. She had turned to face Daniel, eyes heavy with desire and let her towel fall slowly to the floor.

He crossed the room in two strides. This time he didn't resist or hesitate, instead his lips sought out hers and his hands moved across her expectant body. He'd seemed renewed and desperate as he pushed her back towards the bed. Once again Rachel felt the tiny *frisson* of fear returning, the wildness of the boy almost overwhelming her.

Around his head a halo of moist golden tendrils gave him the look of an avenging angel. Then his lips were on hers, brutal, seeking out her tongue, her lips stretched against her teeth as his tongue probed deeper and deeper.

She knew she was losing control. The lessons she had envisaged teaching Daniel in her fantasies were lost as he pressed her back onto the soft, white expanse of the bed. She lay back under him. For an instant he paused, standing between her open legs, his hands resting on her hips, so that he could look at her. She felt his eyes moving over her exposed, aching body, as if fixing her in his mind, absorbing the images. As his eyes worked down towards her quim he let his towel slide silently to the floor. His magnificent cock was already erect and ready for her. She moaned as his fingers brushed over the mound of Venus.

Gently he opened her body, exploring her with tenderness and curiosity. She let out a shuddering gasping breath, anticipating the sensation of his shaft sliding home. Instead he knelt between her legs. He looked up at her, eyes dark and glittering. She stared deep into his eyes, able to sense his renewed uncertainty.

'Yes,' she'd whispered. 'Please. I know what you want to do. It's all right, kiss me, please . . .'

With no more prelude, his tongue slid between the petals of her sex, his fingers holding her open for his intimate kisses. She gasped and lifted her hips up to meet him, astounded and delighted at his prowess, wondering fleetingly what pretty little country girl he had practised on to become so accomplished.

She was already excited and wet. His kisses fanned the glittering fire in her belly. As his fingers slid deep inside her, she knew, he could taste her desire and smell the musky heat of her body. Her muscles responded instantly, tightening around him. The tip of his tongue found the engorged bud of her clitoris and his lips closed over it with a delicate nibbling kiss. All was lost. A circle of flames burnt up through her, great waves of pleasure swelling and spiralling through her whole body. She cried out in delight and pulled him closer.

His lips moved softly against the little bud, milking it, each kiss, each sucking, delicate caress driving her beyond sanity to the very edges of consciousness. She moaned and writhed, encouraging him on, catching hold of his hair, her fingers tangled in his curls, pulling him tighter and tighter, closer and closer. As she writhed beneath him, the excitement roared through her in an incandescent wave. She heard herself call his name and finally, sated, beg him to stop. Daniel pulled away and she opened her eyes.

His expression was a mixture of triumph and delight. Rachel smiled sleepily and lifted her arms in invitation. Slowly he crept up towards her. She moaned softly as she felt the weight of him on her thighs, the heat of him on her hot, excited, tingling flesh. She pulled herself up onto her elbows as she felt his cock begging for entry at the throbbing lips of her sex. He looked up at her, eyes still diamond bright. He grinned. Once again she was struck by his looks, so young and vulnerable and yet so utterly desirable.

'You planned this, didn't you?' he whispered. There was no accusation, no fear, just delight. She moved closer to him.

'Yes,' she purred, and ran her fingers along his shaft. He shuddered and rolled alongside her on the bed, allowing her free access to his taut sun-tanned body. She let her hands roam feverishly, drinking in his beauty and vitality. His huge eyes were dark and hypnotic. His lips brushed hers tenderly, almost reverently.

She pressed him back into the crisp white sheets and climbed across his chest, her sex leaving moist, fragrant kisses on his skin. Between her thighs she could feel his heat building, his desire almost overwhelming. Gently she moved back until she was straddling his hips and lifted herself to guide his cock inside her.

Daniel watched enraptured as Rachel stroked his shaft against the delicate skin of her inner thighs. Instantly she felt her body opening for him. For a few seconds the crown of his cock nuzzled between her outer lips. She threw back her head, eyes closed, relishing the intensity of the moment. Slowly, slowly she lowered herself down onto him.

He lifted his hips to meet hers. She gasped at the sheer pleasure of feeling him inside her. The sensation echoed through every molecule of her flesh. It felt as if Daniel had filled her to the brim. She could have wept. She was still so close to orgasm that her sex was still contracting with the after-waves of excitement, her inner muscles flexing and sucking on Daniel's thick phallus as it pressed deeper inside her.

They began to move slowly at first. She rubbed her body against his and was rewarded by the sound of his moaning. His fingers and lips moved across her, sucking, lapping, stroking. She let out a mewl of pure pleasure and as they found their rhythm she felt her excitement rekindle with every stroke. She glanced down at Daniel's face. His eyes were closed, his expression almost angelic as he impaled her again and again. Rachel could feel the heat rising again in her belly. Sliding her hands beneath Daniel's buttocks she pulled him still deeper. Below her, his expression was intense and focused.

He was so handsome, so desirable that he looked almost edible. Rachel grinned and thrust forward again, dropping a hand to her crotch. Lifting her body a little she slid a hand between them and circled the base of his shaft. Now her fingers beat out a compelling counter rhythm. Daniel's eyes flashed and she knew by his expression that he couldn't hold back any longer. Gasping for breath he reared up, making her cry out with a mixture of pleasure and surprise. Deep inside, she felt his cock throbbing like a beating heart, filling her to the brim with pleasure. An instant later her own climax ricocheted through them both.

Exhausted, Daniel slumped back onto the bed. Rachel kissed him full on the lips. His response was a dry, soft, sleepy kiss, his eyes were already hooded and weary. She smiled and rolled off him, still cradling his head in the crook of her arm. Within seconds he was asleep, wrapped around her, his boyish warmth comforting and touching. He snuggled closer and in spite of herself Rachel closed her eyes and let his exhaustion carry her into unconsciousness.

When she woke it was late evening, the sun had moved round and cast deep velvet shadows across the bedroom floor. Daniel had already gone and left her sleeping. On the cabinet beside the bed he had left a tiny posy of wild flowers, picked from her garden. She picked them up and stared out towards the sea. For a few seconds her sense of loss was almost overwhelming.

Now, as she thought of that feeling, cloaked from reality by the rich black of ocean night, Rachel shivered. Guiding her car carefully across the last section of the narrow causeway, intense images of Daniel's tanned, muscular body filled her mind, pushing away the last remnants of the dull evening.

In the distance beyond the dunes, she could see Albion

House, a lamp alight in the upstairs window, glowing invitingly in the darkness. Her headlights picked out the crested waves of the incoming tide. Heading towards the sea through the main channel the lights of a small boat, taking advantage of the tide, added a strange magical quality to the darkness as it seemed to sail right up under Albion's walls.

Around the house the sea whispered over the sands. Exhausted, Rachel crept upstairs and slipped into bed, her dreams full of Daniel Grey and his eager caresses.

Outside, the boat made slow, careful progress between the sand bars, the captain watching for the dark solid shadow of Albion on his port bow as they passed by.

Chapter 2

Rachel was woken late the following morning by the sound of the sea. She stretched and slipped out of bed. From the balcony she could see Daniel working in the garden below. He had begun to clear the last quarter of the tangled garden. It was tempting to call to him. As the thought passed through her mind, he looked up and lifted a hand in greeting. She smiled and waved back, wondering what it would be like when they met face to face, though by the expression on Daniel's face perhaps it wouldn't be as uncomfortable as she'd imagined.

Crossing the line between fantasy and reality was a dangerous game. In some ways Rachel could still hardly believe she'd had the courage to take that step. Life since her husband's death had been full of work, Albion, and occasional ill-fated dinners with men whom friends thought suitable, rather than men she would have chosen for herself.

Going back into the bedroom Rachel dressed quickly, suddenly longing to get on with the new painting in the studio. Humming, she trotted downstairs to the kitchen and pulled the kettle onto the stove. It barely had time to boil before the phone rang.

Rachel groaned; Anthea no doubt, wanting every detail of her encounter the previous evening. Who else would it be at this time of the morning? She hurried into the hall, snatched the phone from its cradle and tucked it under her chin.

'Good morning. Please don't disturb me now, darling, I'll call you later.' she said sharply.

An unknown male voice replied, 'I'm so sorry, Mrs Ingram. Would you prefer it if I rang you back later?'

Rachel blushed. 'I'm so sorry, I do apologise. I thought you were someone else. Who is this speaking, please?'

'Julian Morton. We haven't actually met, but I wrote to you a little while ago. Are you sure I'm not disturbing you?'

Rachel struggled to regain her composure. 'No, not at all, how may I help you?' Rachel racked her brain to try and remember what Morton's letter had said.

'I was calling to see if it was still convenient for me to come over this morning. As you hadn't rung . . .' Julian Morton's voice was deep and hypnotic. 'I'd be happy to visit another time if you're busy?'

Rachel coloured, she couldn't remember anything about her ringing to confirm that anyone could call.

'No, no,' she stammered. 'That will be fine. Please excuse me, Mr Morton, I'm a little rushed this morning.'

It wasn't until she'd invited Julian Morton over and hung up, that she realised she couldn't for the life of her remember why he was calling. His letter was still in the bureau, she ought to go and find it before he arrived.

Back in the kitchen as she poured the tea there was a knock on the door. Glancing up at the clock she was astonished to see it was almost ten. Julian Morton had said he'd be over by eleven. Rachel opened the door to find Daniel framed by the porch, silhouetted against a glow of summer sunlight. Instantly she felt a flare of desire that drove away all thoughts of Julian Morton, his letter and his visit.

'Come in,' she said softly. 'How are you this morning?'

Daniel pulled off his straw hat and stepped inside, hesitantly. His expression hovered somewhere between delight and apprehension.

She smiled. 'It's all right. I haven't grown horns and a tail since we last—' she had intended to say met, but instead her mind flooded with intense erotic memories of their afternoon together. She blushed and turned away.

'Why don't you come inside? I am just making a pot of tea, would you like a cup?' she said, stepping away from the door.

He moved across the kitchen with long confident strides and pulled a stool out from under the table. Rachel leant across and passed him a cup and saucer. Their fingers touched – the merest brush. She swallowed hard as the feeling of desire intensified. Looking into the boy's eyes she saw again the longing and the uncertainty simmering there. She reached across and stroked his fingers. His eyes darkened suddenly, like a summer storm and he caught hold of her hands and brought them to his lips. Rachel gasped.

'I've been thinking about you for days,' he whispered. 'I was so afraid you wouldn't want me to come here again.' He shook his head. 'I kept thinking maybe I'd imagined it or worse still that I had taken things too far – misread what you wanted.' He stopped and looked up at her.

'Oh Daniel,' she said lightly, sensing his fear of rejection. 'Why on earth would you think that?'

He stood up, still holding her hands and pulled her towards him. Overwhelmed by the intensity of his need, Rachel nearly pulled back in panic. His strong arms folded around her and pressed her head against his shoulder. He smelt of the sea.

'This isn't right, is it?' he whispered huskily. 'It can't be right. I've been telling myself that all weekend – but I want you so much.'

She felt the panic gripping her throat. What had she started? His desire was raw and uncompromising. His hands lifted to her shoulders, his lips now pressing eagerly into the curve of her neck. She knew she had the power to stop his caresses with a single word, and for an instant wondered if it might be better to push him away.

In her fantasies, in her dark passionate dreams, he had always been her willing and attentive slave, tutored and controlled by her voice and her body's needs. In reality in the cool morning light of her kitchen the living breathing Daniel Grey, alight with desire and passion, was far more unsettling than she could possibly have imagined – and the realisation excited her. Their afternoon together now seemed like another one of her dreams, although she knew the thing she had begun between them was no longer a fantasy, no longer a game. The thrill and the fear heightened her excitement.

Daniel pressed against her more insistently, demanding a response. Her body ached for his touch, even if her rational mind resisted. She did not try to stop him as his fingers tore at the buttons of her blouse. He ripped the thin fabric back over her shoulders, his lips leaving hot desperate kisses over the sensitive skin on her shoulders and collar-bones. His work-roughened hands lifted to cradle her breasts, his eager fingers caressing her nipples, which hardened instantly under his touch. She moaned at the sensation. His progress was relentless. As his fingers moved down to the buttons of her skirt, she felt as if she was drowning, submerged under his overwhelming need for her.

He dragged the fabric down over her hips, jerking the waistband hard to set her body free. Protesting now, she wriggled against him, only to be silenced by his insistent kisses.

'Please, Daniel, please—' she whimpered under the barrage of sensations, unsure whether she was pleading with him to stop or begging him to continue. Trying to push herself free, she held his face with her hands and felt his throbbing, angry pulse beneath her fingertips. The desire she saw in his expression threatened to sweep her away. How could she consider resisting him when every inch of her wanted him so much? She stepped into the flood tide of passion and let her desire take control. Sliding her hands up under his shirt, running her fingers over the tight bands of muscles, she surrendered completely to their mutual need.

She didn't protest as he dropped his hands to her waist and turned her away from him, gently pressing her down towards the table. Glancing over her shoulder she saw the lust in his eyes, an intense dark excitement, and shuddered. Feral, wild, his youth and his beauty inflamed her. His fingers teased back and forth over the damp creases of her knickers, stroking her buttocks, pressing against her outer lips, seeking entry. She knew the fabric was already damp with her juices. She could hear his staccato breaths as he struggled to undress himself with one hand. She longed to turn and help him, but held back, too caught up in the sensation of his caresses to risk breaking the spell.

His fingers drew circles over the rapidly moistening material that divided him from his goal, arcs and swirls that made her shiver with expectation. Suddenly his fingers hooked under the sides and roughly he pulled her knickers down, exposing her completely. She whimpered, her whole consciousness centred on his touch, her body crying out for him. She shuddered as his lips pressed against her spine, tracing a moist web of kisses over her shoulders. His hands circled around her, teasing her nipples, before moving lower still over her taut, sun-tanned belly, his fingers clutching at her thighs, fingers biting into the flesh. He traced a hot, damp, journey with his lips – featherlight kisses, lapping tongue.

She moved instinctively, pressing herself back towards him, her thighs opening for his advance, her hips flexing to let him in. As his fingers parted her outer lips she could smell the musky heat of her excitement and cried out in ecstasy as she felt the light brush of his cock against her buttocks. Her hips flexed again, her glistening sex opening wider still for him, as if her whole being demanded to feel the bulk of his cock slip inside her. She felt his hot breath on her skin and let out a tiny cry as he found his way into the engorged, sensitive folds of her sex. His thumb pressed down hard on the swollen bud of her clitoris and she knew as the first shuddering bolt of pleasure flooded through her body, that she was completely lost.

Across the causeway, watching the hypnotic roll of the incoming tide, Julian Morton sat in his new roadster and glanced down at his watch. Already the water was quite high, filling the meandering, sand-rimmed channels of the eastern salt marshes. He cursed under his breath and consulted the map folded on the passenger seat. Albion House on its promontory was clearly marked. Albion and a little private mooring that was built on the finger of coastline reaching out into one of the channels. Julian lifted his field glasses. Beyond the winding channels, through the salt marsh lay the glittering grey waters of the North sea – and beyond that – just a few hours sailing away, the shores of Holland.

Rachel Ingram's response on the telephone had thrown him. He'd been told she was shy, almost a recluse.

Watching the relentless rise of the tide, he debated whether it might be better to arrange his visit for another day. The last thing he wanted was to be cut off by the incoming water. The coast road was almost deserted this far from the harbour, though one or two people were out walking amongst the dunes. Julian climbed out of the car. He might be better going across on foot. His train of thought was broken by a cheerful voice.

'Good morning. Lovely day.'

Julian turned around. An elderly man with a Labrador emerged from the shelter of the dunes. As he approached the car he tipped his hat in greeting.

Julian forced a smile, slightly annoyed at being interrupted during his deliberations.

'Good morning.'

'Marvellous view.'

Julian decided he might as well take advantage of the situation. 'It certainly is. Tell me, do you live round here?'

The man's expression suggested he did.

'I was wondering whether the causeway gets flooded when the tide comes in?'

The man shook his head and looked Julian up and down. 'Morton, isn't it? The new fellow from out at Medsham Hall?'

Julian nodded and extended his hand. 'That's right, and you are?'

The old man smiled. 'Derek Farnham, Reverend Farnham.

I'm the vicar of Carfax-Staithe, for my sins.' He waved towards the causeway. 'It doesn't flood very often, sometimes at the spring tide, occasionally during storms, I'm told, but otherwise it normally stays well above high-water mark.' He paused and looked at Julian again. 'You do know it's private property over there? Not a public right of way or anything, it leads over to Albion house.'

Julian nodded. 'Yes, I know, I've got an appointment there this morning, I just didn't want to risk getting caught by the tide.'

The old man laughed. 'What, not get stuck there with our lovely Mrs Ingram? She's an artist y'know. They tell me she's quite famous, though I've never seen any of her work myself.'

Julian grinned. 'Famous or not, I still don't fancy being stranded.'

The old man tugged at his dog and nodded. 'Well, you should be all right, Mr Morton. The tide isn't full in until this afternoon and we're not expecting it to be very high today. Perhaps once you're settled in we might see you at St Marks?'

Julian nodded. After the social pleasantries had been exchanged, the old man headed back between the dunes, dog in tow. Watching him stride away along the beach, Julian decided to risk it and, climbing back into the car, drove slowly across the causeway. Although early for his appointment, he'd park up and take a walk around the promontory to get his bearings once he'd crossed over.

The causeway proved shorter than he'd thought, and he realised as he approached Albion House, that what he had assumed from the map were open rolling dunes, were in fact part of the grounds of the house. The causeway rose up quite steeply from the water towards the gardens and as he reached the top of the rise he could even see the remains of a boat house beside the jetty in the distance. However the view from the shoreline hadn't prepared him for the house.

In the morning light Albion rose above the last of the white swirling sea mists like a schooner, sailing alone amongst the rolling dunes, its glinting windows staring out towards the open sea. Creepers clung to the clapboard facing on the landward side and odd spires and balconies added to its strange nautical appearance. A great ridge of sand and marram grass stretched out beyond the low retaining wall of Albion's gardens, past battered breakwaters to join the salt marsh. The only way to reach the dunes and the mooring beyond was through Rachel Ingram's garden. Julian adjusted his tie and then reconsidered what he was going to do – it certainly wouldn't do for him to be caught trespassing.

Frustrated, he glanced at his watch again. It was barely twenty-past-ten. He sighed and parked on a semicircle of rough grass and sand close under Albion's walls. Perhaps he'd risk going to see Rachel Ingram now anyway. The worst she could do, he reasoned, was send him away for arriving too soon. He would just explain that he had overestimated the time it would take him to get there.

Locking up his car, he wondered briefly what Rachel Ingram was like. The strange, brooding house above him suggested she was most likely some eccentric dried-up old spinster. Nobody in their right mind could want to live this far away from anywhere, stranded in an isolated rural backwater. He grimaced, aware that his city prejudices were showing. Country life really did not suit him.

Everywhere appeared deserted. The huge front garden was barely more than a vast stretch of scrubby grass and dusty, wind sculpted trees. Making his way slowly round the house, Julian smiled. Overlooked by no one, as silent as the tomb, Albion could have been created with some mad old woman in mind.

At the rear of the house the back door stood slightly ajar. As he approached Julian could just make out low noises coming from inside. Something about the tone of the sounds stifled the call of greeting in his throat – instead he crept closer. Through the half-open door, in the gloom, he could make out a strange movement. As his eyes adjusted Julian stifled a gasp of surprise. A young, blond man, as naked and beautifully shaped as any sculpture, was moving furiously against the table.

It took Julian a few seconds to make out the second figure. Beneath the boy, working eagerly against the curve of his body, was a slim, dark woman. She was bent forward, her back to the boy, her firm buttocks slapping rhythmically against his muscular thighs. The noises he had heard were the woman's soft, animal moans of pleasure as she thrust back against the boy's body. Mouth watering, Julian watched her rounded, pert breasts swaying as the boy forced his way deeper into her. Eyes closed, she braced herself against the table for his exquisite assault.

Julian felt the breath catch in his throat. In the kitchen the woman surged backward against the boy's stroke, pressing herself to him, writhing under him. She was begging him to touch her sex. Her tone was intense, throaty and excited. Julian felt a warm, familiar stirring in his groin as the effects of the tableau worked on him. He swallowed hard, and quickly glanced around to see if he was alone, feeling uncomfortable and foolish, but quite unable to tear his eyes away from the lovers. The woman slid her fingers into the deep recess of her sex and began to stroke herself. Julian hissed in amazement, afraid that he might give himself away.

In the darkness, the woman was approaching her climax, her fingers working frantically with those of her young lover's to bring them both to orgasm. Suddenly, her back arched, her face contorted and her whole body seemed to surge back towards the boy. Julian could sense the boy losing control as he renewed his thrusts, wildly now, eager and instinctive, pushing deeper and deeper into the woman's responsive body.

Breathless, Julian finally tore himself away from the doorway and leant against the wall, trying to compose himself while the colour and heat rose in his face and the painful throb of his unsatisfied erection ached in his groin. Afraid to look back, he hurried over to his car, all thoughts of meeting Rachel

Ingram temporarily pushed aside by the erotic scene in the darkness of the kitchen.

As quietly as he could, still fearing that he might be heard, Julian drove away from Albion House and headed back across the causeway to wait until eleven – tide or no tide, he had no desire to be caught watching the lovers.

In Albion House, Rachel moaned softly under Daniel's weight as he collapsed, exhausted, down onto her. Her whole body twitched and shivered from the aftermath of their mutual orgasm. She could still feel the last of Daniel's contractions deep inside her and sighed contentedly at the sensation. His broad chest was slick with sweat.

There was an intense silence between them, broken as Daniel groaned and slid gently out of her sated body. She turned towards him. His eyes were unreadable in the cool shadows.

'I'm not sure,' he said softly, 'whether I should be apologising.'

She looked up at him, astounded, her body still warm and aching from his attentions. 'Apologising?'

He suddenly looked desperately vulnerable. 'I've never felt anything like this for a woman before. I wanted to know that last time wasn't a one-off, that this isn't some kind of bad joke.' He blushed self-consciously. 'We both know that this isn't right. I work for you . . .' his voice faded.

Rachel had pulled herself up from the table and started to gather her clothes together. She froze and looked across at him, stunned by what Daniel was saying. His words stung her.

'Do you think I'd use you?' she said unsteadily. 'I can't believe you could think that.'

Daniel shrugged. 'I thought it might be a joke. I wondered whether you were going to tell all your friends—'

Rachel flushed crimson, remembering the conversation she had had with Anthea. Staring at Daniel she felt a sudden wave of pain. Perhaps he was right, she had already betrayed him. Tears prickled up behind her eyes.

'How could you think that? Is that what you really believe?' she whispered. 'Can't you tell this isn't a joke? I'm horrified that you think I could be so cruel.'

The boy coloured furiously. In the shadows, looking more twelve than twenty, Daniel resembled an erotically charged angel. His beautiful, chiselled features belying his wild, animal nature.

'I don't really know what you're like, do I?' he said softy. 'I never thought you'd give anyone like me a second look.' He laughed uneasily. 'Not like this.' His voice trailed off.

Rachel struggled with the buttons of her blouse, feeling horribly self-conscious and uncomfortable.

The boy turned. Stepping into a shaft of sunlight from the window his handsome profile was thrown into relief. Rachel's heart tightened. She felt incredibly vulnerable and wondered what on earth she had started. For the first time she had real doubts about letting her desires move from fantasy into reality. To Daniel, she must appear as a worldly-wise woman, taking pleasure as and when she wanted it. He didn't see her as an inexperienced faithful widow but as a lecherous siren. She was horrified as much by his image of her, as his fears that she might just be using him.

But, said a dark little voice in her head, wasn't that exactly what she had been doing? What possible chance did they have together? A working class boy and an educated woman almost old enough to be his mother. Perhaps Anthea had been closer to the truth than she knew. Rachel realised that she had never got beyond the bedroom in her fantasies – she had always seen Daniel purely as a creature of toil and passion, never as a real, living person.

Meanwhile, Daniel continued, 'I've watched you, around the place and thought you were beautiful, something special.'

She looked across at him and forced a laugh, struggling to quell her growing sense of panic. 'I'm not so special, Daniel,

33

I'm just a woman – and this isn't a joke.' She hesitated, painfully aware of the huge gap of culture and years between them.

Daniel smiled, then glanced back towards the open kitchen door. 'I'd better dress and be getting on with the garden.'

She had been so intent on her own thoughts that she had barely noticed Daniel was still naked. His tanned body was breathtaking with its clean sculptural lines, taut bands of muscle, and the dark matt of hair around his exhausted sex. She swallowed hard. Even in her uncertainty there was no doubt that Daniel was truly magnificent, the stuff of which fantasies were made, and for an instant she thought about the canvas she'd begun in the studio.

'No, wait, Daniel, before you go. I wanted to ask you, would you sit for me?'

The boy, who had just begun to get dressed, grinned, as if everything was now simple and uncomplicated between them.

'You mean pose?'

She nodded, afraid that if she spoke she might betray her lingering fears.

'If you want,' he said. 'You mean for one of your pictures, don't you?'

Rachel turned and refilled the kettle. 'Yes, yes that is what I mean. I'll pay you the same rate as for gardening. It will give us a chance to talk and get to know each other better. Maybe you could split your hours between the two jobs.'

He moved closer to her, his hands sliding easily around her waist. 'Don't you mean three jobs?' he purred softly, his mouth nibbling the curve of her neck. She shivered at the intimacy of his tone and touch.

However inexperienced he might be, she knew Daniel sensed the power her desire for him had over her. It would be much simpler to push him away now and reassert her authority – take control – instead she turned and crept into the shelter of his sun-tanned arms, not resisting as he tipped her face towards him and kissed her passionately on the lips. Totally at ease in his nakedness he pulled her closer, filling her senses with the scents of sex, sea and sun. She closed her eyes and drank him in putting all her fears aside.

Chapter 3

At just after eleven o'clock, Julian Morton rang the front doorbell of Albion House. He was rather taken aback when the young woman who he'd seen earlier opened the door to him. She was now dressed eccentrically in a calf-length velvet skirt and peasant blouse which gave her a gypsyish appearance.

He doffed his hat to cover his confusion. 'Good morning, miss. My name is Julian Morton. I am expected. I have an appointment with Mrs Ingram at eleven,' he said briskly. 'I would be most grateful if you could tell her that I have arrived.'

The woman smiled warmly. 'Good morning. I'm very pleased to meet you, Mr Morton. I am Rachel Ingram. I do hope you'll forgive the informality, but my housekeeper only comes in three days a week and the maid is away at her mother's at the moment so I'm my own servant today. Won't you please come in?' As she moved closer to shake his hand, Julian could detect the slightest flush on her tanned face and thought he could detect the smell of the boy's body mingling with her perfume.

Sitting in the car on the far side of the causeway Julian had convinced himself he'd caught the hired help at play, so he was somewhat astonished and at the same time delighted to discover that he had, in fact, been watching the mistress of Albion.

Rachel Ingram indicated he should follow her inside. Utterly composed, she led him into the hallway and took his straw fedora. Her long dark hair was caught up into a bun. Stray tendrils had escaped, giving her features a girlish, vulnerable air. Still smiling, she showed him into an elegant sitting room overlooking the garden and offered him coffee.

'Well, Mr Morton,' she said, returning from the kitchen with a tray, 'we have very few visitors out here. How may I help you?'

'We?' he enquired pleasantly, taking the cup she offered him.

Rachel Ingram blushed slightly and then laughed. 'I'm so sorry, it's an old habit. I'm a widow, but those basic social niceties are sometimes the hardest to shake off.'

Julian smiled and offered polite condolences.

So, he thought, the golden boy with her in the kitchen was not her husband nor her partner. From the garden he could hear the soft hiss of a scythe and got to his feet to look out of the window.

'It's quite an amazing house you have, Mrs Ingram. Have you lived at Albion long?'

Rachel nodded. 'Thank you. I inherited it from my grandmother last year. I've always thought it was a rather magical place, standing out here amongst the dunes and salt marshes. I often wonder about the man who built the house on what is, after all, virtually an island.'

Julian nodded, though his concentration was not on Rachel's words but the way her body moved. She was as lithe and slim as a dancer. He endeavoured to keep his mind on the conversation. 'Don't you worry about being cut off?'

Rachel shook her head. 'Not really. I used to spend the summers here as a child and in all that time I can never remember the causeway being completely flooded.'

There was a noticeable lull in conversation. Julian realised he was staring and that Rachel Ingram was waiting for him to speak. 'So you've been here a year?' he blustered.

'Six months. And you? Do you live locally?'

Julian picked at his blazer. 'We moved down last month to Medsham Hall. Perhaps you've seen it, up on the coast road?' The conversation was losing its impetus as wave after wave of erotic imagery filled Julian's head. He coughed, struggling to control his thoughts and decided to get to the point.' Actually, I'm here at the suggestion of the pilot out on Carfax Quay. He suggested I contact you about your jetty and the old boathouse out on the headland over there.' He pointed in the general direction of the sea.

Rachel nodded. 'Oh yes. I remember now, you are the gentleman with the pleasure boat.'

Julian watched as a striking young blond man, dressed in working clothes, walked across the garden.

'It seems as if you have another visitor, Mrs Ingram.'

Did he see her blush? Julian thought so, and felt a strange sense of pleasure at her momentary embarrassment. He had no doubt that the blond boy was the one he'd seen earlier in the kitchen.

'Oh no, that's my gardener, Daniel,' she said hastily, 'he's trying to do something with the chaos out there. Rather an uphill struggle, I'm afraid.'

Julian forced himself to keep his expression neutral. The boy was her gardener? He was astonished, but managed to continue, 'He looks a useful sort of fellow. Now, where were we? Oh yes, the jetty. At present my boat is moored in the salt marshes at Carfax but it's hardly an ideal arrangement. We have to use a skiff to row out to her every time we want to use her, and maintenance and such like would be far easier on a permanent mooring. The pilot said the channel here has a draft deep enough for a boat her size. He didn't think you had a boat of your own.'

Rachel smiled pleasantly. 'No, I don't. I would have to think about it, but in principle I don't have any objection. How often do you use the boat?'

Julian shrugged. 'At few day trips, mostly at weekends. A little maintenance in between painting and things like that. I promise we'd cause very little interruption to your solitude.' He glanced at Rachel's face remembering what the local vicar had told him on the far side of the causeway. 'One of the people from the village told me that you are something of an artist.'

Rachel coloured. 'That's right. The local paper did an article on me when I first moved down here, I'm afraid. I'm surprised anyone remembers.'

Julian leant forward and said softly, 'I think you underestimate yourself, Mrs Ingram.' He was rewarded by the slight flush returning to Rachel's cheeks. She really was quite delightful.

Elaborating on the vicar's story, Julian continued, 'I've been told you are very good and quite famous. I feel rather a philistine for not realising who you were. My sister and I are both keen collectors. Perhaps we could see some of your work at some time in the future?'

Rachel poured herself a cup of coffee. 'I'd be flattered.' Her tone was polite rather than enthusiastic. Julian felt compelled to try another tack – he really wanted to get to know Mrs Rachel Ingram very much better.

'My sister and I are new to Carfax-Staithe and so I'm afraid we don't know many people locally. Perhaps you would care to have dinner with us some time?'

'It appears we are both newcomers, Mr Morton.'

How pointedly she side-stepped his invitation. Julian Morton was completely enchanted.

'Apparently so. I do think we outsiders ought to stick together.'

She smiled. 'If you will excuse me, Mr Morton, I have quite a lot of work to do this morning. I'll be happy to ring you once I've reached decision about the jetty.'

She stood up, indicating that their meeting was at an end. Julian couldn't help noticing the curve of her breasts pressing against the thin cotton shirt, and thought about the way he'd seen them earlier, flushed with passion, nipples hard and dark. He closed his eyes, trying to push the image away, but instead, deep within his mind, he heard her moan and beg her young lover to stroke her wet, gaping sex.

'Indeed. That would be splendid. And thank you for seeing me at such short notice.'

Rachel had already moved on, ready to show him out. As she reached the door she looked back over her shoulder. Framed in the doorway she looked exquisite and Julian knew he had to find a way to possess her. She was astonishing and excited him in a way he hadn't felt for years. How glorious it would be to feel the heat of her eager body writhing under him. He longed to explore every inch of her slim delicate frame, take her again and again, making her cry out for more . . .

Falling into step beside her, Julian struggled with his thoughts, trying to re-establish the priorities he had arrived with, as Rachel led him through the shadowy corridors of Albion. He felt compelled to find a way to stay a little longer.

As they reached the front door, Julian said. 'This may seem terribly impertinent but I wondered if I might see some of your work now?' Frantically he fished around for a plausible reason why he might want to.

'You see,' he stammered. 'It's my sister, Petra's, birthday quite soon and I don't anticipate being able to get up to town beforehand, with the estate and everything. She adores painting, perhaps you have something that might be suitable as a gift?'

Rachel stared at him and then smiled. Julian coloured. The reasoning sounded as strained and unlikely to him as it must do to Rachel Ingram.

'Of course, if it's too much trouble,' he continued, not meeting her eyes, 'I quite understand. If you're busy I could call back at another time.'

After a few seconds she shook her head. 'No, of course it's no trouble. If you'd like to follow me. My studio is this way.' She led him back through the house and out into a little courtyard at the rear of the house. She smiled as she directed him through another door. 'It's more or less self-contained. Although you can get to it from the main house, this is the

41

quickest route – if you'd like to go up.'

At the top of a flight of narrow stairs the landing broadened out into a large sunlit room. All the rooms in Albion had spectacular views and Rachel's studio was no exception. Julian Morton walked across to the broad window and looked out. The view was to the north-east over the maze of salt marshes that surrounded the house. Below them was Rachel's garden and beyond that, on a man-made promontory, the narrow jetty that had brought him to Albion. It was astonishing, he thought, that something so mundane had opened the door into Rachel Ingram's life.

Around the room were the trappings of a working artist: easels, brushes, stacks of canvases protected by dust sheets, a huge battered work bench strewn with drawing materials, everything permeated by the smell of turpentine and linseed oil.

Julian turned back to face Rachel. 'What a wonderful studio. No wonder you became an artist. The view from here would inspire anybody.'

She moved across the room to join him. 'Actually it's a terrible distraction, I have to tear myself away from watching the water and the sky to concentrate on what I'm supposed to be doing. My grandfather was a watercolourist and had the studio built when he retired here. Now, I've got one or two things up here that might be suitable.' She paused thoughtfully and then pulled a small watercolour from a stack of open shelves. It was a simple, delicate rendering of the view from the studio window.

Julian smiled appreciatively. 'I see you don't always fight the distraction of the view, this is really rather good.'

Rachel laughed. 'As you've just moved to Carfax I thought perhaps your sister might like a local view? Or would you prefer something more instantly recognisable as an Ingram?'

Julian lay the watercolour back on the shelf. 'I feel even more ashamed now, I didn't realise you were a name.'

'Hardly a name. I'm quite well-known in America, but not

so well-known over here. I used to illustrate my husband's books. Wait, there's something here that might be more suitable, this is more of my usual style.'

She pulled another unframed canvas from amongst the stack against the wall. Julian took it from her. It was a pagan landscape of windswept trees and stormy skies, rendered in a naive style with rich, jewel-bright colours. In the centre was a unicorn, caught in a shaft of sunlight.

Julian stared across at her, astounded by the power of the painting. 'This is absolutely amazing – and so different from the watercolour.'

Rachel smiled modestly. 'Do you think your sister might like it?'

Julian nodded dumbly. It was almost too good, and he was afraid for an instant that his voice might give away his motives for wanting to stay – which had nothing to do with painting. He certainly hadn't expected anything of this calibre.

'It will do beautifully,' he said at last. 'If you're sure you're happy to sell it?'

Rachel nodded. 'Absolutely. I've done several on the same theme.'

Julian set the painting down carefully on the work bench. 'I'd be very interested to see some of your other work.' It was a line he had rehearsed seconds before they had mounted the stairs, now he was surprised to realise he actually meant it.

Rachel grinned, almost as if she guessed he was delaying the moment of departure. The air between them crackled with expectation.

'Are you sure I'm not boring you, Mr Morton?'

Julian pulled a face. 'Please, call me Julian.'

He glanced around the room. None of Rachel's paintings hung on the walls but were stacked upright on the floor or piled on the shelves. In the centre of the room on an easel was a large canvas draped with a dust sheet.

'What about this one?'

Rachel dismissed it with a wave. 'It's a new work in progress, barely more than a rough sketch at the moment. I've got one or two things here, that might interest you.'

She started to sort through the other paintings, as if eager to distract his attention from the picture under the cloth.

Julian moved closer to it. 'May I look?'

To his surprise, Rachel, who had been completely at ease until that moment, blushed furiously and started to protest. Curious, Julian lifted the cloth without waiting for a definite reply and then smiled broadly.

The picture was no more than the sketch as she had said, but even so it was a picture of stunning passion. She had begun a life study of the boy, his tumbling blond hair plaited and magically changing into the stems of plants as it spread across the canvas. Caught in a tangle of shadows his beautiful body subtly blended with the trees. Rachel had transformed her young lover into a sexual icon set amidst an erotic pagan woodland.

Julian turned back towards her. Images of the boy pawing at Rachel's glorious body suffused his imagination.

Almost as if she could see the thoughts forming inside Julian's head, Rachel gnawed at her lip, her eyes suddenly dark and glassy. When she spoke her voice was unsteady and she wouldn't meet his gaze.

'I did warn you it was just a sketch,' she mumbled uncomfortably. 'If you're happy with the painting of the unicorn I can arrange to have it framed.'

Julian moved closer to her, relishing her mixture of embarrassment and vulnerability.

'I do apologise. But I have to say your latest work is really quite stunning,' he said softly. 'Something so beautiful ought to make you famous.'

Rachel looked up at him. 'It wasn't really meant to be seen by anyone else,' she said quietly.

'I'm sorry, is it a private commission?' asked Julian archly.

Rachel nodded, seizing on his explanation. 'Yes, yes it's a private commission. Now, if you're sure you're happy with the unicorn we'll go back downstairs. I'm sure you are a very busy man, Mr Morton.'

'Julian.'

She nodded and scurried away from him like a frightened rabbit. Julian smiled to himself and covered the sketch of the boy. The pursuit and seduction of Rachel Ingram was going to give him a great deal of pleasure.

Downstairs in the hall, Rachel quickly regained her composure. Behind her, Julian Morton followed more slowly.

'Once the painting is framed, if you'll give me a ring, I'll come over and collect it,' he said, conversationally. 'And we really should talk about the price.'

Rachel nodded. 'Have you got a card?'

'Of course, I'm so sorry. I should have given it to you earlier. Here.' Julian opened his wallet and passed the card to Rachel. It read, simply: *Julian C. Morton* embossed in black on thick creamy card with a telephone number printed beneath his name.

Rachel glanced at it briefly before laying it on a side table.

He could sense she wanted him to leave. Instead he hesitated at the door, trying to catch her eye.

'I wonder whether you might reconsider my invitation to have dinner with us some time? I'd be delighted if you'd accept it as a small gesture of thanks for Petra's present.'

Rachel hesitated. 'I'm not really a very social animal—' she began, handing him his hat.

Julian smiled. 'Please, I insist. Petra and I are both finding the social life in Carfax hideously oppressive. It would be a real pleasure to have jolly company for a change. Do say you'll come. What about this Friday?'

Rachel laughed. 'I would hardly describe myself as jolly company.'

Julian grinned. 'Nonsense. Anything has got to be better than our new neighbours. We invited them over for supper on Saturday. All they talked about was the weather and the price of skate.' He paused and caught hold of her hand. It delighted him to finally touch her. 'I absolutely refuse to take no for an answer.'

Finally Rachel looked up at him with a smile. 'In that case I'd be delighted,' she said, extricating her hand. 'I will brush up on the price of fish so I'll be able to make small talk.' And with this she showed Julian to the door.

As he reached the corner of the house Julian turned back to look at Albion. Rachel Ingram was now striding across the lawn towards her glorious pagan boy. Julian smiled to himself, all thoughts of his precious boat and renting the jetty had vanished. What a strange thing fate was he mused, climbing back into his car. He must remember to prime Petra about it being her birthday. Dropping the car into gear he headed back across the causeway, oblivious to the tide rising up alongside the weather-worn stones.

'So how did it go?' Anthea purred down the phone an hour or so after Julian had left.

Rachel laughed. 'How did what go?'

'Your assignation. When you didn't come back to the flat last night, I thought . . .' Anthea's voice faded leaving a conspiratorial question in the air.

'I came home. How on earth could you think that awful man was my type? The good news is that I've just met one of my neighbours. The one who wrote to me?'

'Not the boat man?'

Rachel giggled. 'How very clever of you to remember. He came over to discuss using the jetty, bought a painting and invited me to dinner.'

This time it was Anthea who giggled. 'Good Lord, that was fast work. Maybe it's all that country air. What's he like?'

Rachel smiled. 'You'd approve. He's forty-ish, distinguished-looking, tall, with a sort of hawkish face but interesting eyes.' She smiled and curled herself onto the chair beside the phone. 'Which he couldn't take off me – he was terribly flirty.'

At the far end of the line, Anthea laughed. 'He sounds absolutely perfect. When's your dinner date?'

'Friday night, but you don't have to worry about my virtue, apparently his sister lives with him.'

Anthea groaned. 'What a bore. Look, I really have to dash, Pip has just turned up to take me to Langmores for lunch and is pacing up and down like a caged tiger. I'll ring you later in the week.'

Julian Morton was singing when he pulled up on the broad driveway outside Medsham Hall. He chose to ignore the crumbling masonry, the missing tiles and the peeling window frames that had occupied his entire mind since he had first arrived at the damned house.

Dropping his jacket and hat into the arms of the waiting butler, he took the stairs up to the first floor two at a time, his rich bass voice turning effortlessly into a resonant whistle. A door on the landing opened and his sister, Petra, dressed in a grey silk peignoir and a beaded cloche, stared at him. She took a long pull on her cigarette holder as he approached.

'Well?' she purred mischievously. 'You look like the cat that's got the cream. Can I safely assume from the stupid grin on your face that you've got the use of the jetty?'

Julian pressed a kiss to each of her cheeks. 'My dear, it's better – much, much better.' As he walked passed her he undid his tie and pulled it off. In Petra's room, on a *chaise longue* under the window, lay a slim girl in her early twenties. She was dressed in a sheer cream lace camisole, cream stockings and little grey, T-bar shoes. It was possible to pick out every line and curve of her slim body. She made no attempt to cover herself at Julian's arrival.

Julian lifted a hand in greeting and then turned his attention back to Petra.

'Izzy still here? I thought your little princess was back off to London this morning?' he said, plucking the stopper from a decanter on the sideboard and pouring himself a drink.

The girl on the *chaise* stretched artfully. Her movements were sinuous and charged with a thousand sexual possibilities. Through the thin camisole Julian could make out her breasts, which were as tiny as bee stings but topped with pert, cherry-pip nipples.

As she rolled over onto her belly she said, in a tiny voice, 'I can speak you know, Julian.'

Julian grinned. 'Next thing, Izzy, you'll be telling me you can read and write as well.'

Petra glared at him. 'Jealousy is a terrible failing in a man,' she snapped. 'Actually I've invited Izzy to stay for the rest of the week.'

Julian tipped his head on one side. 'I see. And is the lovely Izzy planning to earn her keep by servicing the Lord of the manor, or is she reserving her favours for the Lord of the manor's butch little sister?'

On the *chaise*, Izzy pouted. 'Why is it you two always talk about me as if I'm not here?'

Both Petra and Julian turned towards her, while Petra continued, 'She doesn't like men, they're nasty and rough and want to stick things in her.'

Julian snorted. 'Not many things – besides it seems such a terrible waste. She's a little poppet. What about if I promised to restrict the number of things I wanted to stick in her to say, two or three. Would she sleep with me then?'

Petra snorted and poured herself a drink. 'I very much doubt it. You are remarkably chipper – how did your meeting with Mrs Ingram go?'

Julian settled himself back into an armchair and closed his eyes. Instantly he saw Rachel Ingram, naked, bent over the kitchen table. He shivered.

'Better than I could have possibly imagined. She is quite perfect – oh, by the way, she is coming to dinner on Friday night and it's your birthday, if she asks. I was going to say you will love her but I'm rather hoping that you won't.'

Petra pulled a face and settled herself on the *chaise* beside

Izzy. Her hands idly cupped one of the girl's tiny breasts and stroked at the little peaks beneath the cream silk. Izzy moaned softly.

Julian sighed. 'Why is it you never let me play with any of your friends?'

'Because, darling,' said Petra with a grin, 'you already have everything else. A girl has to have some little thing to call her own.'

Julian grimaced. 'Well, thank you. I get a crumbling pile, a trust fund tied so tight that it is strangling the life out of me, and meanwhile you get all the fun. Come on, Petra, just let me borrow Izzy for an hour or so. I've got this appalling need that just has to be sorted out. What I need is a medicinal screw.'

Petra laughed. 'You really are a bore, Julian. Go and find a friend of your own, Izzy is spoken for.' As if to emphasise the point she slid her hand down over the girl's belly. Instantly Izzy's legs opened and Petra's hand cupped her sex. Julian groaned and screwed up his face.

'I promise not to break her. And you've got her all week. Come on, Petra, be a sport. Just this once.'

Petra sighed. 'Oh, all right, but don't be long. I'm going to go into town and when I get back I want to find her all washed and nicely buffed up. And don't ask me again.'

Julian grinned and held out his hand to Izzy. 'Come on, sweetie. Let's go to my room. Petra wants to get ready to go out, and besides my bed is so much bigger than hers.'

Petra pushed another cigarette into the holder and lit it. 'Not to mention your ego,' she said in an undertone.

Izzy sighed and slithered off the couch. Julian caught hold of her hand before Petra could change her mind and led the girl along the corridor.

Once they were in his rooms it took Julian very little effort to persuade Izzy to undress. Kissing her gently on the forehead he slipped his fingers under the shoe-string straps of her camisole and slid it down over her shoulders.

49

Despite the softness and warmth of her compliant little body he found it hard to concentrate. Every time he closed his eyes, Izzy's face and body were transformed into those of Rachel Ingram. Under the cream silk Izzy was slim, but unlike Rachel her body was almost boyish, her waist gliding down to narrow hips with little difference in size. Her sex was dusted with a light powder puff of white-blonde curls that barely covered the pink, moist slit of her quim. Her tiny breasts – as he had anticipated – were topped with delectable little pink peaks. He nuzzled one with his lips, drawing it in to his mouth. Izzy shivered and despite Petra's suggestion that she preferred female flesh, she moaned most convincingly.

Gently, Julian guided her back towards the bed and arranged her amongst the tumble of white linen. Her delicate skin was almost the same colour as the sheets. This might be a therapeutic screw but there was certainly no need to rush it, he thought, unbuttoning his shirt slowly.

Izzy watched him from behind big brown eyes with languid curiosity. Her legs were open, knees bent so that he caught a glimpse of the moist little prize between her thighs. She grinned at him, running a cat-pink tongue around her lips, as he slipped out of his trousers. Her eyes moved hungrily along the throbbing curve of his engorged cock.

'I thought you didn't like men, Izzy?' he said, leaning forward to plant a kiss on the junction of her sex. She smelt divine. He slipped his tongue lower, parting the lips of her sex, brushing her clitoris, his senses awash with the intense perfume of her body.

Izzy mewled and lifted herself up onto his tongue. Her fingers locked in his hair, pulling him closer so that it felt as if he was being drawn inside her.

'That's what Petra likes people to think,' she moaned, opening her legs wider to give Julian greater freedom to explore, 'but to be perfectly honest the only thing I can't stand is to be ignored – and you two are terrible for that.'

He pulled back and pursed his lips, blowing a steady stream

of air onto her pleasure bud, while his fingers traced the plump outer lips of her quim. 'You can hardly complain that I'm ignoring you now.'

Izzy snorted and wriggled under his fingers. 'Only because you want something. But I have to admit you're good very at this – oh yes, touch me there again.'

Julian grinned and ran a fingernail down over the little hood that protected her clitoris. She moaned appreciatively.

'You really ought to thank Petra,' he said, opening her lips so that he could examine her more closely. 'I used to spend hours watching her seduce her friends.'

He replaced his finger with his tongue and lapped and circled her pleasure bud, slipping his hands under her slim buttocks so that he could lift her up to his waiting mouth. The effect was instantaneous, Izzy thrust upwards, forcing her pussy towards him, moaning feverishly.

If only all medicine was as entertaining as this, Julian thought, plunging his tongue deep inside her. She tasted delicious. Sliding a finger into her, he was delighted to find not only was she amazingly tight – her quim nibbled at him like the mouth of hungry fish – but she was so wet and hot that it made the breath catch in his throat. With her body gyrating against his lips, thighs nipped tight against his head, he could sense that it wouldn't take much to bring her to the moment of climax. He lapped at her again and again, running his nose down over her clitoris so his tongue could dip deep inside her.

Just as he thought she had reached the point from which there was no return, he lowered her down onto the bed. She looked up at him with an angry pout.

'Don't stop now,' she murmured. 'I'm almost there.'

Julian grinned. 'I know, just trust me, I know what I'm doing.' With one hand still resting on her waist, he eased her thighs apart and guided his cock inside her. Feeling her body open and then close around him was as wonderful as he had anticipated.

He pushed deeper; her sex felt like damp velvet. Thrusting rhythmically he leant forwards and pressed a chaste kiss on to each of her pert little nipples. She gasped and lifted her legs to encircle his waist. Carefully, he slid a hand down over her belly to find the little bud that served her so well and continued to rub and stroke it, until poor Izzy was practically sobbing with pleasure.

Deep inside her, he felt the first tiny contraction of orgasm – her sex tightening eagerly around his cock – and then the feeling hit him again in a series of great waves like a fist milking him dry. Relinquishing all pretence of control, Julian threw back his head and let the sheer joy of Izzy's body take him away. Snorting, he drove into her again, and again, and at the very point when it seemed as if every thought, every reflex was centred on his cock, buried deep inside the warm wet pit between Izzy's legs, Julian had a blinding flash of Rachel Ingram's face as she made love to her handsome young gardener.

The image intensified every sensation, every feeling, until he wondered whether he might die from sheer pleasure. As the waves closed over him it was all he could do to stop himself from calling out her name. Finally he rolled off Izzy and collapsed in a sweating, breathless heap alongside her.

The little blonde girl grinned and then kissed him gently on the nose.

'That was rather good,' she said in a sleepy voice. 'It seems a bit of a shame I have to go back to Petra's room so soon.'

Julian groaned. 'You better had – she'll never forgive me if you don't.'

Chapter 4

Rachel wiped her hands on a rag and stood back to admire the progress of Daniel's portrait. Although she had been a little taken aback by Julian Morton removing the dust sheet, she had been flattered by his praise. Looking at the way the work was developing she knew that he was right – it would be something very special when it was complete. On a dais in the corner of the studio, Daniel stretched like a cat. A shaft of sunlight caught his muscular body, adding an almost unearthly glow.

Rachel dipped her brush in a jar of turpentine to clean off the paint.

'Why don't you take a break,' she said, picking up a silk robe that hung over a chair. 'I'll ring for some tea.'

Daniel yawned. 'I'd not thought sitting still would be so tiring.' He stood up and ran his hands along the back of his neck to ease out the tension. Eyes closed he stretched again. Rachel was transfixed. He looked like something from Greek mythology. As she stared at him, somewhere on the periphery of her concentration she heard the phone ring. It rang once, twice and then stopped.

A few seconds later her housekeeper, Mrs Weirs, called up the stairs. 'Mrs Ingram? There's a telephone call for you from a gentleman called Mr Morton. Would you like me to tell him to call back later?'

'No, no, I'll take it,' Rachel said quickly, turning away from the naked boy. 'Oh, and Mrs Weirs, would you please send Molly up with a pot of tea?'

Across the room Daniel was wrapping himself in the robe. Rachel had had him sit for her every afternoon since she had arrived back from London. Familiarity, she thought with a wry smile, most certainly did not breed contempt. The only problem was that with her housekeeper and maid back in the house, she and Daniel had had no time or opportunity to be alone without the risk of disturbance. The tension bubbling low in her belly was almost unbearable.

Rachel hurried downstairs, across the courtyard and into the hall, then picked up the receiver. 'Hello?'

Julian Morton laughed. 'Hello, Rachel. I was beginning to think that perhaps you were too busy to talk to me. I just rang to remind you about our dinner engagement this evening.'

Rachel smiled. 'As if I'd forget. What time are we dining?'

'Around nine. I'll drive over to collect you at eight so we can indulge in cocktails on the terrace.'

'That's very kind, Julian, but there really is no need, I can drive myself.'

Julian laughed again. 'No need to be so damned independent, Rachel. Indulge me. I've just bought this most glorious new motor car and I would like an excuse to give her a run.'

Rachel smiled. 'In that case I would be delighted to accept your offer. I've had your sister's picture taken to the framers, so I'll bring it with me.' She paused. 'Your sister will be there this evening, won't she?'

'Don't you trust me?' Julian chuckled. There was a pause and then he added, 'Of course she will. Petra is looking forward to meeting you, so your reputation will remain as pure as the driven snow.' Before Rachel had chance to reply he continued, 'Which brings me to my next point, your young gardener.'

Rachel felt her colour rising. 'What about him?' she said in a low voice. It was odd that he moved from her reputation to Daniel. Did she detect a note of amusement in Julian's tone? Had the local gossip spread as far as Julian Morton already?

'I am looking for someone to work here at Medsham Hall.

He's not in the market for another job is he?'

With a sigh of relief Rachel said, 'I'm not sure. He works for Ted Grey, who does all sorts of work – odd jobs, gardening, building, that sort of thing – all over the village.'

Julian made a thoughtful noise. 'He sounds exactly like the sort of chap I'm looking for. You wouldn't have this fellow Grey's address handy would you?'

Rachel frowned. 'I think he lives in Church Lane. My housekeeper suggested him. I could ask her.' She paused and glanced back towards her studio. 'Or I could ask my gardener to pass on a message if you like.'

'If it's no trouble.'

Rachel shook her head. 'No trouble at all.'

'In that case I won't stop you from getting on with your work. I'll see you this evening at around eight.'

Rachel smiled. 'I'll look forward to it.'

As she dropped the phone back into its cradle, her housemaid appeared with a tea tray. Rachel nodded her thanks. 'Thank you, Molly, I'll take that up.'

Molly lifted an eyebrow as Rachel extricated the tray from the girl's hands. Rachel had no doubt that neither her housekeeper or her maid approved of Daniel posing for her and wondered what stories had already percolated through to the village as a result.

Upstairs, Daniel was sitting by the window looking out over the sea. He glanced up at the sound of her footsteps, catching hold of the neck of the robe so that it covered his chest. When he saw it was Rachel he smiled.

'I thought you were Molly – or Mrs Weirs. It wouldn't do for them to see me like this.' His voice faded. 'Well, you know what I mean,' he said quickly, as if she might expect an explanation.

Rachel set the tray down on her work bench and realised with a start that the expression on Molly's face might have been envy, not disapproval. Molly was seventeen, perhaps eighteen, much closer to Daniel in age than she was. Their being attracted to each other would be the most natural thing in the world. Rachel took a deep breath.

'You're right. Do you like Molly?' Even as she said it Rachel realised a small green-eyed monster had slithered up unbidden from some dark corner of her soul.

Daniel grinned. 'I haven't given it a lot of thought. She's not much more than kid, is she? When I first came to work here she was out in the garden every ten minutes, bringing me drinks, making sure I'd got something for me dinner – making cow eyes at me—' he stopped and coloured dramatically. 'Not that I want to get her into trouble or anything.'

Rachel looked away and began to pour the tea. As she did so, Daniel stepped up behind her and slid his arms around her waist. He nibbled her ear and ran his tongue down her neck. She shivered.

'Why? Does it bother you? Molly is nothing more than a silly little girl,' he purred.

Rachel closed her eyes: a silly little girl who under other circumstances might well have been Daniel's lover. She did not resist as Daniel turned her round and pressed a delicate kiss to her lips. She could feel the heat of his body through the thin robe and moaned softly. He was glorious. It was impossible to resist him.

He began to unbutton her blouse. 'My mother would have said your maid, Molly, was a bad sort. I don't know what she would have made of you, Mrs Ingram.' His voice was teasing and intimate. 'Mind you, if she'd still been alive I might have ended up a teacher after all – and it wouldn't be so bad then, a school master and his lady artist.'

Struggling to retain some semblance of control, Rachel said quickly, 'By the way, I might have some work for you and your step-father. The man who just called, Julian Morton, he's looking for a handy man.'

The words weren't enough to stop Daniel's eager caresses. He cupped her breasts and brushed his thumbs over her nipples. They hardened instantly under his touch, making Rachel gasp.

'Right,' he whispered. 'I'll tell him when I see him.' Lifting her chin up he kissed her more fervently, his tongue demanding to be allowed between her lips. Rachel intended to protest – this was too dangerous, they were likely to be discovered by the servants, the door to the studio was still open – but it was impossible. Every fibre of her body ached to hold Daniel in her arms. As she returned the kiss his hands moved down from her waist to her thighs. As his tongue explored her mouth he began to lift up her skirt, exposing more and more of her legs. She moaned and dragged the robe back off his shoulders, lapping at his salty skin, relishing the sensation of his strength against her.

He smiled lazily, eyes alight with passion, and then lifted her up onto the edge of the bench. 'Or is it that you like me better as a gardener, Mrs Ingram?' he said with a sly grin. 'Do you like me because I'm strong and rough and earthy?'

She smiled at him, desire rippling along her spine. 'I think,' she said with a tremor in her voice, 'that I would want you whatever you were.' She stroked his nipples, electrified by the way they hardened under her fingertips. His finger slid back between her thighs, tracing the mound of her quim. His touch lit a thousand flares inside her mind.

'That's good,' he purred.

Rachel groaned and lifted herself up so that he could slip her knickers down, while all the time his lips worked back and forth across her neck and throat, his kisses leaving a white hot glow of sensation in their wake.

'You feel good,' he moaned.

She knew she was already wet. From the moment Daniel had walked into the studio and undressed, almost every thought she had was centred on what it would feel like to run her hands over his broad chest, kiss his full lips – feel his throbbing cock buried to the hilt inside her.

He pushed her skirt up around her waist and ran his thumb

down between the lips of her sex, seeking out the little pleasure bud that nestled between them.

'Oh yes,' she murmured as he found it, 'touch me there, that feels so wonderful.' The words were completely involuntary.

Daniel pulled back. His eyes were dark with expectation. 'Whatever you say,' he whispered. 'Just tell me what you want and I'll do it gladly.' As he spoke he opened the lips of her sex wider still so that he could explore the soft folds and creases. His thumbs stroked down over her clitoris again, making her shiver with pure pleasure. Gently he eased her towards the edge of the bench.

'Let me see your breasts,' he whispered thickly. With shaking fingers Rachel pushed her blouse off her shoulders and pulled the white camisole she was wearing down after it. He grinned.

'God, you're so lovely, teacher or gardener I couldn't want you more,' he whispered and drew one nipple deep into his mouth. The sensation catapulted Rachel to the edge of the precipice. Frantically she tore at the belt of his robe, her hands working as if they had a mind of their own. Beneath the thin fabric his cock was already rock hard, jutting towards her like a rapier blade.

Her mouth began to water as her fingers closed around him, drawing him nearer, guiding him into her. When his cock brushed the sensitive inner petals of her quim, she felt a rush of joy so intense that she thought she might faint.

Daniel needed no further encouragement and gently eased his shaft home, his hands linking around her buttocks, so that he could pull her even closer. Blindly following where desire led her, Rachel wrapped her legs around his hips, so that as Daniel began to move, her thrusts were an intense echo of his rhythm. With his fingers still working on her clitoris, Daniel buried his face between her breasts, his breath warming and moistening her skin.

It seemed as if it was an age since she had felt him inside her. The waves of tenderness and elation that rippled through her were accompanied by a growing flame of pleasure that glowed between her legs. On and on the boy thrust, taking her again and again to the very edge of oblivion until finally neither of them could hold back any longer. Gasping they tumbled head long into a seething, bubbling sea of pleasure.

When it was over Rachel was so stunned by the intensity of the sensations Daniel had fired in her that she could barely breathe.

He kissed her gently and then withdrew his exhausted cock from her body. Rachel felt a wave of loss at relinquishing her hold on him.

'Do you think the tea is cold?' he said with a grin.

She laughed, pulling her skirt down over her hips. 'More than likely – and I think the sitting is over for today too. I don't think I could hold a brush after that.'

Daniel cuddled close to her, his lips seeking hers with a flurry of tiny, playful kisses. 'You'll just have to work harder on Monday, then.'

Rachel stared up into his stormy blue eyes, wondering how she would be able to manage without seeing him until after the weekend. She wondered if she dare suggest he come to the house before Monday. His expression was alive with passion and delight. How she could have let herself get caught up in something so potentially complicated, so addictive . . . she fought to still the fears that threatened to bubble up and engulf her.

'You're right,' she said with false heartiness and pulled away from his compelling embrace. 'Here—' She turned her attention to the tea tray and poured them both a cup. He was right about the tea too – it was stone cold.

Ted Grey – Daniel's step-father – reined in the chestnut mare and climbed down off his cart. He glanced round as he tied the traces to one of the posts in the garden fence. There was still a lot of work to be done at Albion. Rachel Ingram said she wanted a proper garden and he would do his damnedest to ensure she got one – at a price.

Another summer working for the lovely Mrs Ingram and he might be able to afford to buy himself a van – and if the rumours in the village were right about the boy, Daniel, Lord only knew what the lad might get for himself.

Ted grinned and ran a hand over the stubble on his chin. Mind you, folk always liked to talk, and people in Carfax-Staithe were like villagers the land over – if there wasn't a story someone would take it upon themselves to invent one. Probably nothing in it – more's the pity. A good-looking young lad like Daniel could do a good deal worse than end up as stud dog to some rich bitch.

He'd done the same himself when he'd worked up at the old Manor. Ted grimaced at the memory. Miss Stapleford had been a damn sight older than Rachel Ingram and a lot less attractive. He'd had to close his eyes and think of the barmaid in the Grey Mare when he'd ploughed that particular dry furrow. Even so, when the old girl passed on, she'd left him a little something for services rendered.

Ted hitched up his trousers, pushed up the sleeves of his collarless shirt and headed across to the gravel to the tradesmen's entrance around the back of Albion house. The sun was already well past its zenith. He pulled the pocket watch out of his waistcoat. Time he and the boy got home, though he had arrived a bit early. Maybe if Mrs Weir wasn't about, that lass, Molly, would make him a pot of tea.

He grinned salaciously. If Daniel had any sense at all he'd be servicing the pair of them. Damned pretty little wench that Molly with her great big jiggling breasts and wide, smiling mouth. For a few seconds Ted imagined rubbing his cock between young Molly's jolly tits – a nice thought. He felt a familiar and far from unpleasant stirring in his groin.

Removing his cap, Ted knocked on the frame of the open kitchen door. Molly, who had been working at the sink, looked up at him. Her expression was sullen.

'And what d'you want, Ted Grey?' she snapped. 'I'm real busy.'

Ted aped pain. 'Now that's no way to talk to your elders. That face of yours would turn cream sour. I've come to pick Daniel up. Is he about?'

Molly snorted and dried her hands on her apron. 'He's still upstairs with Mrs Ingram, and I'm not going up there to fetch him if that's what you think.'

Ted grinned. 'Never know what you mind find, eh, Molly?' he said with a sly grin. 'Is the old dragon about?' He looked left and right around the dark confines of the kitchen.

'You mean Mrs Weirs? No, she's already gone off home. Her upstairs is going out to dinner tonight, so Mrs Weirs went early. Left me here on me own to finish up. Old cow.'

Ted stepped inside and pulled out a chair at the kitchen table.

'In that case how about a pot of tea then, my pet, while I wait for my boy? I'll keep you company till he shows himself. Can't have a lovely girl like you left all on her lonesome. Seems such a terrible waste.'

Molly slammed the enamel bowl into the cupboard under the sink but Ted could tell she was flattered by his attention.

'You ain't half got a nerve, Ted Grey. Cup of tea, I ask you!'

He shrugged. 'I've been telling young Daniel he ought to ask you out. I said to him, "How could you be blind to that young Molly – prettiest girl in the village. Fancy working with a girl like that and not asking her if she like to go out for a stroll—"'

Molly blushed furiously and slid the kettle onto the stove.

Ted pressed home the little advantage he had gained. 'I told him some handsome fella will come along and snap you up from under his nose.' He paused, eyes working hungrily over the girl's ripe body. How nice it would be to feel her working away under him. He lifted an eyebrow. 'I'd ask you out meself but you're far too pretty to fall for an old 'un like me.'

Molly giggled and then peeked up at him under her long eyelashes. He was delighted to see that her cheeks were still pink.

'I didn't know Daniel had even noticed me,' she began and then changed tack. 'You aren't that old, are you?'

Ted smiled. 'Old enough, my pet. But, then again, an old man knows what he's doing. We know what a woman needs and wants. You ask any woman if I'm not right. Young men are fast and furious, out to pleasure themselves, whereas an old dog like me can afford to take his time.' He paused for effect, his eyes never leaving Molly's. 'Fellow like me can make a little lass like you glow, you know. Make you feel so good that you cry out for more—'

He wondered for an instant if he had taken the conversation too far. Molly had frozen to the spot but then she grinned and took two cups off the rack over the stove.

'Is that right?' she said.

Ted nodded. He noticed that the girl's nipples had hardened, pressing forward provocatively like two thimbles against her thin cotton dress. Before he could take the conversation any further he heard voices in the main house.

Molly looked up and the sullen expression instantly returned to her face.

'Seems like Mrs Ingram has finished with your Daniel for the day,' she said in a sarcastic voice. 'So you won't be getting that cup of tea after all. Shame really, there's some nice Madeira cake in the tin.'

The door to the kitchen opened and for an instant Daniel and Rachel Ingram were framed in the opening. Ted knew in that split second that all the rumours were true. Rachel Ingram was dressed in a soft lawn blouse tucked into long grey skirt. Her lightly tanned skin was suffused with a deep, earthy glow and her eyes flashed like the moon on water. Tendrils of hair had escaped from her bun framing her small features. Her whole body seemed to shimmer with desire. Ted felt a flash of hunger. Compared to Rachel Ingram, Molly was just another cheap bright bauble.

Daniel, his step-son, stood just behind the mistress of Albion House, but there was nothing about his demeanour that suggested subservience. His eyes were mellow with passion spent, his body completely at ease. Ted's desire for Rachel was replaced by an intense stab of jealousy. All this Ted Grey took in and experienced in the instant between Rachel opening the door and her realising he was sitting at the kitchen table.

As she caught sight of him her expression became more guarded.

'Good afternoon, Mr Grey,' she said pleasantly. 'Have you come to collect Daniel? I hope we haven't kept you waiting too long? Has Molly offered you a cup of tea?'

Ted smiled and got to his feet, wondering if his voice might fail him.

By the stove, Molly frowned. 'I'm just making him one, ma'am.'

Rachel smiled. 'Good.' She looked back at Ted. 'I was talking to the gentleman who owns Medsham Hall this afternoon. He's looking for someone to do some odd jobs for him and I gave him your name. I hope you don't mind.'

Ted shook his head. 'Not at all, Mrs Ingram, not at all. I'm very flattered that you thought of me. I'm glad to hear you're pleased with the services we provide.'

Rachel coloured very slightly and Ted felt a surge of delight. As with Molly he felt compelled to push home the advantage. 'We like to think we keep our customers well satisfied, don't we, Daniel?'

His step-son flushed crimson and then nodded. 'I'm just going outside to fetch my jacket,' he mumbled.

Rachel Ingram appeared to have less trouble retaining her composure.

'The gentleman's name is Mr Julian Morton,' she said in a low voice. 'Now, if you will excuse me.' She glanced at Daniel. 'I'll see you next week.'

Sitting on the cart on the way home, Ted Grey found it very difficult to get his mind off Rachel Ingram. A woman of her calibre was wasted on a boy like Daniel. He let the reins go slack and pulled a hessian bag out from under the seat.

'Here,' he said in a gruff voice. 'Open me a bottle of beer, will ya, Dan? I'm real dry today.'

Daniel took the bag from him and rummaged about inside. Ted would have liked to ask his step-son about Rachel, but thought better of it – he had another idea that gradually took shape as the horse plodded slowly over the causeway and down onto the beach.

'I thought we'd stop off at the Cutter tonight and have a drink or two before we head home. Maybe have our supper in there an' all.'

Daniel shook his head. 'Not for me, Ted. I can walk home from the Cutter, if you like. To tell you the truth, I'm all in.'

'As you like,' Ted said suppressing the note of triumph in his voice. 'But you'll have to get yourself some grub when you get in.'

Daniel nodded.

Ted slapped the rein down across the back of his horse and urged her into a brisk walk. Daniel was too much of a Methodist – like his mother, God rest her soul. The boy didn't really hold with drinking, and on the odd times he did join Ted at the pub insisted on washing and changing first. The Cutter Inn was on the harbour, not that far from Albion. Ted squared his shoulders, perhaps, once Daniel was safely home he might pay Mrs Ingram another little visit.

He took the bottle of beer from Daniel, closed his lips around the neck and tipped it back. Maybe he'd go and ask Rachel Ingram what she thought she was playing at with young Daniel. Perhaps if he was really lucky, she might offer to show him. Ted grinned and took another mouthful of beer. He wasn't a bad-looking chap for his age, and after all, one bit of tinker's rough was much like another if she had a taste for that kind of thing. And if she didn't want to entertain him, maybe he'd take another crack at Molly, the little housemaid.

Sitting beside him, Daniel, lulled by the gentle rhythm of the cart swaying, was gradually closing his eyes. Ted snapped the reins again. Daniel jumped and pulled himself upright.

Glancing across at his step-son, Ted said, 'Have a hard day did ya', boy?'

Daniel, his gaze fixed between the horse's ears, nodded.

Ted grinned. 'I don't know – you young 'uns have got no staying power. You better get yourself off home and have an early night. No need to wait up for me. I don't plan to be home until late.'

Julian Morton sat at his dressing table and made another attempt to pull his tie into shape. Behind him, Petra, dressed in an exquisite green silk shift dress, lay her cigarette down in the ashtray and said, 'Here, let me.'

Julian turned round. 'New dress?'

Petra pouted. 'How very cruel of you to notice. Yes, it is. I had to have something new, I've worn everything else to death.'

Julian lifted his eyebrows.

'Don't look at me like that, Julian, besides it wasn't that expensive and it's for your benefit.'

'How so?'

Petra pulled the bow tight. 'To impress your dinner guest. If she asks I'll tell her I got it for my birthday.'

Julian snorted. 'Have we managed to save face with tonight's menus as well?'

Petra sucked her teeth. 'I put Izzy to work on it. She and that simpleton you employed as cook have done a sterling job. The only thing is, I'm really not certain how much longer I can continue to whip the proverbial silk purse out of a succession of very unpromising pigs' ears.' She paused, her eyes still on his bow tie. 'We need new china and silverware. I'm hoping your Mrs Ingram doesn't notice that nothing matches. What's she like by the way?'

Julian got to his feet and pulled on his evening jacket. 'Bohemian, beautiful – and from asking around locally, apparently quite wealthy . . .'

'And?'

Julian poured himself and Petra a glass of sherry. 'Widowed.'

Petra laughed. 'Oh, darling, you are so predictable.'

Julian grinned. 'But not so our Mrs Ingram. The first time I had the pleasure of seeing her was in her kitchen being rogered senseless by her man of all works over the scrub-top table.'

Petra stared at him. 'Is that a joke?'

Julian drained his glass. 'Fortunately not.'

Petra was still staring at him. 'My God, in that case wheel her in. I thought I might die of boredom in Carfax.'

Julian topped up their glasses. 'Perhaps that's the very reason Mrs Ingram succumbed to the hired help. Whatever, I shall endeavour to uncover her motives.'

'And offer yourself in his place no doubt?'

Julian struck a pose, the back of his hand resting on his forehead. 'You know what a martyr I am, Petra, darling. In my role as Lord of the manor I shall attempt to rescue the poor unfortunate waif from this woman's clutches and throw myself onto the sword.'

Petra giggled and then snorted, 'Julian, you really are quite outrageous.'

Rachel Ingram glanced in the mirror before slipping on her dress. The little grey shift was heavily beaded, with shoe-string straps and a fringed hem. It was the only thing she had, she thought ruefully, that could be considered even vaguely fashionable. She had kept her long hair, where most fashion-conscious women had had their tresses reduced to sleek bangs or Eton crops. She added a pair of earrings and then sat down in front of the dressing table to put on the lightest touch of rouge and lipstick and outline her eyes with a smudge of kohl. She picked up a perfume bottle and sprayed a dash of cologne behind her ears. Staring into the mirror she found herself thinking about Daniel.

The doorbell rang, breaking her train of thought. She waited for a second or two, straining to hear if Molly had answered it. It was barely half-past-seven – surely Julian hadn't arrived early. The bell rang again – it seemed that Molly was elsewhere. Wrapping herself in a silk stole, Rachel hurried out onto the landing in time to see her maid scurrying across the hall to the front door.

She couldn't see who the caller was but heard Molly's side of the conversation.

'You've got a nerve, this isn't the tradesman's entrance, you know.'

Something the visitor said made Molly giggle and then she turned, and seeing Rachel hurried up the stairs. When she reached the landing Molly glanced back over her shoulder into the hall below.

'It's Ted Grey, ma'am. He says he wants to see you. Would you like me to show him in or shall I tell him to go round the back?'

Rachel sighed. Ted Grey was an opportunist – she wondered what it was he wanted.

'Show him into the sitting-room, Molly. I'll be done presently.'

'Right you are, ma'am. Would you like me to bring the sherry?'

Rachel smiled, imagining Ted Grey's great paw wrapped around a sherry glass. 'No, thank you, Molly. I doubt very much this is a social call, and I'm certain Mr Grey is more a beer man.'

Molly nodded. 'By the look of him he's already had one or two of those.'

By the time Rachel got downstairs Ted Grey had removed his cap and made himself at home in the sitting room, sprawled out in one of the large armchairs by the French windows. When Rachel walked in he got to his feet hastily.

'Good evening, Mr Grey. How nice of you to drop by again. How may I help you?'

To her surprise Ted Grey grinned. There was something about him that was slightly unnerving and Rachel wondered for a second if she had been wise to send Molly back to the kitchen.

'Evening, Mrs Ingram,' he said in a low voice. 'Nice of you to see me. I've come to talk about young Daniel.'

Rachel felt a ripple of apprehension. His tone was conspiratorial.

'I see,' she said briskly. 'Well, I have no complaints about his work. I am extremely pleased with what he has done with the garden.'

Ted Grey stepped closer. 'And what about what he's been doing in the house?' he said with a leer.

Rachel stiffened. She could smell beer on his breath. His dark eyes were bright with drink and lust. What perturbed her too was that she couldn't believe Daniel would have told Ted Grey about their relationship.

'What has Daniel said?' she said as evenly as she could.

Ted snorted. 'Him? He's told me nothing at all, tight-lipped little bugger, but there's been talk and when I saw you with him tonight I knew the rumours was right.' He stepped closer. 'If I'd had an idea that was the sort of labour you had in mind, Mrs Ingram, I'd not have sent him over here.' He lifted a hand and touched her cheek. 'I'd never knowingly send a boy to do a man's job.'

Rachel was so stunned that she was rooted to the spot. Ted Grey's hand lingered for a second on the curve of her cheek before dropping away.

'I think,' said Rachel unsteadily, 'that you had better leave, Mr Grey. I can see you have been drinking, so we'll put your impertinence down to beer and say no more about this. Please go now, before you cross the border from merely impertinent to downright rude.'

To her horror, Ted laughed. 'You're all the same you women,

tell a man no when you really mean yes. You society types are always worst – have to hold on to your dignity, don't you? After all, it would never do to admit you like a bit of rough, would it? We must be a real treat for you after all those poncy chinless wonders. You don't have to worry, lady, your secret is safe with me.'

As he spoke he lunged forward and crushed her in his arms, forcing his lips against hers. Rachel gasped, almost unable to believe what was happening. Ted's hand lifted to cup her breasts, his thick fingers pawing her tender flesh. Desperately Rachel struggled to push him away. His leg slipped between hers, while his mouth gnawed and sucked at her lips, demanding entry.

Finally Rachel found the strength to jerk away from him.

'How dare you!' she hissed, straightening her dress, her eyes bright with fury. 'How dare you? Get out of my house this instant—'

Ted grinned and wiped the back of hand across his mouth. 'Say what you like, I know your type. People in the village know what sort of woman you are – or if they don't, they very soon will do.'

Rachel felt her stomach contract. 'What do you mean?' she said unsteadily. 'If this is some feeble attempt at blackmail, Mr Grey, you have chosen the wrong woman. I really don't care what people think of me.'

Ted shrugged. 'So you say, but I was just saying that Carfax is a small place, rumours spread real fast.' His eyes moved down slowly over her body. 'And look at you, all breathless and hot. You don't have to tell me how you like it – I know. If you put up a bit of struggle you can convince yourself I took what yer didn't want to give, but we both know it would be a lie. I think you're a wench who needs a man with a bit of backbone, not some bloody boy. I could slip my tongue up inside that little fanny of yours and lick you till you begged me for mercy. I could make you hum, Mrs Ingram – and as for this,' he cupped the intimidating bulge in the front of his breeches with both hands, 'let me tell you, lady, this is a treasure well worth struggling for.'

Rachel ran her fingers over her hair, her eyes firmly fixed on Ted Grey's sweating red face.

'Get out,' she hissed. 'Or I will get the constable onto you.'

Ted snorted. 'And what are you going to tell him? That you're fucking my step-son senseless and got shirty when I suggested you share a bit of the same with old Ted?' He grinned. 'If he turns up on my doorstep, I'll tell him myself.' Ted picked up his cap from the arm of the chair. 'I'll show myself out, and if you reconsider my offer, let me know. I'd be only too happy to oblige you—'

After he left, Rachel stood in the middle of her sitting room, trembling.

Molly opened the door. 'Are you all right, Mrs Ingram?' she said.

Rachel took a deep breath and nodded. 'I'm fine, thank you, Molly. I'm just going upstairs to finish getting ready. Please let me know when Mr Morton arrives.' Without meeting the maid's eye she hurried upstairs, her heart thumping wildly in her chest.

Chapter 5

When Julian Morton arrived at Albion he was rather surprised to find that Rachel wasn't ready, and even more surprised by her appearance when she finally descended the stairs. Although she looked quite delightful she had the most peculiar look in her eyes that he could only describe as haunted. She apologised profusely for her tardiness.

'Would you like a drink before we leave?'

Julian smiled. 'Why not?' He paused. 'You look as if you could do with one. Is everything all right?'

Rachel smiled but he sensed the good humour was painted on.

'Yes, thank you. I've just had rather a busy day.' Her voice faltered slightly, and he noticed that her hands were shaking as she poured them both a large brandy.

Julian settled himself down in an armchair. 'Are you sure? If you're feeling unwell we could easily arrange to dine another evening.'

Rachel held up a hand to silence him. 'Really, Julian,' she said more forcefully, 'I'm fine. I'll just get my shawl and your sister's painting and then we can be off.' As she was about to hand him the glass she stopped and looked up at him. Her eyes were bright with unshed tears. 'Actually I have just had the most awful run-in with a chap from the village. He seemed to think I might—' she paused, as if she was aware that she was crossing some unmarked boundary of good form.

'Yes?' Julian encouraged, his curiosity aroused.

Rachel took a deep breath and then laughed. 'He seemed

71

to think I might be in the market for a romantic liaison. It was all rather unfortunate and left me a little shaken up.'

'I see,' Julian said, in a tone he hoped would make her continue. He was intrigued to find out who else might consider Rachel Ingram a good proposition.

'And to make matters worse,' Rachel continued unsteadily, 'he concluded his rather crude proposition by making a lunge at me.'

Julian suppressed a smile and gathered his face up into a more appropriate mask of outrage. 'The bounder. No wonder you look so pale. I hope you put him in his place?'

Rachel sighed and took a long pull on her brandy. 'Actually, I threatened him with the constable.'

'Bravo,' said Julian. 'I'm pleased to hear it. Would you like me to have a word with him?'

Rachel coloured. 'I don't think so, though thank you for offering. I'm sure the matter is at an end. Now if you'll excuse me, please make yourself at home while I get my things and then we can be off.'

Julian got to his feet. 'Of course.'

He watched Rachel leaving and took a sip from his glass. Her face was slightly flushed, she looked hot and excited. Julian couldn't help wonder who her unwelcome beau had been. He could easily see why such a man might risk taking a grab at Mrs Ingram – the prize would certainly be worth the effort, but then again, he suspected she might respond better to a more considered approach.

When Rachel returned, carrying her stole, he hurried to help her on with it. Standing so close behind her he could smell her perfume and catch a shadowy glimpse of her breasts where they nestled under her dress. He shivered, and then very gently put his arms around her. He felt her stiffen, but persisted.

'Please don't think me forward, my dear, but you look as if you could do with a little comfort.' He spoke in an undertone. 'You're probably in shock.' He felt her tension easing and

72

turned her round, so that her head rested on his shoulder. 'There, there, my dear. It must have been quite awful for you.'

As she allowed him to draw her closer he felt the delicate press of her nipples hardening against his chest. Gently, before Rachel had time to think or protest, he tipped her chin up towards him and very softly kissed her on the lips.

She shivered and pulled back slightly. 'I'm not sure this is a very good idea,' she said thickly.

Julian smiled. 'Nonsense, just trust me.' He caught hold of her hand. 'Let's finish off this brandy, go to Medsham and have a wonderful supper, give Petra her painting and try to put this nasty experience behind you.'

Rachel smiled and stepped willingly into his arms. 'And are you planning to comfort me again?'

Julian pulled her close and brushed her lips with his. 'Why, my dear Mrs Ingram, you can depend on it.'

Despite Julian's chaste little kiss, Rachel did not arrive at Medsham with any intention of allowing herself to be seduced. Medsham turned out to be a glorious folly whose grand proportions and stunning silhouette belied the rather dilapidated interior.

They were greeted at the door by Julian's sister, Petra and her friend, an attractive little creature called Izzy. Rachel was immediately aware that Izzy and Petra were far closer than most friends. Petra embraced Rachel warmly and handed her a champagne cocktail from the tray being carried by the butler.

'Do come in to the sitting room and tell me all about yourself,' she said, taking a long pull on her glass. 'Julian tells me you are an artist.'

Julian took the wrapped canvas from Rachel and handed it to her. 'Indeed she is. Happy Birthday, Petra.'

Rachel smiled. 'You'll be able to judge for yourself. It's one of mine.'

Petra sat down on a threadbare *chaise longue* and ripped off the paper. She looked first at the canvas and then back up at Rachel and Julian who were still standing in the centre of the room.

'This is quite beautiful,' she paused as she pulled the wrapping away. 'I recognise the . . .' Petra stopped again, some kind of revelation dawning. 'My God, I've got a book with a picture very similar to this in it. You're not *the* R. Ingram, the illustrator?'

Rachel nodded.

Petra got to her feet and held the canvas at arm's length. 'You really should have told me, Julian. Rachel is famous.'

Julian wrapped his arm casually around Rachel's shoulders. 'I think she likes it.'

Petra laughed. 'Like it? I absolutely adore it.'

'Let me look,' said Izzy. The little blonde girl wriggled under Petra's outstretched arms to look at the painting, and as she did, to Rachel's complete surprise Petra kissed the girl full on the lips. Izzy giggled and responded by kissing her back. It was so unexpected that Rachel felt her stomach tighten.

Glancing up at Rachel, Petra continued, 'It's quite the loveliest thing I've ever been given. I think this calls for more champagne.'

Rachel didn't resist as the butler refilled her glass, and as she sat down on the sofa Julian sat down alongside her. Izzy and Petra were still looking at the painting. Petra slipped her arm around Izzy's waist as they admired it. Rachel found the show of affection between the two women oddly disturbing.

Julian pressed a single kiss to Rachel's shoulder. 'I knew she would appreciate it.'

Rachel turned to stare at him. 'I thought Petra was here as a chaperone.'

Julian laughed. 'Who, Petra? Good lord, no, whatever gave you that idea? She has the morals of an alley cat. Now, would you like to go out on the terrace or would you prefer it if we stayed in here and watched these two get terribly drunk and paw each other?'

Rachel shook her head in disbelief and then smiled. 'I thought when you arrived this evening that you might be a knight in shining armour come to rescue me.'

Julian aped affront. 'Me? Most certainly not. Oh no, most definitely not. I'm a charmer and a rake – a hedonist of the first water. I'm purely intent on seduction and fornication. I was rather hoping you might be a kindred spirit.'

Rachel giggled. 'What on earth made you think that?'

Julian shrugged. 'Call it a hunch. Let's go outside and look at the terrace.'

Arm in arm they walked out through the French windows into a beautiful, overgrown garden. Below, beyond rolling fields and the dunes, was the sea. The view was quite astonishing.

'It's so beautiful here,' Rachel said in delight, as she rested against the balustrade that divided the terrace from the garden beyond.

Julian groaned. 'Oh damn, I wish you hadn't noticed. I find it all rather too bucolic for my taste. Give me streets and rooftops any day.'

'But I thought you'd just moved here?'

Julian, who was standing behind her, moved a little closer and rested his hands on the top of the wall, one either side of hers, effectively pinning her in his arms.

'Inheritance can be a terribly cruel business, my dear. Medsham Hall is held in trust for my family and I, unfortunately, was the next in line.' He brushed his lips against her neck. 'My, my, but you do smell wonderful. Can't I persuade you to play with me?'

Rachel turned round so that their faces were barely more than an inch apart.

'Play with you? Really Julian, I don't know what you mean. I am a respectable widow,' she said in a firm but not altogether serious tone. Julian Morton's attentions were desperately flattering and he was very good-looking. His humorous attempts at seduction were the perfect antidote to Ted Grey's frantic pawings.

'Oh,' he said with mock dejection and kissed her gently. 'Go on, please say you'll play with me.'

'What had you got in mind?'

Julian grinned triumphantly. 'Whatever you like. What do you fancy? I could be the willing slave to a cruel unfeeling mistress or you could be a nymph and I could chase you through the garden, completely captivated by your beauty.'

Rachel found it impossible to suppress a gale of laughter. 'Are you serious?'

'Never more so, come though,' he said, catching hold of her wrists, 'these are not the kind of decisions easily made on an empty stomach. Let's go inside and eat and play your seduction over a good bottle of vintage claret. I'm sure Petra has some wonderful ideas.'

There was an awful lot of good wine served with dinner – and Rachel found herself mellowing as the night progressed. Petra and Julian were boisterous hosts, and the wine flowed like water, but despite the good-natured laughter, Rachel could sense a strange tension growing around the table. Julian's joking remarks about seduction gradually seemed to be changing from fantasy into a distinct possibility.

'Bondage,' said Petra, finishing another glass of wine as everyone else finished their dessert. 'I absolutely adore it, all that wonderful tooled leather and the crack of the whip. Simply delicious.'

Rachel, who until that point had remained fairly unforthcoming, preferring to listen to her hosts, said. 'My husband liked bondage.'

Julian, eyes alight, turned towards her. 'Really? How enchanting. But a more important point is, did you enjoy it?'

Rachel shook her head. 'Not really. André was a wonderful man in some ways, but he was very overbearing. I could never—' she stopped, realising the rest of the table had turned to listen to what she had to say. She reddened, wishing she had had a little less to drink. 'I found it impossible.'

Julian grinned and clapped his hands. 'That's it then, I

shall teach you the joys of submission.'

Rachel felt her colour draining. 'I really don't think—' she began.

Julian lifted a hand to silence her. 'Enough, enough, I insist, but first I must ask you some pertinent questions. Do you find me attractive?'

Rachel nodded, her discomfort balanced by the odd sense of mischief that permeated the dining room.

'Good, and presuming we were properly introduced, say in London at Fenleys, over champagne cocktails and a boring little finger buffet, would you – if we began to see each other regularly – eventually sleep with me?'

Rachel stared at him in astonishment. This was a style of truth and consequences she had never envisaged playing with anyone.

Emboldened by drink she nodded. 'Probably, eventually, yes.'

Julian leapt up from the table and clapped his hands with delight. 'Bravo. Then all we are doing is accelerating that process. Now come along. I really can't wait to begin.'

Rachel stared at Petra. 'Is he serious?'

Petra smiled and lifted her glass to her lips. 'Never more so.'

In the doorway Julian beckoned to Rachel. 'I said come along.'

Rachel got to her feet. 'This is complete and utter madness.'

As she reached his side Julian pulled her to him and kissed her, hard. 'No, no, not complete and utter madness, Rachel darling,' he whispered, 'this is divine madness.'

Grabbing hold of her wrists, he led her upstairs. What had seemed like a rather silly, if somewhat dangerous, game downstairs was quickly turning into something else. At the door to his bedroom, Rachel pulled back.

'Julian,' she said thickly. 'I'm really not sure that I want to do this.'

He frowned and lifted a finger to trace the outline of her

77

breasts where the thin material of her evening dress clung to them.

'Please don't disappoint me or yourself,' he murmured. 'I can show you so many wonderful things if only you will let me.' He moved closer still and unfastened the button at the neck of her dress. With alarming ease he slid the dress down over her shoulders, his lips working all the time along her throat and collarbones. Rachel – in spite of her fears – felt her body responding.

How like André, so commanding and perfectly in control. She shuddered – Julian Morton was nothing like André, and she knew from making love with Daniel that men didn't necessarily have to have the upper hand. She stared at Julian and wondered if, after so many years of marriage, given a situation where the man took control, she had been programmed to respond without thinking. It was a disturbing thought.

Julian pushed the fabric lower, taking with it the straps of her camisole top. With a gentle touch he cupped her firm breasts and lifted first one and then the other to his lips. He planted a tiny, almost innocent kiss to each hard peak. Despite her fears Rachel felt a wave of heat rise low in her belly.

'My God,' he purred, 'you are so lovely.' As he spoke he tugged her dress down over her waist and hips, leaving the camisole in a silken cummerbund around her narrow waist. Rachel's first instinct was to try to cover herself – despite the fact that her body was baying for satisfaction she was far from wanton.

'Julian, please,' she stammered. Julian looked up at her as he guided the dress down over her thighs.

'Oh come, come now, my dear,' he whispered. 'We both know that this is what you want. I can see it in your eyes.'

Rachel stiffened as he settled on his knees and pressed his face to the outside of her white silk knickers. She looked up, avoiding his intense dark eyes and then gasped as he nuzzled at her, his face working over the mound of her quim. His breath warmed her skin, making her gasp. A second later his lips closed in a kiss, tongue darting out to moisten the thin material.

Breathlessly she struggled to retain some shred of control but knew it was impossible.

Julian Morton could hardly believe his luck – Rachel was everything he could possibly have imagined and more. Slowly, he slid her knickers down, exposing the ripe, full lips of her sex. At every stage of his rather theatrical seduction he wondered if she would call a halt and back away, but it seemed he had underestimated her. He wondered if she was naturally submissive.

With a growing sense of confidence, his tongue parted the heavy, outer lips to find the prize within. Her clitoris was like a tiny, plump olive. Lapping back and forth across the engorged ridge, he was delighted to feel her shudder, while below his fingers made their way into the tight, wet confines of her body. She tasted and smelt divine. Her pussy was already slick with gossamer threads of excitement. Slowly he pulled away and got to his feet. Her eyes had darkened to deep, crystal pools. Her state of undress made him shiver with anticipation. Her breasts were naked, though the camisole top encircled her waist. She still had on her stockings, held up by little garters, and high button shoes – God, the woman was as tempting as a banquet. His mouth began to water as he led her wordlessly over to the end of the four-poster bed that dominated the centre of the room.

She stood and watched him with those bright eyes whilst he pulled two ties out of the wardrobe. Catching hold of her wrists he bound first one and then the other to the uprights of the foot of the bed. He longed to ask her about previous lovers – what other men had been privileged enough to breach those exquisite curves?

Only when she was secured did he sense a tiny ripple of fear in her body. Picking up two more ties he busied himself with her ankles – it took him less than five minutes to render her helpless, totally at his mercy. As he stepped back, he could see a delicate flush rising on her skin, see the excited, short breaths making her shoulders lift and knew without a doubt she had been on this exquisite journey before.

He ran his hands down over her breasts. Her nipples were as hard as tiny gems.

'Well, Rachel,' he purred, 'it seems you are willing to play after all.'

She glanced back at him over her shoulder. Her face was pale, the haunted expression he had seen early in the evening had returned.

'I'm afraid,' she said in a tiny voice.

Julian smiled. 'No need, my dear. I can guarantee your pleasure – and mine. Did your husband like to tie you up?'

Rachel shivered and nodded.

Julian smiled and gently kissed her shoulders. 'And I gather from your expression that it gave you very little pleasure?' The idea of some faceless brute of a husband taking her against her will, tying her up and seducing her added another layer to Julian's fantasy. Slowly, he crossed the room and picked up a cane carpet beater that had taken his fancy when he had first arrived at Medsham. 'Well, my dear, don't worry, tonight you are in the hands of a *maestro*. Now, there was something else – ah yes.'

He took a handkerchief from the dressing table and blindfolded her. He could feel the tremors of fear and expectation as he tightened the knot. A bead of sweat had lifted on her top lip. Julian grinned, weighed the beater thoughtfully in one hand and then with a flourish brought it down across Rachel's naked buttocks.

To his delight she shrieked, flexing against the ties. Her whole body seemed to be suffused with the red hot flash of pain. He struck again, for the first time realising that he could see her reflection in the dressing table mirror. She looked exquisite straining against the bed posts. With his own excitement building, Julian brought the beater down again. He was almost mesmerised by the way her pert breasts thrust forward as the sensation exploded through her. My God she is stunning, he thought, what a waste that something so beautiful should be squandered on the hired help.

His hands trembled, pleasure building like a head of steam in his belly. As he drew back the carpet beater his heart was racing. Julian grinned savagely and brought the beater down again, making Rachel scream out, the muscles in her backside tightened like bow strings while a cloud of colour was spread up over her buttocks and back. He hit her again.

She moaned, taking her body weight on her arms as she braced herself for the next blow. He closed his eyes, fighting the desire to abandon the beating and take her there and then. Another stroke, another cry, and her body writhed and twisted against the restraints. She looked so ripe, so desirable. It was no good, Julian couldn't wait any longer. Throwing the carpet beater to the floor he unbuttoned his flies and encircled her waist with one arm, pulling her back towards him.

Her body was hot and gloriously compliant. As his fingers dipped into her sex he couldn't suppress a gasp of pure delight. Rachel was so wet that her juices were trickling out onto her thighs. As he circled her clitoris he could almost see the ripples of pleasure spiralling out from under his fingertips.

Helpless to resist him, Rachel moaned under his caresses. Her breasts were flushed, nipples hard. He rolled and twisted them back and forth under his fingertips, making her sob with pure delight.

'You look glorious,' he purred into her ear. 'So lovely. But perhaps you've had enough, perhaps you'd like me to stop?'

Rachel shuddered, desperately pressing herself back against his hands and body. 'No, please,' she hissed, 'please don't stop – fuck me, do it now – please . . .'

Julian laughed. 'Oh how nicely you beg and what a dirty little mouth you have there, Mrs Ingram.'

He shivered as he guided his cock into that glorious sopping well between her thighs and, with a single thrust, drove it home.

She mewled, surging back against him. Deep inside he felt her sex tighten around him like a fist. His fingers slid back to stroke the pleasure bud that nestled between the outer lips of her quim. As he brushed the sensitive hood she let out a little throaty gasp and forced herself further onto his cock. Her hips began to move back and forth, working with him, like liquid silk.

It seemed as if he could sense this was the moment when she finally abandoned all pretence of control and gave herself to him. On and on they thrust, Julian aware that her excitement matched his measure for measure. It was all he could do to hold back the waves of pleasure that broke over him, and then suddenly he felt her stiffen. He could almost see the orgasm rising up inside her like a flood tide. Unable to control himself any longer Julian plunged over the precipice, letting sensation and pleasure sweep him away into a dark moonlight sea.

In the kitchen at Albion House, Molly was folding the last of the linen when she heard a knock at the kitchen door. A second later, before she had chance to answer it, it swung open and Ted Grey was framed in the opening. He grinned and held out a bottle towards her.

'You're working late, gal,' he said. 'Thought you might like a little something to wet your whistle.' He smiled wolfishly.

Molly grinned. 'You made me jump, I thought you were long gone,' she said.

Ted pulled out a chair and opened the bottle while she got two glasses from the cupboard. He'd have to go slowly. Molly was young and he had no desire to frighten her off.

After his summary dismissal by Rachel Ingram he had gone back to the Cutter for a few pints and as he had stood by the bar, found that his mind returning again and again to Albion house. He had hoped that Rachel Ingram might be back home by now but from a quick look round the house he had discovered only Molly. He'd watched her for a while before knocking, timing his entry so that her work was done. Peering through the kitchen window his pulse had quickened as he watched her moving about unselfconsciously, stretching and bending, her full breasts straining against her uniform.

Molly glanced at the pile of linen she had ironed and stacked neatly on the kitchen table.

'I really ought to put these away,' she said.

Ted pulled out the chair beside him and patted it invitingly. 'Plenty of time for that afterwards,' he said, handing her a full glass.

Molly took a long pull on her beer and then looked at him from under lowered eyelids, a hint of mischief playing on her full lips.

'After what?' she said, ignoring the chair and sitting on the table facing him.

Ted grinned. Maybe this wasn't going to be as difficult as he imagined. He reached up and began to unfasten the buttons on the front of her dress. As each one gave it revealed a little more plump pink flesh.

'What do you think?' he said thickly.

Molly giggled and skittered away from him. Posing provocatively against the range she began to undo the buttons herself, her eyes never leaving Ted's face.

'Oh, I know exactly what you're after, Ted Grey,' she said in a low, earthy voice. 'I knew from the first time you came over here. Mrs Weirs the housekeeper warned me about you. And I know if you could you'd have fucked Rachel Ingram, but you can't so you came back for me.'

Ted felt an odd contraction in his guts, and wondered if his motives were always so obvious.

Molly opened her dress, exposing the heavy curve of her breast. They were as plump as cottage loaves, with dark, juicy nipples jutting towards him. He felt his jaw drop. She traced one hardening peak with her finger.

'What are you staring at, Ted? Don't tell me you don't know what to do with a willing woman. We're not all like Rachel Ingram, you know. Why don't you come over here? You told me about older men – how long is it since you've fucked a younger woman?' she said slyly. She lifted up her skirt, revealing an acre of plump thigh. 'Or are you one of them men who just likes to look?'

Ted licked his lips, got to his feet, and pushed the chair away, his eyes firmly fixed on Molly's ripe body.

Rachel opened her eyes and realised with astonishment that she was curled up alongside Julian Morton in his double bed. She blinked, unable to remember being untied, unable to remember sliding in under the sheets with her host and talented seducer. It would be easy to blame the wine she had had with dinner to explain her behaviour – it had certainly lowered her inhibitions – but the truth of the matter was she had enjoyed Julian's virtuoso performance. Her whole body still glowed with a lingering sense of satisfaction. She lay back amongst the snowstorm of pillows and stared up at the ornate ceiling.

What on earth had happened to her? Alongside a thread of guilt and self-consciousness was the knowledge that she had relished everything that had happened and was excited by the sense of abandonment that Julian had unleashed in her.

Her movements disturbed Julian. He rolled over and slid an arm under her shoulders. Pulling her closer, he nuzzled tenderly at her breasts. Without looking up, he said, 'Well, my dear. Did you enjoy our little game?'

Rachel blushed furiously as his lips closed around one of her nipples. 'Yes and no,' she said in a low voice.

Julian pulled away and grinned. 'How very like a woman.' He hauled himself up onto one elbow so that he was looking down at her. It gave Rachel a chance to study him. His chest was broad, with a sprinkling of hair in the valley between his nipples, a dark line of curls leading down beneath the sheets.

The soft light flattered his hawkish features making him look like a pirate or a highwayman.

He lifted a finger to trace the curve of her lips. 'Tell me that I gave you exactly what you wanted.'

Rachel shivered and then smiled. 'Oh, you did, what worries me is that I didn't realise that that *was* what I wanted.' She pulled the sheet up over her chest. 'This is happening far too fast.'

Julian grimaced. 'Oh, please don't say that. It was glorious – stunning. And,' he added mischievously, 'something I'd like very much to try again – this time without the carpet beater. Unless, of course, you prefer it that way?' As he spoke he caught hold of one of her hands and guided it beneath the bedclothes. Her fingers brushed his cock which was as rigid as a tent pole. He guided her fingers around it.

'See what you've done to me,' he said with a lazy grin. 'My firm friend is equally as enthusiastic about meeting you. He doesn't think this is too fast at all. In fact,' Julian continued, encouraging her to slide her hand up and down along the length of his shaft, 'he thinks you aren't moving fast enough.'

Rachel shook her head in disbelief. 'Julian, stop it! I hardly know anything about you, I'm stunned to find myself in bed with you . . .' Her voice faded.

Julian pouted. 'Oh Rachel, please don't tell me it was all a terrible mistake and that you wish you'd never set eyes on me. I'd be terrible hurt – particularly whilst you've got my cock in your hand.'

Rachel laughed – it was impossible not to. 'No, no that's not what I was going to say. I'm just not sure that I'm ready for this. I am not this sort of woman. I do not make a habit of leaping into bed with virtual strangers.'

Julian groaned and returned his attention to her nipples, while his hand slithered down over her thighs. She knew she was still wet, and resisted the temptation to open her legs and let him begin again. He looked up at her and frowned.

'Oh no? Regrets? A conscience suddenly rearing its

unwelcome little head?' His hand moved back over hers and he encouraged her again, by example, to slide her fingers up and down his throbbing shaft. 'You really are a heartless creature. I know, how about if we consider this whole episode as a kind of philanthropic act of charity, consider it as easing an old man's pain.'

His fingers eased back between her thighs, his thumb brushed her clitoris, rekindling the embers of the fire he had lit earlier. She fought to resist the feelings but found it impossible. Slowly, her legs opened under his busy, insistent fingers.

Julian grinned. 'Besides, I thought all you Bohemian artist types were wanton, carried along by the passion of the muse from lover to lover, exploring human nature at its raw animal roots. Well, all the ones I've met have always been like that.'

Rachel smiled. If only he had stopped talking she would have been tempted to succumb. Instead she rolled away from him gently. 'Maybe you've just been lucky. Until recently I'd only ever made love with my husband.' Julian stared at her. It seemed that he was looking into her soul. 'Though since he died,' she said, not quite meeting his eyes, 'I have met someone else.'

'Lucky chap. Anyone I know?'

Rachel reddened. 'No,' she said emphatically. Julian was the last person she wanted to find out about Daniel.

Julian sighed and rolled over onto his back. 'I'm not sure whether to be terribly impressed or terribly disappointed. I thought you were a one of those deliciously fast women my friends warned me about.'

Rachel glared at him, amusement mixed with genuine hurt. 'How dare you!'

Julian laughed. 'Don't be so stuffy. Under the circumstances it seemed rather appropriate. Tell me about your husband, or is it crass and unfeeling of me to ask?'

Rachel shook her head, though she wasn't altogether certain the gesture reflected her true feelings. 'No, it's not crass, but in a funny way it all seems such a long time ago now, though he's only been dead for eighteen months. André was a great deal older than me. And I suppose he probably was part of the fast set.' She paused, seeing her marriage briefly through the eyes of experience. 'I'm sure he married me for some rather dark sexual motives. I was barely more than a child and extremely innocent. My father was a clerk in André's publishing house. I'd begun to draw and paint quite competently by then and somehow André found out about it and I was invited to bring in some of my work for him to look at. Looking back I realise that he practically bought me. We were married within six months.' She paused and looked up at Julian. 'And I now realise that, for many years, André kept up his various liaisons with mistresses and street walkers—' she stopped, feeling a flurry of emotions that made her voice tremble.

Julian was staring at her. 'And what about with you?'

Rachel laughed to disguise her pain and the welter of memories that threatened to bubble up and drown her. 'I'm under no illusions, I may have been his wife, and I'm certain he loved me in his own way, but really I was just a talented pet bird kept in a gilded cage, taught to perform for my master's pleasure.'

Julian wriggled away from her, pulled on a dressing gown and clambered out of bed. 'Would you care for some tea?' he said, padding across the floor.

Rachel nodded incredulously. He seemed completely unconcerned that she had been talking from the heart. He tugged at the bell-pull beside the dressing table.

'Good.'

Rachel struggled to retain some sense of composure. 'So this—' she lifted her hands to encompass the room and the events that had taken place in it, '—is completely out of character for me. I'm worried that I've gone too far too fast.'

Julian grinned at her over his shoulder. 'Don't worry, it's our little secret. I won't tell anyone, except perhaps Petra and

Izzy and a few of my closest friends. Now, would you care to stay the night or would you prefer it if we had some tea and I drove you back to Albion?'

Rachel hesitated for just long enough for Julian to add, 'Of course, whatever your decision we have time to make love before you leave, or alternatively, if you would like to stay, before I show you to the guest room.'

Rachel laughed. 'Julian, is there any chance we can begin this friendship again from scratch? I really do think it's moving too fast.'

He laughed. 'You do? What a shame. Of course, if that's what you want. What do you say that I call on you tomorrow morning to discuss the jetty? Or would you prefer me to write and introduce myself?'

Rachel smiled.

Julian picked up his shirt from the floor. 'You might like to slip this on before the butler arrives. I'm not sure what happened to your camisole.'

Rachel looked down – it was still bundled in a warm, moist band around her waist.

Julian crept back into bed beside her and gently pulled the shirt over her shoulders.

'You know you really are quite, quite beautiful,' he whispered, stroking her breasts beneath the soft cotton. The shirt smelt of him, a soft, compelling mix of masculine sweat and cologne. Rachel shivered and did not resist as he pulled her closer. His lips brushed hers, his hand sliding back under the sheets to cup her sex.

'Say you'll stay tonight, Rachel. We'll forget about moving to the guest bedroom,' he murmured. 'And I have to tell you that not only am I terribly glad that we moved fast, but I promise that we can begin all over again in the morning – a clean slate.'

It was too compelling an offer to resist. Gently, Julian pulled her down in the bed, his fingers working their magic in the soft folds of her quim.

'What about the butler?' she whispered as she felt the brush of his cock against her thigh.

Julian snorted as he rolled on top of her. 'He's not my type.'

Chapter 6

Rachel was relieved when Julian suggested he drive her back to Albion before breakfast – she wasn't certain that she had the front to sit at the table with Petra and Izzy. The butler had arrived a few minutes after she and Julian began to make love and had been dispatched, through the closed door, with instructions to return an hour later with tea and toast. By the time he reappeared both Julian and Rachel were reasonably respectable, if a little breathless.

The sun was just rising as Julian guided his car onto the causeway that led across to Albion. They had driven in silence from Medsham. Now, as Albion appeared amidst a swirl of early morning mist, Julian turned towards her.

'Were you being serious when you said you would like us to begin again?'

Rachel nodded. 'Yes, last night was really far too much, far too soon.'

Julian pulled a face. 'Oh, Rachel, it seems such a terrible waste. Does this mean you will invite me to tea and we'll have to sit and make cow eyes at each other over the cucumber sandwiches?'

Rachel suppressed a smile and held her face rigid. 'Of course, Julian, and after a decent period of time you may take me to church, local dances and for long, bracing walks along the dunes.'

Julian growled. 'I'd much rather throw you down in the sand and roger you senseless. Though I suppose that is out of the question now, until I get to know you better?' He moved closer. The seam of humour did little to disguise his want for her. He looked so desirable in the new daylight, wearing the white cotton shirt he had dressed her in earlier. Unbuttoned at the throat, it revealed a sprinkling of dark curls. His hair, shot thought with grey, was unkempt and tousled. Everything about him, including his subtle air of dominance, offered an enticing sexual promise that was hard to resist. His hand settled on her thigh, sliding up to explore the contours of her sex through her evening dress.

Rachel gently removed his hand. 'I'd keep your mind on the road if I were you, the causeway is quite narrow here.'

Julian groaned theatrically. 'And if I am patient and agree to this absurd bargain, how long before I can make love to you again? And what about guarantees? Should I insist on having something in writing? What if I try to be good – and perhaps I ought to warn you I'm damned boring when I'm being civilised – and in the meantime you run off with someone else?'

Rachel laughed at his feigned discomfort but also felt a flurry of desire that surprised her. How, realistically, could she deny herself the pleasure that Julian's body could offer after the events of the night before? She looked across at him and took a deep breath, trying to order her thoughts.

'I'm not saying we can't make love, what I'm saying, I suppose, is that I want to get to know you better, not just fall into bed at the drop of a hat. Last night was completely out of character for me. I'm not . . . I'm not . . .' She stopped, struggling to find a suitable word or expression to describe what she meant.

Julian grinned. 'Rest assured, I do know what you're not, Rachel. Look, it seems as if your hired help is already on his way to work – wanting to make an early start, no doubt. Would you like me to pick him up?'

Rachel reddened in horror as she glanced up and saw Daniel through the windscreen, head down, making his way across the causeway. As the car drew level he looked round and stared into the car. Rachel felt her colour and discomfort intensify. The boy's face was an impassive mask as he touched his hat in salute.

She glanced across at Julian, who was wearing a tight, amused smile.

'It's going to be very hot today,' she stammered. 'Perhaps he thought it would be better if he made an early start.'

Julian nodded. 'Good show. I like a chap who takes his work seriously.'

Rachel wondered if she could detect a hint of sarcasm in his voice.

Under the walls of Albion Julian cut the engine and turned towards her. 'I hope you enjoyed your evening at Medsham. I certainly enjoyed having the pleasure of your company. Perhaps we can do it again some time.'

Rachel glanced behind her. Through the rear window she could see Daniel approaching the house. 'Thank you,' she said quickly, 'I had a lovely time.'

Julian grinned and caught hold of her arm. 'How terribly polite we both sound. I thought the very least I might have expected was a kiss. Or are we already pretending that nothing happened last night?'

Rachel leant forward and brushed her lips with his. The kiss was almost chaste in its brevity. 'I've got no intention of pretending last night didn't happen,' she said in an undertone. 'But please, I really have to get back inside before my gardener arrives. What will he think?'

Julian snorted and pulled her tight against his chest. 'Who cares? What on earth does it matter what he thinks?' he murmured, and kissed her fiercely.

Rachel was torn between surrendering to Julian's kisses and scurrying into the house. Julian tightened his grip on her and pulled her closer still so that she had little choice but to respond. From the corner of her eye she saw Daniel rounding the back of the car and her heart sank.

Extricating herself from Julian's arms she almost leapt from the car and hurried towards the safety of Albion. Just as she got to the front door it swung open. Molly, her housemaid, stepped out onto the stoop.

'Morning, Mrs Ingram,' said Molly, slyly, looking her up and down. 'I thought I heard a car.'

Rachel nodded, afraid to speak and then hurried upstairs to her bedroom. As she reached the landing she turned and looked down into the hall. The girl was staring up at her with a knowing grin on her face.

'Please don't disturb me.'

Molly nodded and hurried back into the shadows as if she was afraid Rachel might rebuke her.

In her bedroom Rachel pulled off her clothes and dragged on a robe, struggling to keep control of her thoughts. She felt terrible that Daniel had seen her coming home with Julian. She glanced at her reflection in the mirror – she even looked guilty. Her whole body smelt of Julian, her hair, her clothes, even her mouth still held the lingering imprint of his kisses. She went into the bathroom, hoping Molly had had enough sense to keep the boiler going, and ran herself a bath. She wanted to be clean and have had a few hours sleep before she came face to face with Daniel.

The warm water washed the remnants of Julian's lovemaking from her body but it wasn't so easy to wipe them from her mind. Her buttocks still ached from the kiss of the carpet beater, and every time she closed her eyes she could hear the swish of it cutting through the still air in Julian's bedroom. Worse still, the images combined in a stunning amalgam with the sensations of Julian's hands on her body and the dark compelling rhythm of his cock as he plunged into her again and again. The images rekindled an ache so fierce that Rachel was almost tempted to go and find Daniel. His name forming in her head brought her, painfully, back to reality.

Pulling the curtains closed, she climbed into bed and let sleep claim her. Her dreams were full of turbulent erotic images. First there was Julian and then Daniel, and then a glorious combination of both men, each one struggling to take her further and further out into the realms of pure pleasure. Just at the moment when she thought her fantasy might take her to the point of no return her mind was flooded with images of Ted Grey, lunging towards her, lips slack and wet as his hands lifted to her breasts. She shuddered.

Half awake and half asleep she slid her hands down between her legs, her fingers desperately seeking relief, brushing the little bud that would bring her to orgasm. With one hand stroking her pert nipples, her other circled her clitoris. It was no more than a few seconds before she tumbled into the spiral dance that led to release and, with her passion spent, she finally fell into a deep dreamless void.

Julian Morton picked up his newspaper and stretched sleepily whilst the butler cleared away the breakfast things. In daylight the dining room looked dilapidated. Julian sniffed and tried to ignore the air of genteel decay. It was barely eight o'clock – early by his standards – and Petra and Izzy were no doubt still fast asleep. He wondered fleetingly if Petra might be willing to lend him Izzy for a little early morning entertainment. His encounter with Rachel Ingram, deeply satisfying though it had been, had left him hungry for more. What a shame she had insisted on going back to Albion. What a day they could have had together.

He allowed his imagination to take flight. If only she had stayed. Her body was everything he had anticipated, firm, warm, lithe – and far more willing than he had ever dreamed it would be. He would, of course, respect her wish to get to know him better – in fact he was banking on doing just that.

He smiled, remembering the look in her eyes and the way her body had responded to his with such delicious abandon. She might say she wanted them to begin again and get to know him each other better, but surely she would find it difficult now that they had made love to deny him, or herself, the pleasure they had experienced? She was a woman whose desires obviously bubbled close to the surface and needed to be harnessed by a stronger, older man. And he hoped, rather like Pandora's box, that once her desires had been unleashed, she would find it hard to get them back under control.

'Excuse me, Mr Morton,' said the butler, breaking his train of thought. 'There is a Mr Grey to see you. Would you like me to show him in?'

Julian looked up. 'Grey?'

His butler nodded, his features revealing a modicum of disdain. 'I believe he is a local tradesman, sir. He said something about you requiring someone to work on the house?'

Comprehension dawned. 'Ah yes, Mrs Ingram recommended him. Would you show him into the study?'

When Julian first saw Ted Grey he knew instinctively the man was a rogue. Although the odd job man stood respectfully to attention in the middle of the study, clutching his cap in a show of deference, Julian was not fooled. The man's dark brown eyes moved busily round the shadowy room absorbing every detail.

'Good morning, Mr Grey, how very good of you to come so quickly. Would you care to take a seat?'

Ted Grey looked him up and down. 'By the look of this place I didn't get here soon enough.'

Julian nodded grimly. 'I'm afraid my great-uncle, the late Sir Charles, did rather let the place go.'

Ted snorted. 'I'd say he did. Guttering's gone. Plaster's shot, and the roof—'

Julian sighed. 'I know. I was hoping you might be persuaded to take on the job of trying to get it round?'

Ted Grey fixed him with his bright, feral eyes. 'You did, did you?' he sniffed. 'My terms would be that you pay me as I go – in cash. I've a feeling that you've got champagne tastes, Mr Morton, and a bread-and-butter income.'

Julian laughed. 'You're very impertinent for a jobbing builder, Mr Grey.'

Ted snorted. 'Maybe so, but I've seen your sort before, Mr Morton. Best if we lay our cards on the table, wouldn't you say? If you had the money to get Medsham fixed properly you'd not consider taking on the likes of me to do the work.'

Julian rang the bell that would call his butler. 'What an astute chap you are, Mr Grey. Perhaps you and I could have a look round and then discuss what we can do about papering over the cracks over a pot of tea.'

Ted nodded. 'Sounds a fine idea.'

Rachel wasn't certain what woke her – a change of the light, a noise – it was hard to tell. She stretched and opened her eyes. To her surprise, Daniel stood beside the bed looking down at her. His eyes almost seemed to glow in the gloom. His wild blond hair framed his beautiful face, making him look like a wraith from some magical realm and for an instant she wondered if he was part of a dream. As she stirred he moved closer. Her first instincts were to pull the sheets up over her chest.

'Daniel,' she said, struggling to control her voice. 'What are you doing up here. I told Molly—'

The boy's expression dried the words in her mouth.

'What's the matter?' she whispered, as if there was any doubt.

Daniel snorted. 'I saw you with that man. I thought you were mine,' he said in a thick, unhappy voice.

Rachel stared at him, sensing his hurt and betrayal. She swallowed hard, looking around for her night dress – in her hurry to get into bed she hadn't bothered to put it on after her bath.

'Daniel, please,' she said gently. 'This really isn't the time or the place.'

To her surprise, the boy lunged forward and kissed her hard. She gasped, every fibre of her body responding instantly, as if his kiss was a spark on dry tinder. As his lips pressed to hers, tongue begging entry, he jerked the sheets out her hands, exposing her breasts.

'I thought you were mine,' he repeated. 'You must think I'm a complete fool. You stayed out all night with that man – did he have you too?'

Rachel was stunned. How could she deny what was so patently true?

'Daniel,' she murmured, torn between her pain and the desire that his raw passion ignited in her belly. 'Please don't do this. Let me get dressed and then we can talk.'

His hand cupped her breasts, mouth working over her neck and shoulders until his lips closed over their dark pearls. She moaned, rising up to meet his caresses, astonished that his touch could arouse her so easily. As she thrust herself towards him he pushed her back down onto the bed.

'You're no better than a whore, leading me on like you do. Have I to share you?' he snorted, pulling away, undoing his shirt, tearing at his clothes. Rachel was so stunned she could barely speak.

'Is that the kind of game you want to play, Mrs Ingram – having a boy and a man at your beck and call?'

Without his shirt his body seemed to glow with vitality. Despite a tendril of fear that lingered in her belly, Rachel knew that she couldn't fight the desire that roared through her.

She struggled to speak. 'Listen to me, please, last night was a mistake, I've already told Julian—' she stopped wondering how she could possibly justify her actions. 'I had too much to drink, Daniel, I—'

The boy silenced her excuses with a barrage of hurt, angry kisses. He clambered onto the bed, his hands moving frantically over her body if he was desperate to reclaim her for himself.

The heat and power of his body moving so ferociously against hers made Rachel gasp with sheer pleasure. Forgetting her panic she ran her hands over his muscular back, pulling him closer, relishing the sensation of his skin next to hers.

He struggled with his breeches, jerking them down. Rachel felt his cock brush her belly, as hard and intimidating as a steel rod. Freed from the restraints of his clothes he dragged the sheets aside. Desire, fury and pain mingled as he forced her thighs apart and plunged his cock deep inside her. She cried out his name as her body closed around him and he plunged into her again and again. Instinctively she wrapped her legs around his waist, his break-neck rhythm purging the memory of Julian Morton, and igniting an arc of pleasure that threatened to drown her. His anger and his hurt stripped away every emotion, leaving only raw passion.

Afraid to think, Rachel surrendered, allowing herself to be drawn into the anonymous, swirling maelstrom. On and on they plunged, rolling and thrashing around the bed like wild animals engaged in a fight to the death.

Between her legs, the excitement built up in intense, white-hot waves, gathering and intensifying, forming and reforming, while the boy thrust on and on, his head thrown back, eyes tight closed, until suddenly she couldn't hold the tide back any more and the damn burst. Pleasure flooded out from the junction of their two bodies, tearing through her mind like a tidal surge.

She knew Daniel felt it too and that instant it seemed as if they were two halves of one being, fused together on an endless voyage towards release, tossed backwards and forwards at the mercy of an ancient current. Finally the waves began to subside and Rachel found herself gasping her way back to reality.

As soon as they were still, Rachel wished that it could carry on forever. In the white-hot, empty spaces of passion there was no need for words or explanations, pain or guilt. Sensation was the only language they needed.

Wordlessly, Daniel rolled over and scooped her up in his arms as if he was afraid to let her go. She couldn't bring herself to look into his face, terrified of what she might see there.

Taking a deep breath she tried to search for words that would comfort them both, but before she could say anything there was a knock at the bedroom door.

'Mrs Ingram? Are you awake, ma'am?' said Molly from outside on the landing. 'I know you said you weren't to be disturbed, but Miss Anthea has just arrived from London. I've shown her into the sitting room downstairs, but she says she wants to come up and talk to you.'

Rachel stiffened and then coughed to clear her throat. 'Thank you, Molly. Would you please tell her I'll be down in just a second.'

She turned back to Daniel, who was looking at her with his sharp blue eyes. 'I really have to go,' she murmured.

He said nothing. For an instant it seemed as if they were frozen in time. Daniel reached up to trace the line of her jaw. His touch was so gentle that it made Rachel's heart ache.

'I thought you were mine,' he said with such sadness that Rachel felt grief prickle up behind her eyes.

'Oh, Daniel,' she murmured and closed her eyes to stop the tears. He held her close to him, cradling her head against her shoulder. She felt helpless, an intense wave of pain and regret lifting up from deep inside her. Gently she extricated herself from his arms.

'I have to go down and see Anthea,' she said, 'but we need to talk.'

Daniel slid off the bed and picked up his shirt from where he had abandoned it.

'Do you think we have anything to say?' he said in an undertone. 'Haven't you already made your choice?'

Rachel struggled with the tears. 'No, please,' she whispered. 'Don't leave like this, Daniel, don't hate me.'

Daniel laughed without humour. 'I don't hate you, Rachel, that's the trouble.' He turned and looked at her over his shoulder. 'My trouble is that I love you – and we both know that that will never do. That man who you were with last night

– it would be all right if he fell in love with you and you with him. It would be just perfect.' The boy stopped, eyes alight with pain and longing. 'Maybe it would be better for both of us if I don't come to Albion any more. The heavy work in the garden is almost done. I'm certain Ted could get someone else to finish off the rest of it.'

Rachel stared at him, aware of a great wrenching pain in her stomach. 'Please don't go, Daniel. Come and sit for me this afternoon. We can talk then,' she said in a small uneven voice.

Daniel buttoned his shirt. 'Whatever you say, Mrs Ingram. You're the one who pays the wages.'

Rachel was stunned by the iciness in his tone. He pulled on his breeches and then picking up his boots slipped out between the curtains on the balcony. As the wind caught them she snatched a glimpse of him climbing out over the stone balustrade. Finally alone, she burst into tears.

Ted Grey tucked his notebook and pencil back into the pocket of his jacket, and watched as Julian Morton rang for tea. Their tour of Medsham house was completed. Ted settled himself down in an armchair in Julian's study and let his mind conjure up a picture of Miss Petra Morton, whom he had met on the upstairs landing. She had been wearing a long, white negligee which had done very little to hide the high uptilted contours of her breasts or the shadow of her sex beneath. And as for the other girl, who he had glimpsed briefly through the doorway of Petra Morton's bedroom – Ted fought to suppress a grin. You really didn't need to be a genius to guess what was going between those two, though he'd only seen their sort in pictures before, never in the flesh.

The other girl had been spread-eagled on the bed, wearing a little silk shift. Ted's mouth watered. He could almost see the enticing rise of her quim – and, for an instant, imagined the rather imperious Miss Morton with her head pressed firmly between those creamy white thighs.

'So,' said Julian, interrupting Ted's fantasy, 'what do you reckon, then?'

Ted blew his cheeks out thoughtfully, struggling to focus his thoughts on the job in hand. 'Well, I can muster four men, various trades, but to be honest, Mr Morton, what you really need to get the house back into proper shape is a large fortune and a small army.'

Julian Morton lifted an eyebrow. 'Neither of which, as you so astutely commented this morning, I have. Given that both are beyond me, can you still help?'

Ted grinned. 'I reckon so, but I'll warn you now, Mr Morton, it's cash up front, none of this cheque or credit business. I reckon we can get the place watertight before winter, get the worst of the plaster replaced, tidy up generally. It would be better to do it properly but I can make it sound for you – at a price.' He pulled out the notebook from his pocket, tore off the sheet of paper he had been making notes on, and handed it to Julian.

'That's the work that needs to be done straight away – the gutters and the bad bits of the roof. My price is at the bottom.'

Julian nodded thoughtfully. 'When can you make a start?'

'First thing Monday morning if the price is agreeable.'

Julian sighed. 'It seems like we have a deal then, Mr Grey. I'll arrange to pick up the money from the bank first thing Monday.'

When Rachel finally went downstairs, Anthea was curled up in an armchair in the sitting room. Hearing Rachel's footsteps she looked up and grinned.

'So there you are, I was just about to come up and turf you out of bed.' She paused. 'Darling, you look like something the cat dragged in, are you all right?'

Rachel helped herself to a cup of tea off the tray on the sideboard. 'No, but I'm sure I'll live. What are you doing down here?'

Anthea pulled a face. 'Ouch, are you always this prickly in

the mornings? I had planned to go with Peter Heath to the Rawlingsons' near Swaffham. Everyone's been invited down for Deirdre's birthday party. Anyway, on the way down here, Peter and I had the most frightful spat.' She grinned. 'It was wonderful, I haven't had so much fun for ages. He shouted, he swore – he really is a lion when he's roused, so I made him drop me off at the railway station and I came down here on the milk train. It was all terribly dramatic, and he's *so* jealous.'

Rachel glanced out of the window. In the distance she could just see Daniel working by the wall that kept the dunes at bay.

Anthea snorted. 'Aren't you going to ask me what we argued about?'

Rachel shook her head. 'No, not this morning.'

'You really are in a foul mood. Did you go to dinner with the man who has the boat?'

Rachel was about to speak when Anthea grinned and clapped her hands together.

Something in Rachel's face must have given her away, though she had no idea what.

'Oh, you little minx!! You didn't!' shrieked Anthea with glee. 'Oh, my God, no wonder you look so appalling this morning. What was it like? He didn't have a hairy back, did he – I can't abide hairy backs. Is he gorgeous? Would I like him?'

Rachel slumped into an armchair and took a mouthful of tea. 'Yes, I'm sure you'd love him, actually he's a lot like you.'

Anthea snorted. 'I'm not going to ask you what that means. I was going to ask you if I could spend a few days at Albion but now I'm going to insist on it – when can I meet him?'

Rachel sighed. 'Perhaps not at all. I've already told him last night was a terrible mistake.'

Anthea looked incredulous. 'A mistake? Why on earth did you say that?'

'I'd had too much champagne.' Rachel rubbed her eyes. 'Oh, I don't know. I just want it to be more than a meaningless sexual encounter.'

Anthea lit up a cigarette. 'Sometimes those are the best

kind, darling. So, when can I meet him? What's his name?'

'Julian Morton.' Rachel sighed and turned to Anthea. 'I don't mind you staying for a few days, but once we've had some breakfast you'll have to excuse me. I want to get on with some work this morning. Do you think you can find something to amuse yourself?'

Anthea groaned. 'I'm sure I can find something to do, but only if you promise me to tell me all about Julian.'

Rachel nodded – she would have promised almost anything to be left alone.

Chapter 7

It was nearly midday by the time Rachel finally climbed the stairs up to her studio. Anthea had wanted to tell her every last detail of the row with Peter, and the guest list and intrigues of the house party she had supposed to be joining. It amused and then annoyed Rachel that Anthea gaily assumed that she knew all the people involved or cared about the outcome. Her brief, and much edited, account of the evening spent with Julian Morton had wetted Anthea's appetite – she was desperate to meet him.

By contrast, the studio was tranquil and silent. Outside, the sea was calm, a distant boat caught like a sepia print on the far horizon. Inside, summer sunlight picked out the jars of brushes and tubes of paint, the canvases stacked against the wall. There was the familiar smell of turpentine and linseed oil – amongst these things Rachel was always at her most content.

She pushed the door to, wondering if Daniel would come and sit for her, then glanced at the portrait on the easel. She knew his body so well that she could easily had completed it from memory. While she had been with Anthea it had been easy to keep her mind off Daniel and even Julian, but standing in front of the painting, their faces and their bodies came back in glorious details.

Rachel closed her eyes, struggling to still the muddled thoughts in her head – what was she going to do? She really had no desire to hurt Daniel. When she opened them again she picked up the palette from the bench and squeezed a little paint onto it. Painting might help ease her confusion.

Downstairs in the sitting room, Anthea picked up a magazine and flipped idly through the pages, without really looking at what was on them. Perhaps coming to Albion had not been such a good idea, though it had seemed like a wonderfully theatrical gesture to flounce off on the train, leaving Peter Heath open-mouthed with surprise and indignation. She glanced out of the windows, wondering whether she might take a walk along the dunes, when she heard a car draw up. Perhaps it was Peter Heath come to hunt her down – what a gloriously romantic notion! Pausing to check her hair in the mirror, Anthea hurried out into the hall and practically ran headlong in Rachel's house maid, Molly. The girl eyed her suspiciously.

'Are you expecting someone, Miss?'

Anthea was a little taken aback. 'A friend,' she said sharply and hung back while Molly opened the door. Outside in the sunshine was an elegant blonde woman, immaculately dressed in a pale-blue sailor-suit style dress and matching blue straw hat.

'Good afternoon,' she said, in a cultured voice, stepping into the shadowy hall. 'Would you please tell Mrs Ingram that Miss Morton is here to see her.'

Molly hesitated for a split second. Anthea stepped forward.

'Good afternoon. Actually, Mrs Ingram is busy at the moment. May I help you?' Anthea smiled and extended her hand. 'I'm a friend of Rachel's, Anthea Leven. You must be Julian's sister? Was Rachel expecting you?'

There was an instant as Petra Morton's eyes met hers that Anthea felt an interesting chill run down her spine. The blonde woman had the eyes of a predatory cat. She tightened her grip on Anthea's hand and smiled warmly, the smile not quite disguising the cool, appraising glance she gave Anthea's body.

'No, no she's not. Rather silly of me not to have telephoned

106

first, but I just called by on the off chance. I had planned to ask Rachel if she'd like to have a spot of lunch with me, but if she's too busy—' Petra Morton waved a hand suggesting that she would leave, though the gesture was hardly convincing. Anthea felt the tingle again – she had met women like Petra before and had little doubt in which direction her tastes ran. Petra was quite stunning, with a handsome rather than pretty face. Something about the way she carried herself intensified the odd sensation Anthea had in her stomach.

Anthea indicated the sitting room. 'Why don't you come in? Rachel is working in the studio at the moment, but she will be down later. Perhaps you'd like to wait. I'm sure Molly could rustle up something for us to eat.' Anthea smiled. 'To be perfectly honest I'd be glad of the company. There's not an awful lot to do around here.'

Petra looked heavenwards. 'My God, you're so right. Julian and I are bored senseless, that's why we were so pleased to meet Rachel.' She glanced around the interior of the pleasantly furnished sitting-room. 'Are you sure I'm not putting you to any trouble? I could call back later.'

'No, not at all. We'll eat in here, Molly.'

Molly sniffed with disapproval and vanished into the hall.

Petra took the seat Anthea indicated and then beaded her with her large aquamarine eyes. 'So what do you, Miss Leven? Are you an artist too?'

Anthea leant over and took a cigarette from her bag. 'No, and I would much prefer it if you called me Anthea. Actually I suppose you could call me a hedonist,' she said slowly, watching Petra's reaction. 'I only came to Albion to torment a man who was being terribly boorish, but, sadly, I think my revenge may have back-fired on me, and now I'm stuck here rather than at the Rawlingsons' house party.' She paused, eyes firmly fixed on Petra Morton's face. 'Unlike Rachel, who is terribly industrious and worthy, I'm a rather self-indulgent party-goer with no sense of shame whatsoever.'

Petra laughed, her eyes darkening a shade. 'What a

wonderful coincidence. I'm so glad I called now,' she said in a low voice. 'I'm certain we've met before. Did you say you were going to the Rawlingsons? Do you mean Deirdre and Ralph?'

Anthea nodded. She couldn't help but wonder why Petra had decided to call on Rachel, or what reception she might have received – it was quite obvious that Petra Morton had arrived at Albion with something other than lunch on her mind.

Over an impromptu picnic in the sitting-room they explored their mutual acquaintances – hunts and balls they had both attended, house parties – but all the time Anthea was very aware of an undercurrent of tension that hung between them like mist. Emboldened by the wine, Anthea leant across the little table they were sharing to refill Petra's glass.

'Why exactly did you come out to see Rachel? I wouldn't have thought she was your type.'

Petra laughed. 'Is it so obvious? I'm not really sure why I came. I think Julian is quite smitten with her, and last night,' she paused and lifted the wine to her lips, eyes alight with amusement, 'did Rachel mention last night?'

Anthea smiled conspiratorially. 'She didn't have to, I could see it in her face.'

'Well, I was a little envious – why should the men have all the fun? I woke up with this terrible compulsion to come out here and seduce her. She is very attractive. I suppose Julian and I must be attracted to the same sort of women.' Petra pulled a face and took a cigarette from the case Anthea offered her. 'Though that does sound rather incestuous.'

Anthea sat back in the armchair and blew out a long plume of smoke. 'I'm not sure that Rachel is that keen on female flesh.'

Petra laughed. 'I doubt that she has ever tried it. She is rather naive, but I think that's probably part of her charm, don't you? All the way here I've been toying with ways to convince her to let me take her to bed. Have you ever tried to seduce her?' She leant closer and ran a long, painted nail across Anthea's cheek. 'I'd be terribly interested to know how you got on.'

Anthea suppressed a shiver of expectation. 'No, the thought never really occurred to me. Rachel has always seemed like forbidden fruit. I don't think she has any idea that I might be interested in her.' She smiled. 'Besides which, for years she was out of bounds, safely married to André Ingram, who was a dreadful bore. He liked to fantasise about the three of us in bed together – when Rachel wasn't there, of course – but to be honest I think he got his greatest pleasure from keeping her rather naive and innocent. I believe he thought a discreet *ménage à trois* might corrupt her.'

Petra ginned. 'You slept with André Ingram, Rachel's husband?' she said with barely veiled surprise.

Anthea nodded. 'I'm afraid so, for years – before and after he married Rachel. It's not something I'm particularly proud of, but I was by no means the only one. He had quite a harem of admirers, male and female. Actually, that was how I met first Rachel, through André. He really was a most peculiar man.' She paused and took another puff of her cigarette. 'He liked to be in control – I think that excited him more than anything else. He once took me to a brothel in Paris and then sat in an armchair and watched while I was seduced by the most astonishing coloured woman. He didn't move a muscle, just sat back and watched as this plump woman made love to me.' Anthea sighed. 'I was very young then, too. He always preferred younger women.'

Petra moved closer and outlined the contour of Anthea's mouth with her fingertip. 'And did you enjoy it?'

Anthea smiled and, taking Petra's hand, ran her tongue across the palm.

'I loved it,' she purred. 'It was my first time and I was so nervous, but this woman knew exactly what she was doing. I don't think I've felt anything like it since. And all the time, while she was kissing and stroking me I could see André watching – it was incredibly erotic. I can still remember the smell of her body, like cinnamon and sandalwood. When she had finished with me, André got up and paid her – and then took me out to lunch, with not a word, nothing about what had gone on, what I'd felt . . .' Anthea paused, reddening slightly as her mind flooded with the memories of the little room in the Paris brothel, the huge bed with its metal frame and the sweet, almost overpowering scent of her first female lover. Deep inside, the recollection stirred her passion. She glanced up at Petra, knowing that her face would betray her excitement. 'Perhaps after lunch you might like to come for a walk?' she said in an undertone.

Petra nodded. 'That sounds like a charming idea,' she said with a sly grin.

Julian Morton glowered at his butler. 'What do you mean, Petra has gone out in my new car?'

The man inclined his head slightly. 'I'm very sorry, sir. Miss Petra said she intended to go out for the afternoon, and that I wasn't to disturb you. I had no idea that you might require the car.'

Julian snorted. Not only had Petra stolen his bloody car but Izzy had declined his offer of a little light exercise on the grounds that she had a headache. Julian thrust his hands into his pockets and paced up and down. He had intended to pop over to Albion and invite Rachel out for a drive. Where could Petra have gone – and why? He looked up again at his butler. 'Did she tell you where she was going?'

The man looked blank. Julian sighed theatrically. Being stuck in Medsham alone was sheer purgatory.

'Oh and Mr Smith-Bourton rang while you were upstairs, sir, he asked me not to interrupt you, but to say he and the others would be down tomorrow, as planned,' the butler continued in his obsequious voice.

Julian nodded. 'Good, at least Tippy and the gang will brighten up this hell-hole,' he said, thinking aloud. 'Can you get someone to bring the Daimler round?'

The butler nodded and left. In the excitement of inviting Rachel over to dinner Julian had quite forgotten the invitation he had extended to some of his friends to join him for Sunday lunch. The plan was to take the boat out – perhaps he could persuade Rachel to join them.

Julian loathed his great-uncle's sensible, ageing Daimler. Albion seemed quite deserted when he drew the car to a halt under the shelter of its walls. One thing did catch his attention though – the familiar outlines of his new red roadster, tucked up in the shade. Petra, he thought without amusement. What on earth was she doing at Albion?

Before he could get out to investigate, a young girl appeared from the side of the house, pulling on gloves and adjusting her hat. She looked at Julian in surprise and then with some interest.

'Excuse me,' said Julian indicating the little red car. 'Is my sister here?'

The girl, obviously a servant, sniffed thoughtfully. 'Are you Mr Morton?'

Julian nodded. The girl was rather attractive in a rounded, countrified sort of way. She blushed a little as he looked her over. She really was quite a charming little creature.

'Yes, I am,' he said, doffing his hat.

He could see a hint of amusement in the girl's eyes.

'She's gone out for a walk in the dunes.' She turned and pointed towards the rolling sand that ran behind the jetty and boat house. 'They've been gone about half an hour.'

'Thank you,' he said. For a moment Julian wondered if Petra had designs on Rachel. He wouldn't put it past her, and as the thought worked its way deeper into his mind, he was convinced that was why his sister had come to Albion. He couldn't think of any other reason why Petra would voluntarily go tramping across a deserted beach. It was hardly her sort of thing. The maid had turned and was making her way back across the causeway. Julian grinned and set off towards the

111

dunes. Pretty little thing, he thought, he must remember to ask Rachel about her.

It took him ten minutes to track his sister down, and another two to work out that the woman writhing so fetchingly beneath the large parasol was not Rachel Ingram.

The other woman was naked except for a white silk chemise that was rucked up around her waist. Petra was crouched on a blanket between her legs, lifting her up onto her long artful tongue which slid back and forth across the mound of her gaping quim. In the shadows, the moisture between the woman's legs glittered where it clung to the triangle of curls. Julian felt a pleasant stirring in his groin, and settled himself down to enjoy the spectacle.

The woman gave a throaty laugh and thrust herself up again towards Petra, moving back and forth so that Petra's tongue brushed over her pleasure bud in a gentle, compelling pattern. 'Umm,' she murmured, 'God, that feels good.'

Petra laughed, the sound distorted by the other woman's body.

Just as Julian found a suitable vantage point, the woman suddenly broke away and rolled over onto her belly. He froze wondering if she had seen him. After a few seconds she clambered to her feet and pulled the chemise up over her head. Petra, her lips wet from the intimate kisses, sat back on her heels and looked her up and down.

'You look like a water nymph.'

The woman smiled. 'Really?' she said with a hint of mockery. 'I thought you might be disappointed it was me and not Rachel down here with you.'

Petra smiled wolfishly, 'Hardly. I doubt that she would have been half as keen. Come here and let me look at you.'

The woman gracefully executed a long, slow turn that brought her back within reach of Petra. Her body was long and slender, though her breasts, as they slipped free from the chemise were heavier than Julian had anticipated, they were still quite astonishingly beautiful. Petra knelt forward and planted a single kiss on the dark triangle of her new friend's sex.

'You smell divine, kitten,' she whispered. 'I'm so glad we met.'

The woman laughed and threw back her head as Petra caught hold of her buttocks and pulled her tight against her lips.

'Why don't you get undressed, Petra? The wind feels divine on the skin,' the woman moaned, locking her hands in her lover's hair.

Petra's fingers lifted to part the heavy outer lips of her sex. Her tongue traced the ridge of her clitoris.

'Umm, that feels good too,' the woman murmured. 'Let me undress you. I want you to feel how good this is.'

Petra pulled away, though her fingers remained. 'Anthea, darling, do you really have to talk all the time?' she said with a smile.

Anthea looked down at her, eyes bright with desire. 'Oh come on, Petra, I want to touch you, too. No one will see us from here,' she purred and fell to her knees. Her fingers worked busily at the buttons on the front of Petra's dress, pulling the top down over her narrow shoulders. Her lips followed her fingers, fluttering a starburst of hot, wet kisses over Petra's pert little breasts teasing their peaks into hardness.

Petra moaned with pleasure. 'There might be some sea captain out there with his telescope trained on us,' she said, glancing back over her shoulder towards the sea.

Anthea giggled. 'I rather like the idea of someone watching us. Help me with this catch, I don't want to tear it and my hands are shaking.'

It seemed to be only a matter of seconds before they were both naked. Anthea slid down Petra's stockings, nuzzling at her belly and thighs as the silk slipped down onto the blanket.

Petra rolled onto her side. 'Satisfied now?' she said, posing provocatively. She lifted a finger to trace the outline of her nipple.

Anthea grinned. 'Hardly.' She leant forward and kissed Petra, guiding her gently onto her back, moaning softly as she pulled her closer.

Straddling her companion, she turned so that her sex was above Petra's waiting mouth. As she felt the first caress of Petra's tongue on her body, she bent forward and nuzzled at the soft triangle of curls that lay between Petra's slim white thighs.

Petra's body was as pale as buttermilk and the outer lips of her sex were a delicate shade of ivory, trimmed with a corona of white-blonde hair. The fine down did nothing to conceal the contours of the outer lips of her quim. Anthea slipped a finger between them – inside the moist, fragrant folds were as pale as faded rose petals. She ran her tongue along the deep cleft, savouring the rich fragrance and oceanic tastes.

Petra's clitoris had hardened into a tight, angry bud that she sucked hungrily. Beneath her, Petra gasped in delight and an instant later Anthea felt the woman's mouth close over her own pleasure bud, echoing her touch with little lapping, nibbling kisses. It was ecstasy. Sliding a finger deep into her quim, Anthea felt Petra's body close around her. It felt like liquid velvet, so wet and hot that it almost took her breath away.

Petra copied her caress. Anthea gasped – the other woman's lips and finger seemed to be joined by some magical empathy to her own so that every movement, every touch she began was anticipated and repeated on her own body.

Anthea groaned and pressed down onto Petra's waiting tongue, knowing that she was rapidly reaching that delicious moment where reason departed and only instinct remained. She bent lower and for an instant felt the brush of Petra's breasts against her skin. The sensation set up a ripple of pleasure that refused to be ignored and then Anthea knew she was lost. Her tongue seemed to work without her instruction, fingers moving in and out, stroking and caressing, exploring the silvery reaches of Petra's exquisite body. On and on, deeper and deeper, Anthea felt as if she was caught up in an intricate dance where her every action was mirrored, repeated and renewed, taking her further and further into the realms of pleasure.

Crouching in his hiding place amidst the dunes, Julian Morton was totally captivated. As the first waves of orgasm crashed through the woman's bodies he felt the pleasure as intensely as if the climax had been his own. It took every scrap of self control he had to stop from crying out. Finally, when the women were done and rolled off each other totally sated, he sat for a few minutes – almost as breathless as the lovers – and admired the way their bodies looked in the sunlight.

Both women seemed to glow with an inner contentment that he envied beyond measure; his own hunger lay raw and unsatisfied in his belly. Petra's companion was the one he was most interested in – he certainly had no feelings towards his sister other than envy. He wondered who the other woman was, and, more importantly, how it was that Petra had managed to seduce her, presumably on first meeting.

Still crouched over he made his way back towards Albion. Perhaps, with a little gentle persuasion, Rachel Ingram might be prepared to overlook their absurd agreement and help him ease the terrible ache in his groin.

Rachel heard the footsteps on the stairs and then the sound of studio door opening behind her. She turned slowly from the painting of Daniel Grey and saw, with a strange sense of relief, that he was standing there in the flesh. He was as desirable and beautiful as she imagined him, in a way that – however good an artist she was – she could never quite capture on the canvas. He looked hot and tired and his expression was unreadable.

'Molly's gone home,' he said flatly into the tense silence that hung between them.

Rachel nodded. It was her housemaid's half day.

'I thought I'd wait until she left before I came up,' he said.

Rachel indicated the dais. 'Have you come to sit for me?'

'I came over this morning because I couldn't bear the idea of waiting until Monday to see you—' he stopped and looked up at her, eyes bright with a mixture of pain and anger. She looked away quickly – his reward for his devotion had been to see her arriving home with Julian.

'Daniel,' she said unsteadily, 'I didn't mean to hurt you. I still don't – why don't you sit for me? I could go and make us some tea—'

The boy shook his head. 'What about your visitors?'

Rachel picked up a rag to clean her brush, wishing there was some easy way they could get beyond the odd, stilted feeling that seemed to be crushing down on her chest.

'Anthea,' she said quietly. 'She's staying here for a few days.'

Daniel snorted. 'Not her – the others. Their cars are out front.'

Rachel frowned. 'What others?'

Daniel's eyes flashed angrily. 'You know exactly who I mean. That man of yours. He came back pretty smartish. I thought you might be up here with him.'

'Julian?' said Rachel incredulously, instantly regretting using his name. 'He's here?'

'I thought you must know, him and another woman. She arrived a while back and he turned up about half an hour ago.'

Rachel went over to the window. Everywhere outside seemed deserted. From the corner of her eye she saw Daniel turning to leave.

'Wait,' she said quickly, 'please don't go yet. I wanted you to sit for me. We have to talk.'

The boy stared at her. 'What about your visitors? Aren't you going to go to see them? I'd have thought you'd want to be down there with him.'

Rachel cleared her throat, wondering why Daniel had come

back so soon. It was the most exquisite torture. She caught hold of the bench to steady herself, struggling to find some words that conveyed her confusion and would ease his pain.

'No,' she said softly after a second or two. 'No, Anthea can play host to the Mortons for a little while. I want to be up here with you.'

She saw a flicker of relief in Daniel's eyes and smiled at him. Stepping forward she began to slowly unbutton his shirt. He didn't move, but watched her intently, his eyes darkening as the buttons slid undone. Biting her lips she ran her palm over his chest. He smelt of the sea and wind and raw male energy. The wave of desire that crashed over her was so intense she closed her eyes, struggling to retain some kind of composure.

'I'm so sorry about last night, Daniel. It was a stupid mistake. You have to understand that. I want you so much,' she gasped, almost afraid to say the words aloud in case they lost some of their power.

Daniel groaned and lifted a finger to outline the puckered shadows of her nipples where they pressed through her blouse. It astonished her that one touch, one breath of his body could make her so excited. Between her legs she felt a flutter of desire, and knew that she was already getting wet. It was as if her sex had a mind of its own and was laying a trap to draw him in. She stared up into his stormy blue eyes, unable to find the words to describe what she was feeling, and prayed that he would be able to understand. His expression did not change but she knew he had heard the unspoken plea. He slid his arms around her waist, pulling her tight against his chest, so that every sense was suffused with his essence.

Rachel felt dizzy with desire. He ran a finger under her chin, tilting her face up towards him, and then he kissed her. She moaned softly, moulding herself against him, surrendering all pretence of control, as her mouth opened so that his tongue could slide between her lips. She felt a need for his body that seemed to begin somewhere in her feet and shiver up through her like an icy wind. It was almost as if her body was paying a penance for the sin she had committed, for it reached out to Daniel in a way no words, no logic, no contrition, could conjure.

'Rachel? Rachel, are you up there?'

Daniel leapt away from her as if he had been scalded.

From downstairs in the courtyard Julian Morton called again. 'Hello? Hell-o? Is there anyone at home?'

Daniel dragged his hand across the back of his mouth as if wiping away a vile taste. Rachel was rooted to the spot, her face flushed crimson. They could both hear Julian's progress up the stairs. Rachel grabbed Daniel's arm. 'Please,' she whispered, 'don't go yet.'

Before he could reply the door to the studio opened.

'Ah, there you are,' said Julian with a broad grin. 'I hope you didn't mind my letting myself in, but the place is like the *Marie Celeste*.'

He glanced across at Daniel, who was still standing beside Rachel. The boy looked as if he was curled and ready to pounce. His shirt was still undone to the waist.

'I do hope I didn't disturb you?' said Julian lightly. 'I thought I might pop over to see you, and Petra's car – my car, actually – is parked in the drive. Have you seen her, by any chance?'

Rachel shook her head. Beside her she could feel Daniel's tension changing to anger.

'If you've finished with me for the day, Mrs Ingram,' he said in a tight voice, 'I'll be off now.'

Rachel stepped to block his path. 'Wait a second,' she said quickly and then turned to Julian. 'If you'd like to go downstairs to the sitting room, I'll be down in a few minutes to make us a pot of tea. Petra can't have gone very far. My friend, Anthea, is staying with me at the moment, perhaps they've gone for a walk.'

Julian nodded, his eyes lingering on Daniel for an instant.

'Of course, my dear,' he said, turning his hat in his hands, fingers working along the silk band. 'I'm sorry, I didn't mean

118

to disturb you.' His eyes met Daniel's as he turned to leave. Rachel noticed that Julian was the first to look away.

As the door closed Daniel spun round and caught hold of Rachel by the arms. His grip was so fierce that she almost cried out.

'Is that him?' he growled.

Rachel nodded, too terrified to speak. Besides what was there to say? Daniel seemed to loom over her. Pulling her up towards him he kissed her furiously. Rachel gasped, feeling the intense passion reignite like a flash fire in her belly.

He jerked away from her, eyes as dark and shiny as pitch. 'Then you had better go downstairs and make him some tea,' he said.

Rachel stared at him. 'But I want you,' she said unsteadily.

Daniel snorted and began to button his shirt. 'I know. I shouldn't have come here today – I'll be back on Monday,' he said. Rachel caught hold of a chair to steady herself, torn between letting him leave and begging him to stay. He didn't even turn to look at her as he pulled the door closed. When he had gone Rachel stared out towards the sea and began to tremble.

Chapter 8

'And so I thought,' said Julian, helping himself to another slice of Madeira cake, 'that perhaps, Rachel, you would like to join me on the boat tomorrow? I and a few friends have planned to have a picnic over on the sandbar. They're down for a day or two to enjoy all this country air.' He smiled at the other two women, 'And of course, Anthea and Petra, you're both invited to come along too.'

Rachel's arrival downstairs had coincided with Petra and Anthea's return from their walk in the dunes, and Rachel had found herself obligated to offer them all some tea, when really all she wanted to do was flee upstairs to the privacy of her bedroom. They were now all comfortably installed in the sitting room.

Petra groaned and lit a cigarette. 'Oh, Julian, you know I'm always sick on that damned boat of yours. Take Izzy with you instead, I'm sure she would adore it.'

Anthea looked around for an explanation.

'She's staying with us as well,' said Julian. 'Another little friend of Petra's.'

Rachel caught the artful look that Julian gave Anthea but wasn't altogether sure what it meant.

Anthea nodded and then said, 'Actually, I'm afraid I'll have to decline as well, I'm no sailor either.'

Petra turned towards her. 'In that case perhaps you and I ought to have lunch somewhere instead? We could take a drive along the coast road and stop wherever the fancy takes us.'

The way the women spoke to each other, with a kind of

easy unexpected familiarity, made Rachel wonder if Anthea and Petra already knew each other, but she said nothing.

'Well,' said Julian. 'It seems that everyone's plans are made then. We need to meet down at the quay at around eight to catch the tide.'

Rachel was about to speak, when Anthea said, 'Why don't I drive down to the quay and drop Rachel off? You wouldn't mind me borrowing your car would you, Rachel?'

Rachel felt as if she was being herded into a corner by her three guests. Shaking her head, she said, 'No, I don't mind at all, but I should warn you, Julian, I'm not very good in a boat either.'

Julian laughed. 'Nonsense, it'll be great fun. Besides if we're eventually going to moor her here, it's the very least I can do. A little taste of what you can expect in the future.' He put his side plate down on the table with an air of finality. 'I did come over to see if you might like to go for a drive—'

Before he could finish his sentence Rachel shook her head firmly. 'Thank you, it's very kind of you to ask, but no. I've still got quite a lot of work I want to do in the studio before the light goes.'

Petra got to her feet. 'In that case I think, Julian dear, we really ought to be getting back to Medsham and see how Izzy is.'

Julian nodded, though Rachel sensed he was reluctant to leave.

When they had finally gone, Anthea helped to tidy the tea things onto a tray and followed Rachel into the kitchen.

'He's really rather splendid,' Anthea said setting the tray down on the draining board.

'Sorry?'

'Julian Morton, darling. I couldn't have done better for you myself. He's perfect for you and quite obviously smitten. That's why I said no to the boat trip tomorrow. It'll give you two a chance to be alone together.' She grinned and lifted her eyebrows as she piled the washing up into the sink. 'You ought to employ full-time staff. I'm not used to all this skivvying.'

Rachel stared at her. 'I wish you'd said you'd come as well. He's invited a crowd of his cronies along, so I won't know anybody. Have you met the Mortons before?'

Anthea pulled a face. 'Only in passing. Why? And before you ask, no, Julian Morton isn't amongst the notches on my bed-post.' She grinned again. 'Which is a bit of a shame. He's rather charming. Now, have you really got to do some more work in the studio or was that just an excuse to get rid of them?'

Rachel pulled a chair out from under the kitchen table and sat down, sighing heavily.

'I don't know, I just wanted some peace to think. This thing with Julian. It's all happening too fast. I feel as if I'm being pushed into something I'm really not ready for.'

Anthea sat down on the table beside her and gently kissed Rachel on the head.

'Oh Rachel, whyever not? He seems good company, he's handsome and, let's face it, he's a far better prospect than that pretty little gardener of yours. Did I see him poking around the house today like the spectre at the feast?'

Rachel reddened, feeling as if Anthea had slapped her.

Anthea pulled a cigarette out of the case and stared at her. 'You're not seriously thinking of passing over a catch like Julian Morton to concentrate your efforts on that boy, are you? You must be mad!'

Rachel groaned. 'It's just happening far too quickly, and everything seems so difficult.'

Anthea snorted. 'What's so difficult? You have to choose between a rather dashing chap of your own class, who is a fraction away from being head over heels in love with you, who's quite obviously loaded, or spend your life caged up at Albion with golden boy the gardener because, let's face it, Rachel, you will hardly be able to go anywhere else with him. Which is it to be? The lovely Julian or your gorgeous, penniless bit of rough, who wouldn't know a fish fork from a hole in the ground?' She paused and stared up at the ceiling. 'Well? Come on, Rachel – it doesn't take a genius to work out which would be better for you.'

Rachel ran her hands over her face, imagining the feel of Daniel's body moving against her and the soft heat of his breath on her skin.

'It doesn't seem that simple from where I'm sitting. I don't want to hurt Daniel.' She paused. She already had hurt him. How could she have let herself be seduced by Julian? She sighed. Was it just because he was an older man, a man who, in a odd way, reminded her of André, a man used to taking control? Was it possible that she would ever be free of the old patterns that had dominated her life for so long? As the thought formed in her mind she saw Daniel standing in the studio and knew there was another reason. Daniel Grey had put her in touch with a deep sensual strand in her nature that she never knew existed. He had helped her to become aware of her sexuality, electrified every part of her soul, filled her with a desire that was so strong that it had spilt over into every area of her life. Daniel was as much the cause as the victim of her new-found passion.

She took a long, thoughtful breath. 'No one has ever made me feel the way he does. It's as if meeting him has done something to me. I'm certain if I hadn't met him I'd never have made love to Julian Morton last night, it wouldn't even have occurred to me. It's as if being with Daniel has helped to set me free – he's helped find some part of me that I never knew existed.'

Anthea sighed theatrically. 'Darling, trust me, it's because stolen fruit always taste the sweetest. Your glorious boy is something forbidden, something slightly dangerous – and after all those years of being caged up as André's wife it's small wonder that you hanker after something a little risqué. But that is all it is – a modest little flirtation with danger. Now it's time to creep back under the fence, darling, back to your own kind.'

Rachel sighed. 'If only I was as sure. When I was married to André I was his – he owned me. Everything we did, everything I thought was what he wanted, socially, in bed, he ed, I followed blindly, not realising there could be another way.' She paused again and stared up at Anthea. 'It wasn't until I met Daniel that I realised what making love really means. All those years and I just never guessed. This feels so different. When I'm with Daniel I'm not a possession to be used. When he touches me I want to share what I feel, it's so different from having something taken from me.'

Anthea smiled. 'Trust me, I'm right.'

Rachel shook her head, and finally understood why she thought Julian was like André – they were both takers and if she wasn't careful, if she stayed with Julian, it would be all too easy to lose sight of the things she had learnt.

Anthea opened the pantry door. 'Now, did that cocky little maid of yours leave us a cold supper, or do we have to cook?'

Rachel stared at her, wondering if Anthea had heard a word she had said. 'You can't be hungry, we've only just had tea.'

Anthea pouted. 'It's because I'm bored, I'm always hungry when I'm bored. Why don't I look in the larder?'

It was just after six when Rachel woke the following morning. Her head ached. She stretched, wincing at the effort. She and Anthea had spent a long afternoon and evening raiding Albion's wine cellar and spent the night playing cards and talking. She ran her tongue experimentally around her mouth and remembered with a slight sense of consternation that she had ended up telling Anthea about the events at Medsham in explicit detail.

Slowly, she climbed out of bed and hurried across to the bathroom that adjoined it. Maybe Anthea had been too drunk to remember. Turning on the taps in the shower, Rachel stepped into the icy bore.

On the edge of the quay, just before eight o'clock, Anthea

pulled the car to a halt, winced and covered her eyes with her hands.

'Oh, my God,' she whispered miserably. 'I must have been mad to say I'd bring you down here this morning.'

Rachel smiled and pulled her hat down over her eyes. She didn't feel much better than Anthea. Anthea peered around. 'So where is Julian then? I thought he would have been here by now.'

'Ahoy there, ladies,' called a familiar voice. Both women turned to look out to sea, where a small skiff was being skilfully manoeuvred towards shore. Seated amidships was Julian Morton, resplendent in cap, blazer and white trousers. He waved enthusiastically, while ahead of him the oarsman worked at a steady rhythm to bring the boat alongside the jetty.

'Good morning, ladies,' he said, doffing his cap and hauling himself up the ladder on the quay side. 'We've got the perfect day for it, don't you think?'

He was right, thought Rachel, wishing she had had a little less to drink. Above them the morning sky was palest azure blue, with tails of chiffon white mist clinging to the sea that would be burnt off as the sun rose higher. Julian smiled at Rachel as she got out of the car and took her hand, pressing a kiss to her cheek.

'You look lovely this morning. Everyone else is already aboard. Are you set?'

Rachel nodded somewhat apprehensively. Julian smiled.

'Good show. We'll see you later, Anthea, I hope you have a lovely day with Petra. A shame you couldn't come with us.'

He clambered back down to the boat and then held his hand up towards Rachel.

'Come on, time and tide wait for no man. Watch the ladder, it's a little slippery.'

Rachel knew she had made a mistake as soon as they cast off. Despite the water being flat calm she still felt decidedly queasy as the little boat hauled through the water, and cursed herself again for having so much to drink the night before.

What awaited her on the boat made her feel worse.

As she climbed up onto the deck, helped by Julian, she stared around in astonishment. Lining the handrail of the boat were a fairly large group of young men and women who looked as if they would be far more at home in a nightclub than on the decks of a pleasure cruiser. Julian clambered up alongside her. 'Let me introduce you to my friends.'

From a doorway Izzy appeared, followed by a young man in white shirt and slacks. 'Breakfast will be ready in about ten minutes,' she said with a bright smile, nodding a welcome to Rachel. The man behind her on the ladder grinned and slipped his arm around her waist. As Rachel watched he turned Izzy slightly and kissed her full on the lips, his fingers creeping up over her ribs to cup her breast.

Julian grinned. 'You've already met Izzy – her beau today is Paul Thursford. Now, this is my old school friend, Tippy Smith, this is Lolly Cartwright—' Rachel tried hard to hang onto the names as Julian paraded her round the deck. It was obvious to Rachel that Julian's idea of a pleasure cruise was somewhat different to her own.

She looked nervously across towards the quay – it was too late to go back now.

'I think I'll go and give Izzy a hand,' she said, as the boat began to slowly chug out of the confines of the harbour.

Julian shrugged. 'As you like, but don't be long, Tippy is about to open the champagne.'

Rachel ignored him and headed below. The steps down to the galley were quite steep, and it was dark in comparison to the bright morning sunlight. It took Rachel a second or two to adjust to the gloom. There was a smell of bacon frying in the air which made her stomach heave and then she saw Izzy and Paul.

He had the little blonde girl pinned to the wall, shift dress up around her thighs, hands working eagerly in the shadowy plains between her legs. As Rachel watched in total astonishment, he slipped his arms around her and pulled her

127

up onto him. Izzy, eyes tightly closed, gasped as his cock slid deep inside her. One shoulder of Izzy's little summer dress had slipped down to reveal a tiny, rounded breast. Paul, having got his balance, cupped it with one hand and began to circle the hardening peak. Rachel found it impossible to tear her eyes off them. Rooted to the spot, she could feel her colour rising as Izzy began to move frantically against her lover, thrusting her hips forward in time to the throb of the boat's engine.

A hand dropped onto Rachel's shoulder making her gasp with surprise. Julian Morton leant over her and pressed a single kiss to her neck. He slipped a hand lower to cradle the curve of her breast. Rachel bit her lip – her nipples were hard and ached to be kissed.

'Looks like breakfast may take a little longer than expected,' he whispered with a grin. 'Why don't you come back up on deck and have a glass of champagne and orange juice with the rest of us? Or would you rather we stayed down here and joined them?'

On the quayside Anthea watched the boat sail off out of the harbour and then turned to go back to Rachel's car. Her headache had settled down to a dull, distant throbbing and she really didn't fancy cranking the little roadster into life. To her surprise and relief, she spotted Daniel Grey, Rachel's gardener, amongst the other people on the quay. She waved to him and he lifted a hand in acknowledgement. Rachel was right, he really was very attractive.

'Good morning, Miss Leven,' said the boy. 'You're about early.'

Anthea groaned and then smiled warmly. 'Good morning. Too early for me, really. I wonder whether you might give me a hand with the car?' She pulled the cranking handle out of the footwell, but before Daniel moved another older, thicker set man took it from her. He was taller than Anthea by a head, with flashing brown eyes and tanned skin that gave him a slightly foreign appearance. He had once been a very handsome man, she thought fleetingly, as his fingers closed round the metal shaft.

'Let me,' he said, wiping the handle with a rag from his pocket.

'Thank you,' she said with surprise. 'Very kind of you to help me.'

The man waved Daniel way and then looked up at her.

'No trouble at all, Miss, I'm Daniel's step-dad. Ted Grey's the name.' He grinned and extended his hand. Only good manners persuaded her to take it. As he spoke, his eyes moved over her body like work-roughened fingers. His handshake lasted a fraction of a second longer than was comfortable. Anthea shuddered.

'I'm must obliged for your help, Mr Grey,' she said coolly, stepping away from him.

Ted sniffed. 'No trouble at all. I'd never watch a lady struggle, besides I recognised the car. Mrs Ingram not with you today, then?'

Anthea shook her head, perturbed at being drawn into a conversation with this man.

'No, no she's gone out on a boat for the day.' She pointed out towards the harbour mouth. 'With Mr Morton and his friends.'

Ted's grin widened. 'Fine woman, Mrs Ingram.' He glanced down at Anthea's breasts and licked his lips. 'Not so bad yourself. I expect you know all about her and my boy, don't you?'

Anthea gasped in surprise. 'I beg your pardon?'

Ted Grey moved closer, eyes alight with amusement. 'There's no need to act all coy with me, miss. I'm sure she's told you all the fancy details. All the same you city types. Lonely widows and sex-starved spinsters – I've met them all before.' As he spoke he slid his hand slowly over the barrel of the cranking handle and then turned and thrust it into the car. The gesture seemed incredibly obscene. Anthea felt a knot of fury form in her belly.

'How dare you speak to me like that?' she hissed, glancing over her shoulders to see who else might have heard their exchange.

Ted shrugged, spat into the palms of his hand and prepared to turn the engine over. As soon as it fired Anthea grabbed the handle out of his hands and got into the car.

Ted grinned. 'What, not even going to thank me?' he said, leaning against the door of the roadster.

Anthea glared at him. 'Thank you,' she said tightly.

'If there is anything you ever want,' he said with a leer. 'I'm always ready to oblige a lady.'

Anthea rammed the car into gear. 'I'll bear that in mind,' she snapped and drew away, almost unable to believe what she had heard. Ted Grey was dangerous. She wondered if Rachel had any idea what sort of man Daniel's step-father was.

On board his boat, Julian poured Rachel another glass of champagne and slid his arm around her waist.

'Relax,' he said softly. 'Another half an hour or so and we'll be moored up on the sandbar. Have you ever been there? It's just like a desert island. I used to go out there as a child when I stayed with my great-uncle. Pine trees, a golden sandy beach . . .' he stopped. 'What on earth is the matter? You look quite pale.'

Rachel stared up at him. The atmosphere on deck was tight with expectation. The other people on the deck seemed unnaturally close as if they all shared some strange erotically charged secret. Rachel was so uneasy that she felt physically sick.

'Julian, what is going on? This isn't just a day trip, is it? We both saw Izzy and that man downstairs in the galley. I thought you and I had agreed that we could begin again.'

Julian smiled. 'We can, we can, it's just that I thought you might enjoy a little diversion from all that earnest morality.'

He tipped her face up towards him and kissed her gently. 'Nothing is going to happen that you don't want, I promise you. We're just going to have a little fun, that's all.'

Rachel stared out over the sea; the harbour was just a distant white shape, a flash of brilliance amongst the green and golden coastline. Along the shore a little way she could make out Albion, standing sentinel at the head of one of the channels, looking like a beached schooner amongst the rolling dunes. Ahead of them was the curved shelf of sand that the locals called the sandbar. It was a small, horseshoe-shaped island with a shallow sandy bay in the mouth of the U. The draft in the bay was so shallow that the boat would have to sail out around the back of the hook to make a landing, to be sure they didn't run aground. At very low tide it was possible to walk across to the island from the mainland, but the tides were so treacherous and came in so fast that the unwary could easily find themselves cut off. The centre of the island was dominated by a straggle of pine trees.

Julian piloted the little boat the last few hundreds yards towards a makeshift dock. As one of the crew jumped ashore to secure the bow line, Rachel felt as if she was being crushed under some unseen possibility. When the boat was made fast every one of the passengers – ten or twelve in all – started to scramble ashore, each carrying rugs and picnic baskets. They struck out over the sand towards the pines. The view from the top of the sandbar was quite spectacular but Rachel barely noticed it. Something was about to happen, she could sense it.

Julian took her arm, 'Come along,' he said cheerfully, 'don't dawdle.'

When everyone was in the shade, Julian took out his watch and said with a grin, 'Right, ladies, you have ten minutes to get away – after that you are all fair game.'

Rachel stared at him, while around her the other women, with whoops of delight slipped off their shoes and ran helter skelter towards the cover of the dunes and deeper into the pine trees.

'Julian?' Rachel said, wanting some sort of explanation.

He shrugged philosophically. 'Don't look so disapproving. You don't have to play if you don't want too,' he said with grin. 'It's up to you.'

The other men were spreading rugs on the sand and unfurling parasols, but their activity could not disguise the tense longing in the air – they were keen to be off. Rachel stared into the trees, her stomach quivering. As the seconds passed she felt the adrenaline beginning to build. A cold tingle rose and fell in her spine. The young men began to pace, counting the seconds until they could begin their pursuit – and then suddenly, without thinking, Rachel knew she couldn't stay with them any longer. She kicked off her sandals and ran into the trees as if the devil himself was behind her.

Even as she did it she knew it was a mistake for by running she had consented to play Julian's game. It was madness but she couldn't stop herself. Running away, and the growing sense of fear, seemed instinctive. Her pulse thundered in her ears as she ran left and right and between the wind-contorted trees. Here and there she saw flashes of colour as the girls ahead of her broke up and scattered for cover like a flurry of bright leaves. If she ran too far she would emerge on the far side of the pines and be easy prey.

Behind her she heard a wild banshee shriek and knew that the men were now in pursuit. Gasping for breath she tumbled down into a sandy hollow, completely enclosed by a ring of trees and a jumble of broken branches and crouched down low, praying that the men would run straight passed her. Her heart beat out a frantic tattoo against her ribs, which sounded so loud that she wondered if it might give her away. Covering her head with her hands she waited – and waited.

'So there you are,' said a voice above her. 'You're Julian's new friend, aren't you? Rachel, isn't it? Don't try and run away, I can see you. You'd better come out or I'll come down there to get you.'

Rachel glanced up into the eyes of one of her fellow

passengers. He was a tall, thin man in his late thirties, with sandy red hair. His eyes were alight with lust and desire and she realised with a growing sense of panic she had no idea what his name was, which seemed a ridiculous thing to think of. She got to her feet slowly and began to back away as he clambered down the bank towards her.

He was eight or ten feet away from her when she suddenly turned and made a break for it. As she did she saw to her total horror that there was another man behind her – Paul Thursford who she had seen earlier in the galley with Izzy. He must have been creeping up on her when the first man had been speaking. He lunged forward and grabbed her arms, spinning her round to face the man who had spotted her.

She began to fight them in earnest, as if her life depended on it, aware at the same time that her struggles seemed to have ignited a deep excitement low in her belly, something as feral and ancient as the chase. The ginger man caught hold of her legs and lifted them off the ground. Between them they manhandled her down onto the sand.

Paul Thursford, breathing hard, snorted. 'Looks like we've got a lively one here, Perry. Will you do the honours first or will I?'

Perry wiped his hand across his mouth. 'How about we both mount her?'

Rachel stiffened. 'What?' she gasped in horror.

Perry grinned down at her. 'We caught you, now we can do exactly what we like with you. Those are the rules. Unless of course you object, in which case—' he shrugged and then grinned at Paul. 'Not that we've ever had any complaints before.'

Rachel was so stunned she couldn't find her voice. With rough hands they turned her over onto her belly and then pulled her up onto all fours. Behind her, Paul Thursford ran his hand up between her thighs and slid down her knickers.

'Nice catch, Perry,' he murmured appreciatively.

She knew she was already excited and gasped with a mixture

133

of shame and embarrassment as he slipped a finger inside her and then grunted with delight.

Perry meanwhile undid the front of her dress, and slid a hand under her camisole, cupping her breasts, gently rolling the stiff little peaks between his thumb and forefinger. Rachel closed her eyes and shivered – she had seen his other hand working at the buttons of his flies and guessed what was to follow.

Behind her, Paul Thursford pushed his fingers forward to stroke her clitoris, and as he did so, guided his cock between her thighs. He snorted with pleasure as he found his mark. Rachel was stunned. Her whole body was trembling and hot – she could hardly believe what was happening. Something warm brushed her cheek and without thinking she opened her mouth to take Perry's cock between her lips. He moaned softly and renewed his attentions to her throbbing breasts.

Amongst the trees above them, Julian Morton looked on with a mixture of amusement and pleasure. His demure friend was crouched between the two men, her hands working in harmony with her mouth along the shaft and balls of Perry Comerford, while her hips thrust back frantically to drive Paul Thursford deeper inside her. Between them they had undone her top and pulled off her camisole so that her breasts swayed and trembled like liquid silk. One man's hand slipped back to catch hold of them, another drove his fingers deep between her thighs. Rachel was gasping and moaning with sheer pleasure – as were both the men. It seemed to Julian that he had a convert on his hands.

After a few seconds they found their rhythm, as compulsive as a heartbeat and so smooth that it might have been choreographed. The two men, eyes locked on each others faces, guided Rachel back and forth. Julian smiled; at that moment Rachel seemed to be lost in their passion, an exquisite body to be used and enjoyed. He suspected it was a role she was used to.

Peter renewed his attentions to her sex and suddenly, unexpectedly, Rachel arched up like a taut bow as the first intense waves of orgasm struck, taking both men out over the brink of pleasure. Paul snorted and pulled her back onto him, driving his hips forward like a battering ram. Rachel's cries of delight were stifled by the thrusting gushing stroke of Perry's cock and then – very suddenly – there was stillness. Perry slipped out of her mouth, Paul from her sex and then they got to their feet as a man.

'Are you set to bag another?' said Perry, bent over with hands on his knees.

Paul snorted, struggling to get his breath. 'You bet. Might want another little snort of champagne first though.'

Still huddled on the sand between them Rachel lay as if unconscious, half turned on her back, her breasts exposed, chest heaving as she caught her breath. Julian slid down the bank towards the men, who lifted their hands in greeting as they began the climb back to the picnic.

Julian crouched down beside Rachel, relishing her nakedness and the subdued, exhausted expression on her face. He sat for a few seconds and then very gently opened her legs. She looked up as if she was having trouble focusing. Without a word he leant forward and ran his tongue over the folds of her exhausted, dripping sex. He could still detect the compelling hum of her orgasm deep inside her, a soft resonant glow that excited him.

She tasted divine – a subtle mixture of Paul's spent pleasure and her own stunning, fragrant juices. He lifted her up towards him, tongue working back and forth across her quim.

She moaned softly – he knew his caresses were too intense a sensation for her to handle so close to orgasm, so very gently he parted her thighs a little wider and began to explore the far reaches of her sex. It was so hot and so wet that it made him shiver with sheer pleasure. As a reflex her quim closed around his fingers in a wonderful, fluttering little caress. Unfastening his flies he knelt between her legs and guided his

135

shaft into the silky wet confines of paradise. Her eyes finally flickered into focus and she smiled sleepily as if waking from a dream.

'This is not what I had in mind when I suggested we begin again, Julian,' she whispered.

Julian Morton smiled and kissed her. 'Oh really?' he purred. 'What a pity.'

His hand slid up over her waist and ribs to caress the contours of her breasts. His fingers circled her pert nipples. She moaned softly. He smiled and pulled her up so that she was sitting astride him. His cock seemed to be swallowed whole inside her tight, dripping quim. Locking his fingers in her hair he kissed her fiercely.

'Perhaps we ought to renegotiate the terms of our sexual truce,' he said thickly as he felt her juices trickling out over his balls. 'You look wonderful, I want to fuck you forever.'

Rachel threw back her head, moaning as he kissed and licked her neck. Her skin tasted of sea and sand and sweet perspiration. 'You are a complete bastard, Julian,' she hissed and then ground her sex furiously into his belly.

Julian laughed. 'And there was me thinking you'd never notice. Why don't you touch yourself?' He caught hold of her hand and pushed it down towards the fragrant junction where their bodies met.

'Let me see what you like,' he purred. 'Let me see what turns you on.'

For an instant her eyes locked with his, a flush spreading out over her pale cheeks.

He grinned. 'Don't tell me you've never done it before. I want you to feel how wet you are – it's heaven down there.'

She hesitated for a few seconds and then let him guide her fingers between the heavy outer lips. With no more prompting she began to circle the little bud that lay like a pearl within them.

'Is this what you meant?' she said softly, eyes alight with renewed pleasure. Her fingers quickened and Julian felt the vibrations spreading through her – and then through him, making him gasp with delight.

'Oh yes,' he murmured, straining to push his cock deeper, 'oh yes, that's exactly what I mean.'

Chapter 9

Anthea didn't drive straight back to Albion after she dropped Rachel off at the quay, instead she took Rachel's little sports car on a whistle-stop tour of the village along the coast road around Carfax-Staithe. It felt good to speed in and out of the lanes and byways. She thought about her encounter with Ted Grey – the less Rachel had to do with that family the better, however beautiful Daniel was. The more she thought about it, the more sinister Ted Grey became. Without a great deal of provocation, Anthea suspected he could cause Rachel an awful lot of trouble.

At the head of one of the coastal promontories she pulled the car to a halt and looked out over the sea. In the distance she could see the pine trees on the sandbar – at least Rachel had Julian to protect her now. Shading her eyes to block the sun's glare, she stared out towards the sandy island. She could just make out the lines of Julian's boat against the grey water. Anthea almost regretted not going now, it would be a glorious setting for a summer picnic. Clambering back into the car she started back to Albion. Petra was due to pick her up at lunchtime and she didn't want to be late.

It was still quite early when Anthea parked the car under the shadows of Albion's walls. She hadn't particularly meant to go exploring, but alone in the house time seemed to pass so slowly. Taking a glass of wine for company she went upstairs into Rachel's studio. On the easel was her latest work. Anthea lifted the dust sheet and smiled: Daniel Grey, as stunning and windswept as Rachel could imagine him. Anthea reached out to trace the contours of his broad chest and then realised the paint was still wet – it wouldn't do to spoil anything so glorious, or leave any evidence that she had been spying.

Rachel's brush strokes had transformed her young lover into a stunning sexual icon, pagan and earthy – something barely tame. Anthea shivered, feeling a tiny thrill of pleasure low down in her stomach. If this was how Rachel saw him then it was no wonder that she was so entranced. His skin seemed to glow with an inner light and those flashing blue eyes of his looked as if they could see right inside your soul.

When Anthea heard the studio door open behind her she assumed it was the housemaid, and didn't even turn round.

A slight cough made her jump. Daniel stood in the centre of the studio, dressed in a white cotton shirt and faded cream breeches. Anthea swallowed hard.

Daniel looked uncomfortable. 'Sorry to disturb you, Miss Leven, I saw the car and thought maybe Ra . . . Mrs Ingram might be home.'

Anthea glanced at the portrait and then back at the boy. 'She will be out all day. She's gone for a picnic on Julian Morton's boat. Do you make a habit of letting yourself into the house?'

He shuffled uncomfortably from foot to foot.

'Well?' she persisted.

Daniel glanced toward the dais. 'While I'm posing for Mrs Ingram she said it was all right if I came up. I only came up now because I thought – I hoped – she might be here.'

Anthea looked him up and down and wondered if he was telling the truth. After all, he had seen her driving Rachel's car away from the quayside. Perhaps he hadn't seen Rachel heading across the bay in the skiff – or perhaps he'd come into the studio to spy too.

She pointed towards the easel. 'Have you seen Rachel's new painting?'

'No, Miss Leven, I haven't.'

Anthea lifted the dust sheet off. 'Then I think you better had.'

She watched his face as he stepped up to look at the canvas. His jaw dropped and he reddened furiously as his eyes moved over Rachel's work – and for an instant she thought she detected a look of relief in his eyes.

'Well? What do you think?' she said. He was so close to her that Anthea could see the tight blond curls in the neck of his shirt and the laughter lines that were already beginning to form around his eyes.

He shook his head. 'I don't know what to say. It's beautiful, it's . . . it's . . .'

Anthea turned towards him. 'You have to end this, you know,' she said in an undertone.

Daniel stared down at her. 'I don't understand what you mean,' she said.

Anthea lifted an eyebrow derisively. 'Really? Well, a lot of other people seem to. If you really love Rachel you'll tell her your friendship is over.' Anthea indicated the painting. 'I know she loves you, I just didn't realise how much. You only have to look at this to know what she feels. But if you do truly love her, you'll finish this love affair before it's too late. You have to let her get on with her life.'

Daniel's face darkened. 'You mean with Julian Morton, don't you?'

For a moment he loomed over her and Anthea imagined what it must be like to take him to bed – to see that passion aroused and angry, to feel his cock thrust deep between her legs, his hands on her breasts, her lips alight with his hot, wild kisses. The image was so intense and vivid that she felt herself blush and quickly looked away.

'Yes,' she said, struggling to regain her composure. 'That is exactly what I mean. What can you possibly offer her?' she touched the canvas like a talisman. 'Nothing except this.'

Daniel's eyes were stormy. 'This?' he whispered. 'What do you mean, this?'

Anthea reddened. 'This passion, this foolish, pointless all-consuming desire. Please, Daniel, let Rachel go. She's been so lonely since André died. She ought to settle down and marry someone like Julian and build herself a real life. She needs a life, a family. This painting is part of some elaborate fantasy she has woven around you.'

She stopped to see if her words were having any effect.

Daniel looked first at the painting and then at her. 'You're jealous,' he said suddenly, as if he had seen it in her eyes.

Anthea stepped back, his words like a body blow. And she realised with a sense of panic that he was right – some part of her, some deep, covetous part that she had kept well hidden, even from herself, was deeply envious of Rachel Ingram. She stared at him in astonishment. How was it someone like Daniel could have seen it when she wasn't even consciously aware of it herself?

Daniel moved closer, eyes fixed on the portrait, 'You're jealous of her talent, of this house – jealous of Julian, and, most of all, jealous of her having me.'

A knock on the studio door rooted them both to the spot as if they had been frozen. Anthea, struggling to find her voice, called, 'Yes?'

Molly opened the door and looked first at Daniel and then at Anthea.

'Miss Morton is here for you, miss.'

Anthea nodded stiffly. 'Thank you, Molly, I'll be down in second. Would you please show Daniel out?'

When the boy had gone Anthea stared at Rachel's painting, fists clenched, her nails pressing hard into her palms. Some part of her wanted to smash Daniel's portrait until not a shred of canvas remained.

She swallowed hard and took a deep breath to steady herself. Rachel and Julian Morton now, and no doubt after a decent time they would get married and all this stupidity would be behind her. This foolish, suicidal passion would be just a distant memory.

Anthea bit her lip, struggling to control the tears that threatened to fall. Much as she loved Rachel – and she did – Rachel had always had everything Anthea had wanted – including having had André Ingram as husband. The thought was so old and so shocking that Anthea gasped as if someone had punched her, wondering where the old jealousy had been buried. What was it Rachel had said about Daniel when they had been talking in the kitchen the night before?

No one has ever made me feel the way he does. It's as if meeting him has done something to me – I'm certain if I hadn't met him I'd never have made love to Julian Morton last night, it wouldn't even have occurred to me. It's as if being with Daniel has helped to set me free – he's helped find some part of me that I never knew existed.

Anthea shivered, hearing Rachel's voice inside her head as clearly as if she was standing beside her. It seemed that Rachel wasn't the only one to learn things about herself under Daniel's influence.

She took a deep breath and ran her hands down over her hair and then her dress, trying to tidy away her thoughts and regain her composure.

Downstairs, in the sitting room, Petra Morton was waiting. She looked up as Anthea opened the door and got to her feet.

'Darling, you look very pale. Are you all right?'

Anthea nodded. 'I'm fine, but do you mind if we go out straight away?'

Petra smiled and pressed an airy kiss to Anthea's cheeks. 'Not at all, I thought we could drive up the coast for lunch and then maybe you'd like to . . .' she paused, eyes bright with mischief. 'Well, we'll see how it goes, shall we?'

Anthea nodded and hurried out into the hall to pick up her jacket.

Hidden by the tumble of branches in the pines on the sandbar, Rachel gasped and rested her head on Julian's shoulder. She felt her orgasm building beneath her fingertips like a summer

143

storm and thrust forward instinctively onto his cock. He grunted and pushed deeper, crushing her fingers tight against her body. That last, final split-second of pressure was enough to tip her into oblivion. Her whole body was suffused with a blinding light, driving away every thought accept for the intensity of her pleasure. She threw back her head, riding the waves down and down on a glittering helix of delight. Deep inside she felt Julian's cock throbbing like a beating heart, forcing deeper and deeper into her sopping quim. Knowing that he was coming with her on the wild ride, his instinctive animal thrusts plaiting and twisting with the sensations in her body, made her cry out with sheer joy. She slumped down against him, breathing hard, her senses full of the smell of his sweat and the glowing heat from his body. He pulled her tight against him and thrust one last time, as if he regretted that they had finished. Finally she pulled away, once more aware of the sand against her skin, the crackle of pine needles and the soft sea breeze.

Opening her eyes she was surprised to find Julian staring down at her.

'What a find you are, Rachel,' he said breathlessly.

Rachel reddened. 'You promised me—'

Julian lifted a finger on her lips. 'Ssh, you're not going to complain, are you?'

Rachel's colour intensified. She looked away and eased herself off him. Their skin seemed to have melted together. A slick trail of pleasure oozed out onto her thighs. Julian grinned as she began to search amongst the tumble of branches for her knickers.

'I really shouldn't bother, my dear.'

Rachel glared at him, a red hot plume of outrage kindling in her stomach. 'You planned this, didn't you?'

Julian shrugged. 'Guilty as charged, m'lud.' He caught hold of her hand. 'But look into my eyes and tell me you didn't enjoy it? The chase? That wonderful rush of adrenaline when they found you? Didn't your heart roar when they threw you down to the ground and took you. I saw the look on your face – you loved every second. It's very addictive.'

Rachel plucked her camisole and knickers up from where Peter and Perry had dropped them. They were covered in pine needles and filthy.

Julian's eyes darkened. 'Why don't you just take the rest off?'

Rachel stared at him and then looked up towards the trees where she could hear the excited shrieks and laughter from other members of Julian's party as they found their own route to release.

'What happens now?' she said in an undertone, ignoring his suggestion and pulling her dress straight.

Julian smiled, took the underwear from her hands and stuffed it unceremoniously into his pocket. 'A little Bacchanalian feasting, an ocean of wine, some of my guests will no doubt have a swim in the bay—' He pulled her closer. 'And while we are here on the sandbar I'd like to point out that you women are our slaves.'

Rachel laughed. 'I beg your pardon?'

Julian guided her up the bank between the tumble of fallen branches. 'It's a tradition; you wait, you serve – you do exactly as I and my friends tell you.'

Rachel stopped mid-stride. 'Why did you invite me to come with you today?'

Julian smiled thinly. 'I thought you might enjoy the experience.' He paused, eyes twinkling. 'Or do you always prefer younger, less schooled flesh?'

Rachel was so shocked that she couldn't speak.

Julian grinned. 'Don't be so coy about your young lover. Your liaison with that boy is common knowledge. It's your pretence of restrained genteel passion that amuses me, though I have to admit you do it very convincingly.' He looked back at her. 'It seems such a waste. I thought you might prefer to feel a man between your legs for a change.'

Rachel stared at him and struggled to marshal her thoughts.

145

How had Julian found out about Daniel?

They were walking slowly between the trees now, back towards the picnic. He turned round to face her and grinned. 'Tell me I'm wrong. You need a master, not a slave, Rachel.'

She shivered. 'You just want to take,' she said flatly.

Julian nodded. 'Oh yes, it's part of my nature, just as giving and obeying is part of yours. Remember, I saw you in my bedroom begging me to beat you – and just now with Perry and Peter, you relished being taken by them, reduced to your pure essence, pure sexual magic, like an animal.' He grinned again and added, 'And, I heartily approve, I think we can do great things for each other, Rachel, great things.'

Ahead of them, through the trees, Rachel could see some of the other guests had returned to the picnic area. In their absence the crew of the boat had set up tables and sun loungers under the shadow of the trees around a central table, laden with food.

Rachel tried to keep her eyes down towards the sand. From the other side of the clearing a girl, naked except for her stockings and garters, was being playfully pulled through the trees by one of the men, her wrists tied with the belt of her dress, which her captor had slung over his shoulder. The girl was giggling and resisting but her show of reluctance was far from convincing.

Julian grinned. 'See you bagged one, Harry.'

The man waved a hand. 'Aye, and if she doesn't do what I want I've already told her I'll hand her over to your crew.'

Julian shot a glance at Rachel. 'A very fitting punishment, and one I may consider myself if Rachel here doesn't play.'

Around the table the men had settled themselves down on the chairs and rugs. The women were beginning to serve lunch – most were naked.

Julian turned to face Rachel, and slipped his hand up under her dress. 'See, I told you. A terrible shame to keep yourself hidden away. My friends will think you have something to

146

hide.' With a single upward movement he pulled her dress up over her head.

Her nakedness was met with a cheer of approval from the men on the chairs. One – whom she thought was Tippy Smith – looked up her up and down approvingly.

'Very nice, Julian. Send her over here with some grapes, will you?' He had a young, naked woman crouched at his feet, her torso resting against his legs.

Julian grinned. 'It seems someone wants you already, my dear. Here, don't keep Tippy waiting.' He picked up a plate of fruit from the table and handed it to her.

Rachel walked slowly across the shadowy sand towards Julian's friend. He didn't take the grapes at once, instead his eyes wandered up and down over her body. He leant over, eyes still taking in the subtle details. Rachel coloured – it was impossible not to under such undisguised admiration. In spite of her embarrassment, another part of her was excited and flattered by Tippy's interest. He leant over and picked up a bottle of champagne and a glass from the shadows under his seat.

'Oh, damn it all, Julian, the bubbly is warm.'

Julian, who had settled himself down to be waited on by Izzy, sighed theatrically. 'What do you expect in this heat? There's some more in a lobster pot in the sea, send one of the girl's down to fetch it.'

Tippy waved Rachel away. 'You heard him – go and fetch it, and don't be long.' Rachel turned away. He sounded almost sullen, like a child. She glanced out from the cover of the trees. The water seemed a long way off across a stretch of open sand.

Izzy, who was pouring Julian a drink, grinned at her. 'It's all right, no one will see you. I'll come if you like. We can have a quick dip to cool off. Is that all right, Julian?'

Julian nodded and waved them away. 'Why not? I may join you if it gets much hotter. Go on – and don't forget the bloody champers.'

147

With a giggle, Izzy passed Julian his glass then caught hold of Rachel's hand and pulled her towards the sea. The little blonde girl seemed totally at home with her nakedness and ran enthusiastically towards the blue-grey water.

'Wait,' said Rachel breathlessly, trying to keep pace with her as Izzy plunged headlong into the waves.

Izzy turned and smiled; she looked radiant. Her white-blonde hair and the fine covering of sand that clung to her uptilted breasts made her look like some strange, erotic water spirit.

'Are you having a good time?' said Izzy, as she plunged belly down amongst the shallow waves.

Rachel didn't know what to say. Izzy continued. 'Sometimes the boys are the slaves – that's fun too.'

Rachel stared at her in astonishment. 'You've done this before? I mean, come here to the sandbar?'

Izzy nodded and ran through the shallow water. 'Yes. Last year, when they were sorting the estate out, we came out here twice. Apparently Julian's uncle used to use the island for the same thing – it's lovely isn't it? Sometimes they just play at their house. It'll be better now Julian's moved to Medsham, with all the gardens and everything. Although Petra might have other ideas – Julian complains she cramps his style.' She giggled. 'And messes the numbers up too.'

'I don't understand.'

Izzy bent down and pulled the lobster pot closer. 'She only likes women. It cuts down on who can do what to whom.' She peered up at Rachel. 'But I thought you already knew that? You must have seen her with your friend, Anthea.'

Rachel was stunned. Languidly, the blonde girl rolled over into the surf, splashing herself with water as she hauled the rope that secured the basket. She flicked the water towards Rachel. It hit her skin like a flurry of bee stings.

'Come on,' said Izzy, 'it's beautifully warm.'

Rachel, her mind still on Izzy's revelation about Anthea, slipped down into the water.

Amongst the pine trees Julian topped up his glass of warm champagne and focused his attention on the two women in the sea. They made a beautiful and compelling tableau. Rachel was tall and dark, slim, almost statuesque. Beside her, dancing in and out of the waves, Izzy frolicked like a puppy. He smiled; Izzy was greatly affected by the atmosphere on the sandbar. Under the heat of the sun the air still rippled with quiet expectation. He sipped from his glass. How nice it would be to see his new protégée take Izzy in her arms and sink slowly into the surf. He imagined walking down towards them, to find Rachel kneeling between Izzy's long, slim legs, her face pressed to the girl's tight, glistening sex. He shivered and wondered if he could somehow engineer it. Beside him Tippy Smith held his hands up to his eyes.

'Where the bloody hell have they got to with the champagne?'

Julian pointed towards the sea. 'Our slaves are indulging in a little skinny-dipping.'

Tippy snorted. 'Well, they want to get their arses back up here with the bubbly.' He pulled himself to his feet, pushing aside the girl at his feet, and strode out from the shadow of the pines. 'Ahoy there, ladies, a chap could die of thirst round here.'

Both women looked up like startled deer. Tippy grinned.

'That seems to have done the trick. Damn nice filly, that new woman of yours, Julian. You wouldn't mind if I put her through her paces would you, old man?'

Julian shook his head. 'Be my guest, old chap, you know the house rules as well as I do. Though I was thinking it might be rather nice to see those two together.'

Tippy stared at him for a few seconds and then grinned. 'She goes both ways, does she, this new woman of yours? You were damned lucky to find her in this Godforsaken backwater, if you ask me.'

Julian thrust his hands into his pockets. 'I'm not sure she

does, but I think we can manage to persuade her.'

Down on the beach, Rachel and Izzy strode from the sea cradling a bottle of champagne each. The sunlight picked out the droplets of water on their bodies, highlighting their pale skin with flecks of gold.

Halfway up the beach, giggling wildly, Izzy broke into run. 'Race you,' she shouted.

Rachel threw back her head and laughed and gamely chased after her.

It seemed no more than seconds later that they burst into the ring of trees, breathing heavily. Izzy, still cradling the bottle between her tiny breasts, threw herself down onto a rug. She rolled over and held the bottle up towards Julian, who had seated himself in a deckchair.

'Here we are, master, cool and wet. Just right to drink. Shall I open it?'

Rachel, eyes alight looked up at Julian. 'I'd love a glass, I'm not used to running.'

Julian lifted an eyebrow. She seemed, finally, to be relaxing. 'The slaves are supposed to serve us, not the other way around. Was the water warm?'

Rachel picked up a towel from the pile on one of the chairs and began to dry her hair. 'It was lovely. I've never swam naked before.'

'It was very pleasant to watch.' Julian beckoned to Izzy. 'Come here, my dear.'

Izzy, as pale as ivory got to her feet and stood in front of him. 'What now, master?' she said with a grin.

Gently, he slipped his hand between her thighs and began to explore her sex. Izzy shivered with delight while Rachel looked on in astonishment. Julian pulled a face.

'You're very dry now, sweetie,' he said softly. 'Perhaps Rachel might like to help you rectify the situation. Why don't you go and ask her to make you nice and wet, I'm sure she wouldn't mind.'

Rachel, towel in hand, froze.

Tippy Smith, his interested aroused, leered at the two women with an expression close to hunger.

Izzy glanced at Rachel and then shimmied over to her, pouting provocatively.

Rachel instinctively took a step back.

Julian could already feel his cock stirring into life.

Izzy giggled. 'Oh, come on,' she said in a low, sensuous voice. 'We're slaves, remember, we have to do as we're told.' She lifted a finger to trace the outline of Rachel's jaw and with the other hand gently pulled away the towel that divided them.

Rachel stared at Julian as if hoping he might call Izzy off.

Julian grinned, Izzy was impossible to ignore. Her body exuded an erotic charge like a glowfly. Before Rachel could stop her Izzy leant forward and kissed her gently, her fingers lifting to caress Rachel's nipples. Her touch was as gentle as gossamer but the effect on Rachel was astonishing. It was obvious to Julian that Rachel had never kissed a woman before and he knew from experience that Izzy's lips were gentle but insistent.

At first she stared with horror at her seductress, then she moaned and then finally, as if fighting against everything in her nature, her arms slipped around the blonde girl's waist and pulled her closer. Izzy groaned triumphantly, her lips fixed on Rachel's as she stroked and teased her breasts.

Already her nipples were hard and dark. Julian closed his eyes briefly and swallowed hard: this was everything he had imagined and better. The women's nipples brushed fleetingly and then their breasts pressed closer together. Izzy's lips worked hungrily on Rachel's, showering kiss after kiss onto her open mouth. Rachel gasped as if she was drowning. Julian did wonder if she might pull away – he could sense the inner battle she was fighting.

Next to him, Tippy was watching the women with a glazed expression. Izzy, meanwhile, was gently insinuating her hand between Rachel's legs, seeking out the soft, moist places that glowed like a treasure between them. As her fingers brushed the soft down that framed her outer lips, Rachel let out a thin, high-pitched cry – a stunning mixture of fear and delight. Izzy pressed on, opening the cleft, easing her fingers inside. Julian could barely contain his excitement.

'Touch me,' Izzy murmured, so indistinctly that Julian had to strain to pick out the words. 'Please, touch me, I want to feel your fingers inside me, please.'

At first Rachel didn't move – in fact Julian was convinced that this would be the moment when she would call a halt – and then quite suddenly her hand lifted to cup the girl's tiny breasts, a thumb circling the soft, flushed peak.

Izzy rewarded her with a guttural moan. 'Oh yes,' she purred, 'that's it. That's it. Now, here, this is what I want you to do, make me wet for them.' Catching hold of Rachel's other hand she guided it down between her legs.

Julian gasped.

Rachel couldn't believe what she was doing and almost pulled away. She was astonished by the heat and wetness of the girl's body. It almost felt as if she was touching herself – the soft moist folds and crevices seemed so familiar, and yet so different. It was an odd sensation – closer to curiosity than lust.

Izzy still held her wrist, guiding Rachel's fingers deeper into the throbbing depths of her sex. To her surprise, as her finger slid inside, Izzy's muscles tightened around her. The sensation made her gasp – it felt like a mouth sucking at her. Izzy, meanwhile, had found the little pleasure bud that nestled between the lips of Rachel's quim and artfully drew her fingertip down over the swollen hood. The flare of pleasure quenched her fear, and as it spun through Rachel's mind, it seemed for an instant to block out every thought. She felt hands guiding her down onto one of the sunbeds and it took her a second or two to realise it was not Izzy, but Julian who was directing her. She wanted to cry out, to call a halt, but although her mind protested, every fibre of her body ached for the gentle seduction to continue.

Izzy seemed to slither over her, disentangling herself from Rachel's fingers, pressing tiny, fluttering kisses to her breasts, her neck, her belly, the soft contours of her hips. Rachel struggled to catch her breath and then gasped as Izzy's fingers eagerly parted the lips of her quim and ran her tongue over the engorged ridge of Rachel's clitoris.

It was like a solar flare – Rachel's legs opened wider as if they had a mind of their own. She found herself lifting her hips up towards the girl's hungry mouth, longing to feel more, have more, experience more of Izzy's hypnotic caresses.

The girl moved again, this time circling Rachel so that after a few seconds she seemed to climb seamlessly onto Rachel's chest. All the time her tongue worked its intense spiral of magic on her sex. Slowly, she eased back, working herself onto all fours. Even before she saw it, Rachel could smell the oceanic perfume of the blonde girl's sex – it was like a flower, scarlet and wet with droplets of creamy dew.

Rachel closed her eyes and let her instincts guide her – this was no place for reason. She felt Izzy's thigh brush her cheek and tentatively pressed a kiss to the milky flesh. Izzy's skin tasted of the sea, as if her skin was echoing the flavours and perfume of her most secret places. Revulsion and fear mingled with a hungry animal need, and without waiting to see which would win, Rachel ran her tongue over the plump folds of Izzy's quim. It opened like the petals of a rose and flooded her senses with its rich, pungent musk. Between Rachel's legs Izzy groaned softly and then renewed her attentions to Rachel's body.

It was stunning, each sensation was so new and yet so familiar, different but gloriously the same. Izzy's tongue and fingers were like quicksilver, as if they could anticipate her every need, her every desire. Despite her fear, Rachel found it impossible not to follow Izzy's lead. Without letting her mind free, she kissed and touched, fingers and tongue working up a symphony of pleasure in the other woman's body.

Izzy brought her again and again to the very brink of release until the tension in Rachel's stomach and body was almost unbearable. She realised that Izzy was waiting until the instant when her pleasure matched her own, and then suddenly her tongue flicked like a snake's over the hardened ridge of Rachel's clitoris and she screamed out in astonishment as the pleasure closed over them both.

Before she really had time to think, firm hands pulled the women apart. Tippy, eyes ablaze, loomed over her and without prelude plunged his cock into her glowing sex. She arched up towards him, the power of his first thrust so vigorous that it took her breath away. The way he entered her body seemed so brutal after Izzy's gentle knowing kisses. He pulled her into his arms, manhandling her like a doll onto his rampant shaft.

To her surprise, his brutal, crude attentions rekindled the glowing fire in her sex, catapulting her back into the throes of orgasm. She began to move with him, matching his passion stroke for stroke. Beside them, Julian hunched over Izzy, sliding home into her, making the blonde girl squeal with delight as he dragged her back to the very brink of release.

It seemed to Rachel as if the four of them were linked in some intense dance of desire, on and on they went, pressing down into the cool sand, touching and brushing against each other, until finally they could hold back no longer.

Julian threw back his head and let out a thick, angry grunt as the tide of excitement closed over him. It seemed to be no more than seconds before Tippy joined him, and as the men thrashed and thrust, Rachel surrendered to the hypnotic pull of the erotic tide and plunged headlong into foam-tipped waves of pleasure.

For a few seconds, when they were finished, all Rachel was aware of were the sounds and feelings of passion and then, as the sensation ebbed away she opened her eyes. To her horror, at the instant Tippy slithered out of her a flurry of applause broke out in the semi-circle of observers who had gathered round them. Rachel flushed crimson and grabbed the towel up off the sand to cover herself.

Peter and Perry, the men who had caught Rachel earlier, slapped Tippy on the shoulder and handed him a glass of champagne. Tippy downed it in one and then grinned, rolled over onto the sand and closed his eyes.

'My God, that was good,' he gasped. 'Hot women and cold champagne, what more could a man ask for?'

Rachel wrapped the towel around her, struggling to regain some shred of composure. Julian, still panting and crouched beside Izzy, grinned and lifted his glass in salute.

'What indeed? I'd like to propose a toast, to my new friend, Mrs Rachel Ingram,' he said with amusement.

Rachel kept her eyes firmly fixed on the sand as the audience lifted their glasses in a toast and murmured her name.

Julian settled himself on the sun lounger. 'Now, I think it's time we all ate,' he said indicating the table. 'Perhaps Rachel you'd like to come and sit over here with me and Izzy?'

Rachel nodded dumbly and then said, 'I think I'd like to swim first.'

Julian nodded. 'Of course, but don't be too long, remember you ladies are our slaves today. But I'm sure you won't forget, will you?' His comment was met with general amusement.

Rachel didn't bother to answer him but turned and hurried across the beach to the sea. Her face was scarlet. She had been so conscious of her nakedness when she and Izzy had gone for the champagne, this time she was oblivious, all she wanted was to be away from Julian and the rest of his party. She plunged into the shallow water, wading out through the waves until it was deep enough to swim. After just a few strokes she slowly turned on her back and closed her eyes, letting the sun and water wash away her sense of shame.

Chapter 10

'So, did you have a good time on the boat?' said Anthea, pouring Rachel a glass of sherry. 'You look as if you've caught the sun. Petra and I had the most super lunch down at Wells. I hope you didn't mind my inviting her back. You know how quiet it can be here.'

Rachel smiled without humour as Anthea handed her a drink. Petra Morton, who was curled up in one the armchairs in the sitting room at Albion, smiled knowingly. Rachel just hoped Anthea hadn't invited Petra to join them for dinner.

Rachel had been longing to get home, and it had only been as Julian stopped the car that she realised she'd quite forgotten Anthea was staying at Albion.

Anthea sipped her sherry. 'Why didn't Julian come in with you?'

'He'd got guests waiting for him back at Medsham.'

Petra's eyes flashed mischievously. 'I'm rather surprised he didn't invite you to join them for dinner. Tippy and his crew are tremendous fun.' Her focus sharpened as she added, 'There's always lots of fun to be had by all when they're around.'

Rachel got to her feet, her whole body felt stiff and sore. Even after the events on the sandbar the trip home on the boat had still stunned her. Julian had suggested they sail a little further up the coast to round the day off before going back to Carfax-Staithe. As they sailed in a great arc back towards port, the passengers had a played debauched game of blindman's buff. When the blindfolded player caught someone they had seduced their victim in front of the others. Rachel shivered, remembering the look of glee on Tippy Smith's face as his hands had settled on Perry. The crowd had cheered as the men embraced, hands working eagerly across each other's bodies. She fought to suppress the memory of the way their muscled bodies worked in harmony against the handrail of the deck. Around them the group shouted their encouragement and clapped out a tribal beat.

Rachel had turned away, longing to hide below in the cabin, but Julian had blocked her path and gently turned her round so that she had no choice but to watch the exhibition. Tippy and Perry's excitement spread out through their audience like a fever, men and women fell eagerly into each others arms. It was as if they thought the world was about to end. Within minutes the deck was a heaving mass of naked bodies. Only Rachel and Julian stood back from the melée. Julian caught hold of her arm.

'Why don't we go and have another glass of champagne while the children are playing, there will be plenty of time for us to join them later,' he said, guiding her down into the cool, shadowed galley.

Rachel, grateful to be away from the events on the deck, closed her eyes for a second and then shook her head. 'No, thank you,' she said in a low even voice. 'I think I've had quite enough fun for one day.'

Julian had shrugged philosophically and handed her a glass. 'Suit yourself. Tippy will be staying for a few days, plenty of time for you to change your mind.' His eyes had been alight with mischief.

Rachel shook her head to clear the images and looked squarely at Petra. She had no doubt that dinner at Medsham would involve participating in a lot more of Julian's favourite games.

'Actually Julian did suggest that I join them, but I wanted to get home. If you'll both excuse me, I think I'll go and get changed for dinner.'

Anthea smiled. 'I've asked Molly to serve supper on the terrace, I hope you don't mind?'

Petra got to her feet. 'And I think I ought to be getting back, Julian will wonder where on earth I've got to.'

Rachel nodded. 'Nice to have seen you again,' she said. As she turned to leave she saw a look flash between the other two women – and instantly understood it. It spoke of a dark secret, a tiny white-hot glow of mutual desire. She sighed and made her way upstairs, wondering what else there was that she had missed.

In the privacy of her bathroom Rachel slipped out of her summer dress. Beneath it she was naked – Julian had kept her underwear as a trophy of their day out on the sandbar – and her skin was bruised and scratched. She stared at her reflection. Far from wanting to spend an evening with Anthea what she really wanted to do was to have a long, hot bath and creep into bed.

She turned on the bath taps and poured oil into the tumble of bubbling water; she had no doubt that Anthea and Petra had passed the afternoon in the guest bedroom or somewhere similar. Anthea was positively glowing.

Rachel bundled up her dress, threw it into the laundry basket and climbed into the bath. The water eased around her body as gently as a lover's caress – Izzy's caress. Rachel closed her eyes, blushing furiously as she imagined the little blonde's tongue working its way across the moist folds of her sex, igniting a flame that had roared into a fire of passion. She could almost feel the gentle touch of the woman's fingers as they circled her nipples, delicately stirring them into life.

She sank lower, letting the fantasy claim her. She closed her eyes, relishing the relaxing effects of the warm water. Its embrace felt so much like Izzy's fingers. She shivered, a little ripple of expectation threading its way through her. Her reverie was disturbed by Anthea banging on the door.

'Rachel? Can I come in, darling? I want to hear all about your trip with Julian.'

Rachel instantly snapped back to reality and groaned. 'Go away, I'm in the bath.'

Anthea giggled. 'Come on, open up. Don't be shy, it's only me.' The bathroom door opened just a fraction. Rachel sank lower under the cover of bubbles.

'I promise not to peek. I'm just eaten with curiosity. Did he propose?'

Rachel laughed, thinking about Julian's intense, erotic games on the island. He proposed all right, he proposed all kinds of things but certainly not marriage.

Anthea slipped through the opening in the door and perched on a stool, discreetly averting her eyes while Rachel pulled the shower curtain around the bath.

'Can't this wait – I won't be more than ten minutes?'

'No,' said Anthea emphatically. 'I want to know everything that happened. It seemed so romantic sailing off together into the sunlight. I thought he might pop the question. He's perfect.'

Rachel sighed. 'You have a very peculiar idea of what makes a perfect man.'

Rachel had decided that she wouldn't tell Anthea what had happened on the sandbar. She wasn't certain she even really wanted to think about it, let alone repeat it aloud.

Anthea groaned. 'Please – you have to tell me.'

Rachel wondered how little of the truth she could get away with.

'We played games and then had a picnic,' she said, trying to fill the expectant silence.

'How romantic. When are you going to see him again?'

Rachel tugged the curtain aside and stared at Anthea.

'This is ridiculous. Why do you want me to settle down with Julian Morton, of all people?'

Anthea pulled a cigarette from her bag and lit it. 'I don't know, it just seems like the perfect ending to a summer spent out here in the back of beyond.'

Rachel snorted and lay back in the bath. 'He's a complete and utter cad,' she said flatly.

Anthea giggled. 'So much the better, you don't want a dull man, do you? So, when *are* you going to see him again?'

'I don't know. I said he could ring me.' Rachel paused, wondering how far she dare go with this conversation. Hooking her robe off the chair beside the bath she wrapped it round her and tied the belt tight before pulling the curtain aside.

'Are you certain that this is to do with Julian? Aren't you more interested in trying to stop me seeing Daniel?' She watched her friend's face for some kind of reaction. Anthea coloured lightly.

'Or,' Rachel continued crossly, 'has all this frantic matchmaking got something to do with being able to see Petra whenever the fancy takes you?'

Two scarlet roses flared on Anthea's cheeks. 'What on earth do you mean?' she said quickly.

Rachel picked up a towel and rubbed her hair briskly. 'Do you really want me to answer that?' she said in an undertone.

Anthea got to her feet and took a long pull on her cigarette. 'How did you find out?' she said in a quiet voice.

'What worries me more is why I had never guessed before.' Rachel sighed. 'You must have thought I was very naive. Was it that you didn't trust me enough to say anything? All that nonsense with all those men in your life. Or is it that you like both?'

Anthea smiled wolfishly. 'Something like that. Most men find it incredibly erotic to think about two women making love, and then of course they like the challenge of trying to convert me. They think that given the right man – them of course – they can save me forever from the attraction of female flesh.' She paused as if considering how much to say, and then continued. 'How little they know. It is the most glorious, purest form of pleasure I've ever experienced. No fumbling, no not knowing what to touch or how to touch it. It's like self love . . .' she paused and then stared at Rachel, who could feel the colour rushing into her cheeks.

'My God,' Anthea hissed in astonishment. 'You already

know, don't you? Is that what you were doing out on the sandbar? My God – what?'

Rachel turned away. 'I have to get dressed now,' she said quickly, cutting Anthea short. 'Tell Molly we'll eat in half an hour.'

When Anthea had gone Rachel rubbed the mist off the bathroom mirror and stared thoughtfully at her reflection. Slowly she slipped off her robe. Her hair had curled into soft, damp ringlets, framing her small face. Her breasts were high, her belly taut and yet unmistakably feminine. Anthea was right, making love to Izzy had been a complete revelation. She could almost taste and smell the girl's body above her, pressing her sex down onto Rachel's waiting tongue, her breasts brushing her belly. Rachel shivered, quite unable to keep the intense images at bay.

Deep inside she felt a phantom echo of excitement and almost without thinking ran her hands down over her breasts and belly to the warm, glowing spot that lay between her legs.

Wisps of gossamer-fine moisture clung to her fingers as she drove them deep inside. Closing her eyes, she imagined Tippy and Julian looking on while she and Izzy made love.

She could feel the little pleasure bud hardening. Her fingers brushed it tentatively and at once a trembling arch of pleasure spiralled out from the epicentre. She circled it again, pressing down harder this time, relishing the little spiral growing in intensity as it moved out from the spot beneath her fingertips.

For a brief second she wondered what might happen if Anthea opened the bathroom door now. Would she fall into her arms, pull her close so that Anthea's fingers could follow the same intense pattern as her own, their lips locked in a passionate kiss? Or would she open her legs and guide Anthea onto her knees, her hands eagerly pressing Anthea's lips to her sex, letting the woman's tongue lap and nibble at the same glorious spot? She shivered, astonished by the wild fantasies her mind was conjuring.

A flicker of movement in the mirror registered somewhere

in her mind and she half turned towards the bedroom door, expecting Anthea to walk into the room. To her total surprise, the curtains on the balcony parted and Daniel stepped across the room towards her.

'How long have you been there?' she gasped in horror.

Daniel smiled. 'Long enough. I've been waiting down at the boat house for you to get back.'

He caught hold of her hand, still nestling in the pit of her sex and lifted it to his lips, drawing her fingers over his tongue. She started to tremble as he pulled her into his arms and lapped hungrily at each finger in turn. He looked deep into her eyes and then let her hand drop back to her side, turning her gently so that they were both caught in the cold, misty eye of the mirror. His hands curled round her, working slowly across her body.

'I saw the painting today while you were out on the boat. It's beautiful. I had no idea you felt . . .' he paused, voice fading away as if he needed to gather his thoughts. 'I was afraid that Julian Morton might have given you all the satisfaction you needed.' He stroked a finger around one pert nipple, bringing another ripple of pleasure to the surface. 'Looking at the painting I knew I was wrong.'

Rachel swallowed hard as he pressed his lips to her neck. 'Please Daniel, Anthea is waiting for me downstairs . . .' She knew her words wouldn't stop him – and besides, her excuses were half-hearted. She wanted to share the excitement that had been building in her belly. His tanned arms, a stark contrast to her pale skin, held her tight against him, trailing a finger down towards the cleft of her sex. She moaned with delight, not just enjoying the sensation but also the stunning, living portrait of the passion reflected in the looking glass. She pushed back against him, rubbing her backside into his groin. He groaned and thrust forward, the sensation of his rough breeches against her flesh setting her mind alight.

He spun her round, kissing her fiercely, tongue forcing its way into her mouth. The passion that had been building inside her suddenly burst through the surface like a volcanic eruption. Lips locked to his, she bit his tongue and clawed furiously at his clothes, propelling them both back against the bathroom wall. The kiss of the cold tiles against her skin made her gasp with surprise as they sank slowly towards the floor. Her need was so great that it seemed to roar in her ears like thunder. She fought with his buttons, ripping his shirt open, hands dropping from his bare chest to his flies.

All the time, as she fought to undress him he kissed her, his hands kneading her flesh, nipping and stroking at her breasts, driving her further and further towards the bright fire that called her. Dragging his trousers down to his knees she trapped his cock between her fingers and tried to pull him into her.

He was immovable. Pushing his trousers down to the floor, he knelt beside her and guided his cock into her mouth. It was a gesture so charged with sexual energy that she shivered. Everything about his stance said he owned her, he dominated her mind and her body and now he wanted to prove it. The strange thing was she didn't feel threatened by him and knew she wanted nothing more than to give him the pleasure he sought.

Looking up towards the mirror she was captivated by the image. The artist in her marvelled at the stunning composition, the way the glass caught their passion and desire – and then the thought faded, replaced by the hungry need that glowed inside her. Eagerly, her lips and tongue lapped and sucked at the throbbing bulk of his shaft, hands lifting to cradle his balls. Something about the way he held her head against him made her feel as if she had totally surrendered herself to his desire and his body. Without thinking she uncurled so she lay alongside him, head still buried in his groin, allowing him to explore every inch of her feverish body.

'Sweet Jesus,' he murmured as he slid a finger into her quim.

She could imagine what he could feel – a molten furnace,

red hot and desperate for a lover's touch. He groaned as she ran her tongue around the end of his shaft, crossing back and forth so that the very tip of her tongue dipped into the single eye. She could taste his excitement, salty and warm in her mouth. His whole body seemed to be humming with pent-up desire. She began to slide her hand up and down over his foreskin, gently guiding it back and forth in time with the caresses of her mouth. He gasped, flexing his muscles to stay the rising tide of pleasure. His cock wept tears of joy onto her tongue, filling her mouth with the rich taste of desire. Her hand worked back to cup the bulk of his balls, her thumb pressing up against the roof of his shaft.

He moaned and she sensed he was struggling to control his growing excitement. Just as she thought he might explode into her mouth her jerked her head away and, grabbing her wrists thrust them up above her head, pinning her to the cold, wet floor. She licked her lips.

'What do you want now?' she whispered.

Daniel grinned as he climbed onto her. 'I've got everything I want right here.'

Straddling her thighs he brushed his moist cock over her belly, seeking entry.

'Let me help,' she murmured, struggling against the grip he had on her wrists.

The boy shook his head, eyes dark with desire. 'It'll find it's own way,' he whispered and moving down a little, nuzzled the swollen crown between the outer lips of her quim. The sensation made her gasp with delight. He held it there for what seemed like an eternity, teasing her, making her strain up towards him so that she could drive him deeper.

'Please,' she whispered, 'Please . . . don't make me wait, let me feel you inside me, I want you . . .'

Daniel grinned again. 'I know,' he said and slowly, fraction by fraction, he slipped deeper into the moist confines of her body.

She let out a thin wail of delight as her sex tightened round him, holding him fast, making every nerve ending in her body flare white-hot. This was what she wanted. This boy, more than Julian, more even than Izzy, had the power to ignite a flame in her mind and body that threatened to burn her up, to engulf her and leave only charred ruins in his wake.

As he drove into her she arched up to meet him, impaling herself again and again on his cock. Her body seemed to catch light at that instant. Nothing else remained in her mind except for the sheer overwhelming pleasure of feeling his body in hers. Every sense was full of him: she could taste only his kisses, smell only his body, see only his face, hear only his breathing, touch only his skin . . .

She mewled in terror, afraid that she would be lost forever in his embrace. It was no more than an instant before the first great wave of release tore through her, and then there was another and another, each so intense that they were almost painful. As the after-tremors hit again and again, like surf crashing upon a desolate beach, she wondered if she would go mad with the sheer intensity of the sensations Daniel lit in her. As she arched up for the final stroke she felt him lose control. He lunged forward, biting her shoulders, fingers clawing at her breasts, as if he too felt the pull of oblivion.

Finally they lay still amongst the tumble of damp towels, still joined, both hot and breathless. Lazily, eyes heavy with spent passion, Daniel pushed her hair off her face and kissed her tenderly.

'Your friend Anthea told me that I was to finish this,' he said softly. 'Leave you in the hands of Julian Morton. I came to ask if that was what you wanted.'

Rachel sighed. 'Oh Daniel, how can you ask me now? I don't know what to say to you.' She felt the boy's body tense. 'I keep thinking that this is madness, but when I'm with you I can't imagine living a life without you.' She paused, trying to work out whether he understood the paradox she was wrestling with.

He stared down at her. 'Just tell me you love me.'

166

Rachel shivered, wondering if love alone would be enough to sustain them. If they could stay there, as they were now it would hold them forever. She touched his face, praying he would understand what she was about to say.

'If we stay here what life can we offer each other? Would the people in Carfax accept you as my lover? Or my husband? The more I think about it the more impossible it seems. And what about later? I'm fourteen years older than you – what happens when I'm old and you are still young?' She stopped, hardly able to contemplate the pain she might feel if he left her for someone closer to his own age. 'Are you sure you want to be saddled with an old lady?'

She looked up into his dark stormy blue eyes. They glittered with unshed tears, and seeing them made Rachel's pain more intense. She wanted nothing more than to hold him in her arms and send the rest of the world away, but the adult in her knew that that was impossible. 'And even if you say you can now, what's to say that you'll feel the same in a year or five years or ten? What if you realise you've made the most awful mistake?'

Daniel traced the outline of her lips with his finger. 'Do you think I'm so shallow as that?' His voice trembled with emotion. 'I've thought about it endlessly, over and over again. People round here might not like it, but they'll get used to the idea. And as for the age difference?' He grinned unsteadily. 'I keep worrying that you might meet some handsome rich old man who'll steal you away from me, someone who is your social equal. We both have a lot to lose and a lot at risk. I know I'm man enough for you in the bedroom, but what about culture and education and books and . . . I keep wondering if I have enough about me to keep you interested.'

Rachel reached up and kissed him. 'Oh, my love. I don't know what to say. Everything inside me hurts so much—' she stopped and rubbed a stray tear off her cheek. 'I really have to go, Molly will be serving dinner soon. There's no rush for us to make this decision, is there?'

Daniel shook his head and returned her kiss with one that made her flesh tingle.

'I want you to say yes, I want you to say that you'll want me forever, and I'd like you to say it now, but you're right, there is no rush, Rachel. I can wait for as long as it takes.'

Slowly he unpeeled his body from hers. As his sex slid noiselessly from inside her, she felt as if he was robbing her of something precious. Gracefully he picked up his clothes from the floor.

'I'm glad you came to see me,' she said softly. 'I was so worried that you wouldn't come back.' She struggled to keep the emotion out of her voice.

Daniel glanced across at her. 'I couldn't keep away.'

'Will I see you tomorrow?'

For a moment Daniel hesitated and then said, 'My stepfather wants me to help him for a day or two with a job he's taken on in the village. It won't affect your garden too much, I can catch up with the work later in the week.' His eyes held hers. 'I could come tomorrow night if you wanted me to sit for you.'

Rachel licked her lips. The light in the evening wouldn't be good enough for her to paint but they both knew that the painting was just an excuse. She nodded. 'That would be lovely. What time will you finish work?'

Daniel buttoned his shirt. 'I'll wash and eat first and then come over, so I'll be here around eight.'

Rachel nodded and cursed Anthea for using Albion as a bolt-hole – if she hadn't been staying Rachel would have suggested Daniel should come earlier and they could share dinner, a bath, a bottle of wine and a long, slow night of passion. She shivered as her mind spun a dozen different erotic possibilities. Daniel pulled on his boots. Like the prince in Sleeping Beauty he leant over and brushed his lips with hers.

'Tomorrow night,' he whispered. She closed her eyes, reluctant to watch him leaving. When she opened them again the bathroom was empty, only the flutter of the curtains at the bedroom window suggesting anyone had been that way.

Anthea, who was already sitting at the table on the terrace, shook out her napkin. 'You took your time – mind you, it's paid off, you look much better.'

Rachel smiled and took her place while Molly brought out the plates. Molly's face was tight, almost sullen. Rachel wondered if she had seen Daniel leaving.

Anthea poured them both a glass of wine. 'About Petra,' she began, not meeting Rachel's eyes. 'I think I ought to explain.'

Rachel held up a hand to silence her. 'There's no need. I just feel so stupid that I hadn't guessed before.' She glanced up at Anthea. 'Just don't let your feelings for Petra cloud your judgement about Julian.'

Anthea snorted. 'Don't be silly. I don't see why you're so reticent about him. God, I'd snap him up if the shoe was on the other foot.' She tore her bread roll into pieces. 'He's good looking and obviously very keen. The perfect match, I'd have thought.'

Rachel sighed and looked out over the garden towards the sea. She couldn't see the sandbar from where they were sitting, but its influence and the things she had experienced there clung to some part of her mind like mud. If she married Julian – as Anthea was so keen to suggest – what on earth would her life be like? Julian was a pleasure seeker, moving shamelessly from one passion to another. Did she really want to join his debauched entourage? And then there was Daniel, so unsuitable in other ways, but alight with a simple, stunning pure love that glowed like a beacon in the darkness.

'We'll see,' she said non-committally. 'I think it would be better if I took things a little more slowly with Julian.'

Anthea snorted. 'Oh Rachel, you sound so prim. You're not pinning your hopes on making something with the gardener, are you?'

Rachel said nothing, wondering if Anthea had read her mind.

Anthea continued. 'I wouldn't be surprised if we'd seen the last of him. He strikes me as being very fickle.'

Rachel smiled. Anthea was obviously hoping her suggestion to Daniel that he finished their friendship had taken root. Anthea wasn't a mind-reader after all; if she had been she would have known why it was that Rachel looked so much better after her bath.

Chapter 11

Ted Grey was no fool. On Monday morning he set his men to work clearing drains and gutters so that they could make a start on repairing Medsham house. He made sure Daniel was kept well away from the house, fetching and unloading materials – he didn't fancy being in competition with his step-son for any pickings that might be on offer, even though they were plentiful.

Once inside the house Ted decided to take himself on an unofficial tour. Although it was still early the house had a most peculiar atmosphere which intrigued him. Upstairs, whilst looking for damp plaster, he quietly opened a bedroom door and came across a young buck rogering one of Julian's female house guests. The lovers were so engrossed in their own pleasure that they didn't notice him. Caught in a shaft of sunlight the girl was straddling the man's hips, hands in her hair, breasts jiggling up and down in time with her lover's frantic thrusts. The cries of pleasure she made as she rode towards oblivion rang in Ted's ears, making his groin ache.

In a back bedroom, away from the main house, he came across another chap who was buggering his young companion with great enthusiasm. Ted hadn't seen anything like it since he'd been in the army and stood for a second or two watching them strain and sweat, their faces contorted with pleasure, wondering if the men would turn and see him there – and wondering what he might do if they did.

And as an antidote to all that brutal, Spartan passion, on the first floor Ted was delighted to discover Miss Petra Morton still in bed with her little blonde companion. It seemed, he thought gleefully, that by accepting Julian Morton's offer of work he had inadvertently stumbled across a rural Sodom and Gomorra – a house full of debauched secrets and lusts that could well prove to be a wonderful little investment for the future. The only real problem was that unless he was very shrewd he would end up with nothing for all his spying other than the cruel ache in his groin that couldn't be satisfied.

At around ten, when the house began to stir into life, Ted slipped into the dressing room that adjoined Petra Morton's bedroom through a door on the landing, and then very carefully opened the internal door an inch or two. He hoped to see a fine display of female flesh.

As if on cue, in the bedroom Petra Morton climbed stiffly out of bed, as naked as nature intended, and stretched in front of the open window. Ted swallowed hard, struggling to keep quiet – it really wouldn't do to be discovered.

Petra Morton was slim with heavy breasts. Her elegant posture and fashionable hair cut did little to disguise the fact that she was one of nature's predators – she looked debauched. It seemed a terrible shame that a body like that was wasted on other women. She stretched again and as she turned towards the bed, Ted thought she looked like a well groomed cat.

'So, did you enjoy your day out yesterday, Izzy?' said Petra, yawning and running her hands over her torso.

The blonde girl, still curled amongst a tumble of bedclothes, slowly opened one eye. 'You know what Julian's boat trips are like.'

Petra snorted. 'Yes, I do,' she snapped petulantly, 'I was just hoping you'd be a little more forthcoming with the details.'

Izzy, dressed in a sheer white chemise, grinned and rolled over onto her belly.

Ted, crouched in his hiding place, shivered as the girl's breasts rippled under the almost transparent silk.

'What's the matter?' said Izzy in a teasing voice. 'Not the

172

green-eyed god surely, Petra? I didn't kick up a fuss when you said you were off to Albion to spend the day in bed with Anthea Leven, did I? Was she as good as you hoped?'

Petra pulled a face. 'She was just fine, but I want to know about Rachel Ingram.'

Izzy giggled. 'You've really got it bad about Julian's new friend, haven't you? I'd have thought you'd be pleased, after all she's got money. And she makes Julian very happy. They will make a perfect pair—'

Petra rounded on her furiously. 'Stop messing about Izzy, what was she like? Did she take part in Julian's little games?'

Izzy looked hurt. 'There's really no need to shout.'

Petra sighed. 'I'm sorry, I just want to know that's all. Did she play?'

Izzy nodded. 'After a little bit of persuasion from Julian. I think she was quite reluctant, but it was all right in the end.'

'What do you mean, all right in the end? What happened?'

Izzy sat up and crossed her legs, looking thoughtful, as if she had to struggle to remember. 'She played chase. I'm not sure who caught her, but someone must have – she came back to the picnic with Julian stark naked. And then we played slaves and masters . . .' Izzy hesitated. 'You know how Julian loves that one.'

'And?' Petra prompted.

Izzy coloured slightly. 'Julian and Tippy made me make love to her.'

In the dressing room Ted Grey grinned triumphantly as he imagined Rachel Ingram naked, her body at the mercy of the delightful little blonde.

Petra stared at her incredulously. 'You and Rachel Ingram? Are you serious?'

Izzy nodded. 'We had a swim and then Julian complained that I was too dry to make love to . . .' her voice faded. 'Tippy wanted to make love to Rachel, so that left Julian with me – though I think they really just wanted to watch Rachel and I together, you know what those two are like.'

173

Petra hadn't moved. 'My God,' she hissed. 'You and Rachel Ingram?'

Izzy nodded. 'It was lovely and exciting because I knew it was her first time. She was nervous but very curious . . .' She stared at Petra who was still transfixed, '. . . and she was good.'

'My God,' Petra murmured again as if she hadn't heard a word Izzy had said. 'You and Rachel Ingram? I can't believe it. I wonder if Anthea knows about it.'

Izzy slipped off the bed and picked up a robe. 'I very much doubt it, Rachel was terribly quiet on the way home. I can't imagine she's the sort to kiss and tell. I think she rather surprised herself.' Gently, Izzy draped the robe over Petra's shoulders. 'Here,' she said in a low voice, 'you'll catch your death.'

Petra snorted and plucked a cigarette from a box on the side table. 'I wish I'd known about this when I was at Albion with Anthea.' She smiled slyly. 'Imagine the little *menagé à trois* that we could have arranged. I think I might drive out there tonight and suggest it.'

Izzy stared at her. 'What about me?' Her face contorted into a sullen pout.

Petra grinned at her. 'Oh, stop it, for goodness sake, darling. The house is full of people who think you're a gorgeous little thing. You certainly won't be lonely.' She leant forward and kissed Izzy on the forehead. 'Now don't make such a fuss. I'm just going to nip down and see Julian.'

Izzy sniffed and sat down at the dressing table.

Julian Morton was a little disconcerted by all the building activity going on around Medsham. He hoped his guests would have enough sense to be discreet. In his study, sitting at his desk, he was reviewing the state of the family finances. It did not make uplifting reading. Even given that Ted Grey was charging a very reasonable price for the work it would still take most of the ready cash Julian could call upon. He slipped the least urgent bills back into a drawer and spread those that were most pressing in a fan on the blotter, then picked up the phone and dialled Rachel's number.

Her maid took the call and few seconds later Rachel, sounding slightly out of breath picked up the receiver.

'Hello?'

Julian smiled warmly at the sound of her voice. 'Rachel, I hope I didn't disturb you. How are you this morning?'

He heard her take a deep breath. 'I'm fine thank you, Julian, and how are you?' She sounded very formal and stilted.

The smile lingered on Julian's lips as he thought about her in the pine trees on the sandbar, totally sated, her sex wet and open, her breasts dusted with sand, nipples taut and dark, with Izzy poised above her, her lips wet with Rachel's essence. It was a very compelling image.

'I'm fine. I was ringing to see if you might like to join us for dinner this evening? Your friend Anthea would be most welcome to join us too.'

There was a pause. He imagined her cradling the phone in her hands, eyes dark with excitement. She still sounded breathless – perhaps she and Anthea had already discovered they had more in common than they thought. The idea took flight and he fantasised that Anthea was standing beside her, one hand cupping those delicious breasts, the other snaking lower to caress her sex, as plump and ripe as it had looked and felt on the sandbar.

He grinned, perhaps if they came to dinner he could join them – the fantasy developed, getting more and more complex in the tense open silence. Now, in his mind, Rachel crouched above him, drawing his cock deep inside her, while his tongue worked deep in the juicy folds of Anthea's quim. The two women would sit facing each other, their bodies glowing in the evening sunlight. He could almost taste Anthea's sex, almost see their hands caressing each others breasts, lips pressed together in a long hungry kiss. He shuddered, feeling his cock stir into life. Julian took a deep breath, struggling hard to control his mind and asked her again.

'Come on, Rachel, say you'll both come over – it'll be great fun.'

'Thank you,' she said slowly, as if picking her way through her words. 'It's really most kind of you to think of us, but I'm afraid I won't be able to accept.'

Julian groaned. 'Oh Rachel, I'm so disappointed in you.' He scrambled around for a lever to make her accept. 'I was hoping we might discuss the boat. After all, now you've been out on her I thought perhaps we could arrange for her to moor up to Albion.' He paused, letting the words sink in. 'If she's there we could use her more often. I really thought you had enjoyed our day out.'

He could almost hear her embarrassment and smiled again. When Rachel finally spoke her tone was icy.

'I think, Julian, if you remember, we had an agreement that our friendship would move at a slower pace. Yesterday was . . . was . . .' she struggled to find the right words. 'A betrayal of our arrangement.'

Julian laughed. 'A betrayal? That's rather strong. Are you telling me you didn't have fun? I thought you had had a glorious time; so many new experiences in one day. Don't be so straight-laced, say you'll come over and join us for dinner. Tippy would be delighted to renew his acquaintance. He was most impressed by your enthusiasm.'

Rachel made a small, uneasy noise and then said, 'Thank you for the invitation Julian, but actually I have already made other plans.' The phone went dead in his hands. Ruefully Julian dropped the receiver back into its cradle and shuffled the bills back into the letter tray. As the envelopes vanished under a pile of other paperwork he promptly forgot them. It took considerably longer for his fantasy about Rachel Ingram and Anthea Leven to fade.

Ted Grey was beginning to get nervous concealed in his lair – at any minute Izzy could cross the room to the dressing room and root him out. Silently he started to back towards the hall – though his retreat was a reluctant one. After all, he had hoped to see a display of passion, but it wasn't worth the risk of discovery.

The things Petra had said about Rachel had made him think though; a late night trip out to Albion was a different matter. Down amongst the dunes there were lots of places he could hide and watch while Petra Morton seduced Rachel and that other woman, Anthea. He pulled his cap out of his pocket – not a bad idea at all. And afterwards, if the show was up to scratch, he might take another pop at young Molly, the maid. He rubbed his hands down over his belly, trying to ignore the hard press of his cock where it rubbed against his work trousers. It was hungry.

Since Petra left, Izzy had been staring at herself in the dressing table mirror, chin resting in her palm. Just as Ted got to the hall door, she sighed and pulled her chemise up over her head. Her image was caught in the reflection, giving Ted a stunning view of her tiny uptilted breasts, and from behind, he could see the creamy white curves of her back and waist. As he watched she leant forward and ran a finger over one tight pink areola, teasing it into stiffness. She stared at her body thoughtfully and then took a lipstick from a bowl on the dressing table. She twisted it up and ran it around her lips, outlining her generous mouth with a scarlet outline, and then with a sly grin she turned her attention to her breasts and smeared a little of the cream over her nipples. They looked stunning in contrast to her body's pallor. Gently, eyes still firmly fixed on the mirror she began to roll the tips between her thumb and forefinger, admiring the effect.

In the shadows of the bathroom, Ted Grey could barely breathe – perhaps he might stay after all. Silently he crawled back to his original position and waited.

On the stool, one of the girl's hands had worked down over her ribs towards her belly. Ted swallowed hard and closed his eyes, willing her to stand up and let him watch her touch the little, pale, fur-trimmed pussy that he suspected lay between those long legs of hers . . .

Julian was still deep in thought when a knock at his office door brought him back to reality. Quickly, he pulled his jacket down over the embarrassing bulge in the front of his cavalry twills. Petra, dressed in a shimmering negligee, pushed the door open and smiled at him.

'Good morning, darling. I thought I would find you in here. I suppose you know the house is absolutely crawling with workmen? You might have said something.'

Julian sighed. Such a shame Rachel had turned him down. 'I'm sorry, it completely slipped my mind.' He looked her up and down and then turned back to his desk. 'What, disappointed you can't find anything to your tastes?'

Petra's face hardened. 'Why are you in such a foul mood this morning? I thought you'd had a wonderful day out with your Mrs Ingram on the boat yesterday.'

Julian snorted. 'I suppose you've been talking to Izzy. That girl's got a big mouth. Sadly, though, my little *sojourn* with Mrs Ingram doesn't seem to have done me a lot of good. What did you want anyway?'

Petra nodded towards the phone.

Julian got up and stretched. 'Is Izzy still upstairs.'

Petra grinned at him. 'Yes, why?'

'I'm feeling terribly lonely.'

Petra snorted. 'She was just saying much the same thing. Why don't you go up and keep her company while I use the phone?'

Julian was surprised that his sister agreed so readily, normally he had to twist some sort of deal out of her. He was quietly grateful – the ache in his groin was getting almost unbearable. Perhaps her affections had moved on to Anthea Leven – now there was an interesting thought. He waved her towards the desk.

'Be my guest,' he said with a grin and hurried upstairs.

In his hiding place, Ted Grey could feel his mouth begin to water as he watched Izzy in the mirror. She was brushing her hair in a languid kind of way, watching her reflection as if she, too, was captivated by her beauty. With each brushstroke one breast rose, its starburst of scarlet lipstick accentuating the movement, and then, on the downward sweep it seemed to sway and then settle, as if a watery current was passing through it. He couldn't see her other hand but he could guess where it was – buried deep in the warm folds of her quim, a finger working away at her pleasure bud.

Ted was completely mesmerised, his cock aching, as Izzy began another long slow stroke. Her skin seemed almost luminescent. It was all he could do to stop from leaping out of his hiding place and taking her then and there. But of course that was impossible – if he moved or showed himself she would shriek and run away like a startled deer. He would have to content himself with just watching her.

A knock at the bedroom door made him jump. A second or two later Julian strode into the room, without waiting to be invited. Izzy froze, one hand out of sight the other still raised above her head. Her fingers tightened on the shaft of the silver-backed hairbrush.

'Well, well, well,' he grinned. 'What a pretty picture you make.'

Izzy didn't move. 'Does Petra know you're up here? She was going to come and find you.'

Julian nodded. 'I've already seen her,' he said, tugging his tie undone and dropping it onto the bed. 'She gave me *carte blanche*.'

Izzy sighed in exasperation and threw the brush back onto the dressing table. 'You two use me as if I'm some kind of toy to be handed backwards and forwards between you.'

Julian stepped behind her and rested his hands on her shoulders.

'You really ought to be flattered by all the attention.' He

picked up the hairbrush and turned it thoughtfully in her fingers. 'Or perhaps I ought to punish you for being so damned ungrateful.'

Izzy laughed. 'Ungrateful? You must be joking.'

Ted watched them intently, the breath tight in his chest. Julian's eyes had darkened and he could sense the man's growing excitement – what he would give to be in Julian's place!

In the bedroom Julian took a deep breath.

'Not at all, I think you are terribly ungrateful. All the wonderful things we've given you and not a single word of gratitude. If it wasn't for Petra and I you'd still be selling cigarettes out of a tray in that awful little club, turning a trick here and there to help pay your rent. I really think you need to be shown who is master here.'

Izzy grinned. 'Oh, you do, do you?' she said, turning round slowly and getting to her feet. Her sex was framed by a blush of curls. Her nipples were hard now, dark scarlet blossoms still in bed. Julian stroked one finger thoughtfully over the handle of the brush, eyes fixed on her breasts.

'I never realised you were so artistic,' he said slyly, glancing at the open lipstick beside the mirror. 'Is that Petra's too? She won't be very pleased, you know. She's always telling me how she hates people to interfere with her things.'

Izzy giggled and then lowered her eyes provocatively. 'Perhaps I do deserve a little punishment after all. What had you got in mind?'

Julian indicated the stool and then sat down on it. 'I want you to tell me about the worst thing you've ever had to do. Tell me about one of those terrible men who seduced you before Petra and I came along to rescue you.'

Izzy lifted an eyebrow, but Julian waved her on. 'Come on, don't keep me waiting.'

Izzy smiled. 'Once upon a time . . .'

Julian pulled a face. 'I'm serious.'

She took a deep breath, linking her fingers together like a

naughty schoolgirl. In his hiding place, Ted was totally mesmerised.

'There used to be a couple of men who came into the club, they were old friends of the manager. He introduced me to them when I first started to work there. They used to like to fuck me over one of the tables at the club when it was shut. The two of them would arrive early, while I was setting up for supper. They liked it best just before we opened, sometimes they had barely finished when the doors opened. One of them, Giles, he was quite old, used to keep my knickers in his pocket afterwards as a souvenir, then he'd keep touching me during the evening. It excited him to think that I was naked under my dress.' She reddened. 'Will that do?'

Julian shook his head. 'No, not quite. Did they both have you at the same time.'

Izzy picked uncomfortably at her fingernails. 'You're so cruel, Julian,' she said softly.

Julian grinned. 'Did they?'

Ted was delighted by her obvious embarrassment.

Izzy took a deep breath. 'Sometimes they'd have me at the same time, sometimes one after the other.'

Julian nodded. 'And how did they have you?'

Izzy's colour flushed from palest pink to scarlet. 'Giles liked to bugger me,' she whispered. 'And Roy, the other one, liked me to take him in my mouth, and while they were doing it the manager liked to watch them.'

Izzy wriggled self-consciously, her eyes glittering with unshed tears of embarrassment.

Julian stroked her arm gently. His tone was kind and sympathetic. 'That's good. They tell me that confession is terribly good for the soul. Now, if you bend over I'll show you what I do to naughty, ungrateful girls.' He offered her his hand.

Ted Grey, still crouched behind the door of the dressing room held his breath. Izzy stretched and then curled slowly over Julian's lap, easing into position so that she was comfortable. Ted could just make out the soft lips of her quim, peeking provocatively between the arc of her buttocks. He shivered.

Julian ran his hand over the girl's back, and then with a flash of movement brought the hairbrush squarely down across her backside. Izzy shrieked and arched upwards.

'You bastard,' she hissed. 'That really hurt.'

Julian grinned and swung his arm back again. 'It was supposed to, now be quiet and take your punishment like a good girl.'

The next blow was even harder, making Izzy gasp. Tears flooded down her face. The pale, creamy skin on her buttocks flushed crimson. Julian ran his hand over her ribs to steady her, his fingers seeking out her scarlet-tipped breasts.

'Who's an ungrateful little minx?' he whispered as he laid on another stroke.

Izzy snorted. As the blow exploded her legs opened wider to reveal the moisture forming amongst the petals of her sex. Julian brought the brush down again.

'I'm waiting,' he growled.

Izzy let out a tiny, strangled groan. 'I am,' she whispered breathlessly.

'Louder,' snapped Julian, swinging the brush back for another explosive blow.

'I am,' she gasped again. Julian grinned and rolled her onto the floor, the brush still in his hand. As she struggled to get to her feet he pushed her firmly down onto all fours.

'Stay exactly where you are. I haven't finished with you yet,' he said thickly, hands struggling with the buttons of his fly.

Ted fought to keep the sound of his breathing under control. Between his legs his cock was crashing out a rhythm that matched his heartbeat. Another few seconds and he feared he wouldn't be able to hold his excitement back any longer.

Julian's cock was slim and curved like a scimitar. Holding onto Izzy's neck he dropped to his knees behind her and thrust his hand between her thighs. She moaned and bit her lip, while he grinned triumphantly and guided his cock home.

He seemed to be without compassion, driving himself deep into the depths of her body. She mewled and stretched back against him, setting a counter rhythm. Her breasts were taut and flushed with excitement. Julian pulled her closer, one hand settling on her hips, the other moving round to cup her swaying breasts. His fingers twisted and tugged at her nipples making her gasp and writhe. Her eyes were closed, her mouth open in a perfect red oval. Julian's face was contorted into a maniacal grin as he jerked her back and forth onto him. He groaned and thrust deeper still, forcing Izzy's face and breasts down onto carpet. She gasped and began to sob, mouth still open, passion coursing through her as Julian rode on and on.

Ted Grey gasped, oblivious to the sound, as he imagined sliding his throbbing cock deep into her mouth. The image was just too much. Rolling away from the bathroom door, his ears still full of the sounds of Izzy and Julian's wild love-making, he jerked his cock out of his trousers and began to work it frantically – it was no more than an instant before the white-hot waves roared up through him, making him convulse and twitch, as he desperately struggled to remain silent.

When he finally moved back to watch the last throws of Izzy and Julian making love, Julian was just slipping, exhausted, from the girl's body.

Izzy rolled over onto her back and looked up at him. Her skin was still flushed, beads of sweat glinting in the valley between her breasts.

'Julian, do you really think I'm ungrateful?'

Julian snorted as he tucked his cock back into his trousers. 'No, of course not. I'm surprised you've put up with us for as long as you have. By the way, do you know who Petra was going to ring?'

Izzy pouted. 'It always feels as if you two are in some kind of competition. She said she was going to ring that woman who's staying with Rachel Ingram.'

Julian stared at her. 'Anthea Leven? Are you sure?'

Izzy pulled her robe off the bed. 'Yes, of course I'm sure. I think your sister is hoping to seduce your friend, Rachel. You know that she can't bear to be out-done by you.'

'Rachel?' he said softly. 'Are you sure? She's interested in Rachel?'

Izzy seemed annoyed by his questions and pulled the belt on her robe tight. 'That's what I said, didn't I? Are you going deaf?'

Julian shot her an angry glance. 'I don't want her chasing after Rachel in case she frightens her off. I've got plans of my own for Rachel Ingram.'

Izzy pulled a face and then yawned. 'Really? You surprise me,' she said sarcastically. 'Let me guess, you are hoping that she will be willing to bail you out of this mess.' She held up her hands to encompass the house. 'Are you hoping she'll marry you? Have you got around to asking her yet?'

Julian's jaw dropped and he stared at her in astonishment. 'Have you been talking to Petra? Did Petra tell you that?' he hissed furiously.

Izzy laughed and sat back at the dressing table. 'She didn't need to – you think you're so clever, but you're completely transparent Julian Morton, you and your damned sister. Now, if you've finished punishing me would you please be sure to close the door as you leave.'

Julian was speechless. He opened his mouth as if to add something and then, thinking better of it, turned on his heel and left.

In the dressing room, Ted Grey smiled to himself – his work at Medsham was proving more fruitful than he could possibly have hoped for. Quietly, he got to his feet and considered what he had learnt. If he told Daniel that Julian Morton had plans to marry Rachel Ingram perhaps the boy would back off, leaving the way open for Ted to have another try at her.

He grinned, thinking about the soft brush of Rachel

Ingram's breasts under her dress as he had touched her. Of course she had had to pretend to be outraged and upset – her type didn't like to be thought of as too willing. He tugged his jacket straight. He'd take a little ride out to Albion House after work and see what was going on. Maybe if he was lucky he'd get there in time to see Petra Morton's attempts to persuade Rachel into bed too – and then perhaps he would offer his services. As he backed towards the door his mind tumbled headlong into an intricate fantasy revolving around seducing the women at Albion House. The sexual relief of a few minutes earlier was forgotten as the images took on a life of their own. He pulled on his cap, and when he was certain that Julian had gone, he crept back out into the hall.

When Rachel came down from her studio for lunch, Anthea was sitting in the window of the sitting room leafing through a book. Although the French windows were open to catch the sea breeze, it was still almost unbearably hot. Anthea, dressed in thin cotton shift, looked terribly listless perched amongst the cushions on the window seat. She looked up as Rachel came in.

'How's the painting going?' she asked conversationally.

Rachel smiled. 'Fine. You look terribly bored. You know you don't have to stay here – you could ring the Rawlingsons and go to their house party if you want. I'm sure that chap – Peter? – would come and fetch you if you asked him. I wouldn't be offended.

Anthea shook her head. 'No, I was fed up with him anyway.'

Rachel smiled. 'Well, why not go out? If you wanted to borrow the car again, you're very welcome. Why don't you go for a drive along the coast?'

Anthea closed the book with a decisive snap. 'Actually I might just do that. I thought I'd go down to the quay and see if they'd got any fresh fish. Do you think they sell it all first thing?' She stopped, colouring slightly. 'Oh and I hope you don't mind but I invited Petra over for supper tonight.'

Rachel blew out her cheeks thoughtfully, wondering how she would cope now she was certain that Anthea and Petra were lovers.

'Fine,' she said after a second or two. After all she was expecting Daniel and with Anthea occupied entertaining Petra it would be far easier to make her excuses and slip away.

'I was hoping to work late tonight anyway, so you two can have an intimate little dinner *à deux* if you like.'

Anthea's colour deepened. 'Are you sure?'

Rachel laughed. 'Positively, I really loathe the idea of playing gooseberry.'

A flurry of hot air blew in through the open windows. Anthea winced.

'It's so hot today. It must be like an oven in your studio. Why don't you come for a drive with me? You look as if you could do with a break, and you said you were going to work later.'

Rachel nodded. 'Why not.'

Anthea smiled. 'Good, that's settled then. The air's very close – do you think we'll have a storm?'

Rachel shrugged. 'It certainly feels as if there's one about. Perhaps we ought to abandon the idea of a drive and have a siesta instead.'

For an instant Rachel felt Anthea's eyes rest on her body and she shivered without thinking. In that split second she had seen the desire in Anthea's face and felt it register in some deep, unchartered part of her psyche.

'Is than an invitation?' said Anthea quickly, with a hint of amusement in her voice.

Rachel struggled to maintain her smile. 'No, darling, it isn't,' she said gently. 'Now if you'll excuse me, I'll go and tell Molly we're ready to have lunch.'

It was after six when Ted Grey finally called a halt for the day. Daniel, who had been helping to clear the debris away from the walls, stretched, picked up his shirt and jogged across to the cart.

Ted watched him and then called, 'Oy there, boy, what's your hurry?'

Daniel smiled, pulling on his shirt. 'Nothing really, I told Mrs Ingram I'd go over there tonight and sit for her.' His tone was guarded.

Ted suppressed a triumphant grin. He shook his head.

'Not tonight, you won't, my lad. I've told Bob Clark over at Meadow Lodge that someone'll be over there to pick up a load of timber when we've done here. He took it out of the old rectory when they did it up – he's given me a good price.

Daniel tensed. 'Does it have to be me that goes to fetch it?' he said angrily.

Ted nodded and pulled the money Julian Morton had given him out of his waistcoat pocket. 'I wouldn't trust this amount of money to anyone else. And I can't do it 'cos I've got another job to go and price up.'

He counted out the money in Daniel's hand. 'It's all agreed, all you've got to do is go over there, pay Bob, load it up and take the timber back to our place.'

Daniel looked at the notes in his hand.

'Why didn't you tell me before? I've been into town twice already today for bits and pieces. I could have gone on a bit further, got the wood and saved myself a journey.'

Ted shrugged. 'Must have slipped my mind. Don't worry, when you've done come by the Cutter and I'll buy you a pint.'

Daniel sighed and climbed up into the cart.

'Hold up,' said Ted. 'Not so fast. You can drop me off near the quay.'

Sitting side by side with Ted, Daniel slapped the reins and the horse set off towards Carfax-Staithe. Ted pulled a tobacco tin from his jacket and rolled himself a cigarette.

'You want to be careful, sniffing round Mrs Ingram,' he said quietly. Before Daniel could say anything, Ted continued, 'Things will be different once she's married and you don't want to find yourself caught up b'tween husband and wife. I

187

reckon now we've got this job at Medsham, you might be better sticking up here with me. I'll send one of the other blokes over to Albion to finish off the garden.'

Daniel's face was ashen. He stared at Ted. 'What do you mean, married?' he hissed.

Ted snorted. 'Come on boy, surely you must have heard? I mean, you're up there all the time with her. She and Julian Morton are going to tie the knot. I don't think it's official or anything yet, but you must have guessed it was on the cards.'

'You're lying,' Daniel whispered.

Ted snorted, feigning offence. 'Don't be so daft, where's the mileage for me in that one? I heard them talking about it up at the house this morning while I was working.' He pointed to the road. 'And you want t'look where you're going, we'll be halfway up the verge if you aren't careful.'

Ted was pleased to see the angry little tic below Daniel's left eye and the way the boy's jaw had tightened. It seemed that his step-son had swallowed his red herring hook, line and sinker. He stretched luxuriously. 'I have to admit she's a nice-looking woman though,' he said slyly.

Daniel's fists clenched angrily around the reins.

Chapter 12

All afternoon Rachel wished that the promised storm would break. The air was heavy, making her skull throb. While Anthea went out for a drive, she wandered listlessly from room to room, opening and shutting windows, trying to catch a breeze that would clear the heavy air.

Anthea arrived back at just before tea time with a box of fresh fish then disappeared into the kitchen to have Rachel's housekeeper prepare it. When Anthea went upstairs to bathe and get ready for dinner, Molly set the table in the dining room for two.

The tension of the storm seemed to hang in the air like a whisper of cordite, heating the blood, raising a strange sense of foreboding in amongst a promise of passion.

Petra Morton arrived a little after seven, Rachel was immediately aware of the sexual tension that arced between her and Anthea. She shared an aperitif with them before excusing herself. Grateful to be away from the other women, she unlocked the back door to the courtyard for Daniel and headed upstairs to her studio to wait for him to arrive.

Outside, the sky had darkened to the colour of wet slate. Had she bothered to look, Rachel would have seen a solitary figure making its way across the causeway towards Albion, head down, shoulders hunched against the prevailing wind, a dark silhouette against the heavy grey sky.

In the dining room, Petra Morton refilled Anthea's glass. Her eyes were already bright from wine and her gaze lingered for

189

a few seconds on the heavy curve of the other woman's breasts.

Anthea laughed. 'It seems that the storm's on its way.'

Petra glanced towards the windows. 'I love bad weather. It makes my blood boil.' She grinned. 'Talking of which, why didn't Rachel join us?'

Anthea smiled lazily, then dipped her fingers into the wine before lifting them to Petra's lips. 'She told me she didn't want to play gooseberry.'

Petra snorted. 'Really? Did she also tell you she and my friend Izzy made love while they were out on the sandbar yesterday?'

Anthea stared at her in astonishment, 'Izzy? Your friend? No, she didn't say anything about that,' she stopped, remembering their conversation in the bathroom.

Petra smiled wolfishly. 'According to Julian, painting isn't Rachel's only talent.'

Anthea reddened. 'Rachel? I can't believe it. I thought your brother was in love with her – or at least that he would fall in love with her – I . . .' She stared down into her wine glass. 'I really don't know what to say.'

Petra stretched and then ran her hands down over her own body, fingers lingering on the hard peaks of her nipples. 'What is there to say? I had rather hoped we might be able to persuade her to join us.' she grinned again, 'in a little stormy passion.'

Anthea swallowed hard, gathering her thoughts. 'I really don't see Rachel agreeing to that . . .' as she spoke, a great magnesium flash of lightening scythed through the sky outside the dining room window, drowning out her protest. An instant later there was a roar of thunder that made the panes rattle.

Anthea got to her feet. 'We ought to go and close the windows.'

Petra pouted. 'Won't the servants do that?'

Anthea shook her head. 'The housekeeper has already gone home and I've got no idea where Molly is. If Rachel is working she might not think about it. Come on, let's get it done before it starts to rain.'

Petra shrugged and then said, 'Oh damn, I've left the top down on my car. Can we go outside and do that first?' The effects of the wine made standing up a struggle.

Outside, the wind was roaring off the sea and tearing across the garden. Out in the channel, beyond the garden wall the water was being whipped into a froth. Just as the two women drew level with Petra's car, the heavens opened as if someone above them had turned on a hose.

The rain fell in sheets. Petra shrieked in horror as the water soaked through her cocktail dress and flattened her bob to a sleek pelt. Overhead, another flash of lightening lit up the sky as bright as day. Anthea caught hold of the canvas top of the car and jerked it towards her with a wry grin.

'You look stunning,' she said with a gasp, shaking her head like a dog to clear the rain out of her eyes. The rain was so cold Anthea could barely breathe. Glancing down at her own clothes, she saw that the delicate blue silk was almost transparent now it was wet, and clung to her slim frame in cold, wet folds.

Petra laughed crossly and jerked the roof closed. 'You say all the right things. God, I'm frozen to the bone. I can hardly feel my fingers.'

'Don't worry, we can get changed as soon as we get back inside.' Although that was what she said, Anthea felt an almost overwhelming desire to stay outside in the teeth of the storm and make love to Petra in the thunder and the rain. She could hardly believe how the tension in the air heightened the need in her belly, as if one amplified the other. She looked up and stared in Petra's eyes – and knew instantly that her feelings were reciprocated.

Petra grinned. 'We'd drown,' she said with a wink. In the strange storm light she looked more like a wolf than ever. She opened the car door and leant inside. When she re-emerged seconds later she said, 'I brought a friend along, who I thought you might like to meet.'

The lightening flashed again and Anthea stared at the huge,

curved black dildo that Petra held out toward her.

'My God,' she murmured in surprise. 'It looks terrifying.'

Petra ran her finger along the dark curve of the shaft.

'Oh, don't say that, I bought it in Paris. You'll love it,' she said and stepped closer. She ran the cool shaft over Anthea's arm, making her tingle with anticipation.

'Why don't we go back into the house?' Anthea whispered in an undertone.

Petra ran the dildo through her fingers and slid it down between Anthea's breasts. She leant closer and nuzzled and then licked Anthea's lips with her long, serpentine tongue. Her kiss lit another flare of excitement in Anthea that made her gasp.

'Are you sure?' Petra said, her face just a fraction of an inch away from Anthea's. 'Wouldn't you like to make love here, over my car, out in the elements, with the storm roaring overhead?' Her hands eased down over Anthea's belly and thighs – only the wet fabric impeded her progress. Anthea trembled with a mixture of pleasure and cold.

'Yes, I would, you know I would, but you said yourself that we'd probably drown – or die of exposure in the attempt. What if we were struck by lightening?'

Petra giggled. 'How very cautious of you!' Her eyes were alight with mischief as she continued, 'Mind you, the coroner's report would make good reading, wouldn't it? Here,' she caught hold of Anthea's hand. 'Let's go back inside, have a bath and share the champagne I brought over with me.'

Once they were back in the house, Anthea pulled off her dress as soon as she crossed the threshold. Close behind her, Petra followed suit.

'Where to?' Petra said, still cradling the dildo, her teeth chattering. She looked divine. Her skin was pale and creamy and she was dressed only in knickers, stockings and shoes. Her breasts, with their nipples as hard and dark as cherries, jutted forward, begging for attention.

Anthea grinned and then glanced around – it seemed that

Rachel hadn't reappeared despite the storm breaking.

'We'll go up to Rachel's room. I know that there will be hot water in her bathroom. Come on.'

Upstairs, the French windows were still open in Rachel's bedroom. Anthea hurried inside as the wind lashed the curtains into a winding snake, its roar filling the elegant room, while pools of water formed on the wooden floorboards.

Anthea switched on a single bedside lamp and then slammed the windows shut, shivering violently as the wind exploded onto her wet, almost naked body. The room seemed unnaturally still and quiet when the storm was shut outside. As she turned she saw Petra in silhouette, framed in the doorway. In the gloom her eyes glittered and the darkness gave her skin a strange ivory quality. She smiled, leaning provocatively against the frame of the door. Slowly she turned the dildo over in her fingers and then walked towards Anthea.

The expression on Petra's face rooted Anthea to the spot. When they were no more than a heartbeat away, Petra caught hold of Anthea's hair and pulled her closer, her lips as hot as flame. Her desire seemed as raw and untamed as the storm.

Anthea struggled to catch her breath, while Petra's hands, like talons, seemed to be everywhere, touching and caressing, nipping and stroking, driving Anthea wild with a heady mixture of pleasure and pain. All the time Anthea was aware of the soft brush of the dildo against her flesh, cool and unwieldy.

Gasping, she tried to regain some kind of control – she wanted to share what she was feeling, not have it dragged from her. She kissed Petra back, relishing the sensation of the other woman's breasts crushed against her own.

Outside, lightning exploded across the sky, making Anthea jump. It was enough to unbalance them both and they tumbled backwards onto the bed. Anthea rolled over onto Petra and grabbed the dildo. Grinning wildly she drew it into her mouth, running her tongue along the curved shaft to moisten it, and then slipped her hand between Petra's legs. Even through her knickers Anthea could feel that the blonde woman was already wet, the heat of her sex a stark contrast to the waxy chill of her thighs.

Anthea bent forward and kissed Petra on the mouth, then pressed kisses to her collarbone and each nipple in turn. Beneath her, amongst the crush of white linen, Petra smiled lazily. Anthea set up a spiral of kisses that seemed to glow like sparks in the night air, over her lips, her belly, the soft bowl of her hips until finally she placed a kiss on the thin fabric that divided her from the soft curls on Petra's mound of Venus.

Petra snorted and thrust up towards her, offering herself up to the soft sweep of Anthea's tongue. Anthea's fingers locked in the waistband of her knickers and rolled them down, then she grinned and slipped her hand deeper under Petra's firm buttocks, lifting her ever higher. As her tongue pressed softly into Petra's waiting quim, she slid the dildo gently into its wet, fragrant depths. Petra let out a throaty shriek of delight and clenched her buttocks, flexing her hips so that the dark shaft was driven even deeper.

Anthea lapped eagerly at her pleasure bud and began to work the dildo in and out, her tongue matching its rhythm. Petra mewled and thrust forward again and again, giving herself over entirely to the stormy excitement that burned within them both.

'Let me touch you,' she gasped. 'Come closer, I need to kiss you.'

Lazily, her fingers still around the dildo, Anthea rolled alongside Petra. For a moment their lips met, and then Petra curled round like a snake unfurling so that her mouth was level with Anthea's sex. Her tongue darted out, her teeth and lips an instant behind. Anthea gasped, tiny flares of pleasure igniting and glowing white-hot in the dark places between her thighs.

Another lightning bolt lit up the sky like a magnesium flare and Anthea plunged her tongue back into Petra's quim, as if the lightning had been a starting pistol.

The smells and the tastes of Petra's excitement on her

tongue seemed to amalgamate with the crash of thunder and the roar of the wind, driving Anthea's mind out into a wild landscape of passion and pleasure. Her fingers and tongue worked along the dildo, seeking out the rich flavours from the depths of Petra's writhing body, while all the time the blonde woman's intimate, electrifying caresses worked on and on, bringing Anthea nearer and nearer to the moment of release. Her sex was glowing like a beacon, the muscles deep inside closing and tightening around Petra's probing fingers.

Anthea strained up towards her lover. Her body felt as if it might explode, turning her mind and her body into a million tiny luminescent fragments. Suddenly, as the thunder roared in her ears, the fuse finally burned through and she felt as if she was rising up off the bed, up and up into the dark, angry night sky and then, at the very pinnacle of pleasure, she was suddenly sucked down into the torturous crashing waves of the sea. The sensation was astonishing.

Gasping for breath Anthea turned slightly and glanced out into the darkness, just as another lightning bolt scythed the sky in two. For an instant she thought she saw a face staring in at them through the French windows. It was an abstracted, unconnected thought, it had to be a trick of the light, and when she looked again the face had gone.

Downstairs, Rachel couldn't understand why the house seemed empty. She dried her hands on the rag she kept in the pocket of her apron, wiping away the last of the paint. When the storm had struck she had begun closing windows – where were Anthea and Petra? She glanced out into the maw of the storm. Where was Daniel? She prayed he hadn't been caught out in the rain.

Beyond the gardens of Albion House she could see the waves lashing furiously across the inlet, the prevailing wind fighting with the tide as it struggled to go out. If the causeway was ever going to be flooded it would be on a night like this.

She hurried into the hall and to her surprise found the

front door open. At the foot of the stairs were two discarded dresses – Anthea and Petra seemed to have been caught out by the weather. Picking them up, she slammed the door shut and without thinking hurried upstairs to find them.

As she reached the landing she saw the door to her bedroom was open. Puzzled she moved closer and peered inside – and what she saw made the breath catch in her throat.

In the lamplight Petra Morton and Anthea were making love on her bed. Anthea was driving something dark between Petra's open thighs. The curved shaft glistened with Petra's juices. Beside Anthea, the other woman was writhing frantically, gasping for air, her breasts flushed, nipples hard and dark, caught in the arc of golden lamplight. The scene was so extraordinarily compelling that, in spite of her revulsion, Rachel found it impossible to look away.

The two women looked so perfect, so sinuous, like two snakes entwined. As Anthea moved, her breasts swayed like silk. She pulled away for an instant and then her mouth opened a fraction before closing onto the rise of Petra's gaping sex.

Rachel was stunned, feeling a compelling ripple of excitement shimmer through her, beginning somewhere deep in the pit of her belly. Heat rose up inside her like a tide; the whole room seemed to be suffused with passion, as if a scent rolled out from the tumble of sheets in an unseen mist.

Rachel felt her pulse quicken and caught hold of the doorframe to steady herself. She had been waiting for Daniel in the studio, so her mind was already filled with torrid images of passion. The women's excitement intensified the hungry longing.

Anthea moaned as Petra's tongue flicked back and forth across her clitoris. Rachel closed her eyes, feeling as if the woman's caresses, the touch of that snaking, curling tongue, was buried deep in her own body. The ripple of passion inside her grew, making her feel faint with desire.

Out beyond the French windows the storm appeared to be intensifying, perfectly matching her mood.

Rachel wondered for an instant what would happen if the women looked up and saw her there – would she blush, or run, or would she join them? Her colour deepened. Wasn't there some part of her that longed to join them on the bed, to feel their soft bodies moving against hers, enjoy their delicate caresses, which instinctively understood the hunger she had inside?

She bit her lip, imagining those hands working over her breasts, exploring the soft planes of her belly and the delicate, fragrant folds that ached to be caressed. Beads of sweat broke out in the valley between her breasts. Her whole attention was focused on the writhing bodies, their intense pleasure drawing her like a magnet.

Lightning flared again and for an instant Rachel's concentration was broken – the room was lit up like high noon and she thought she saw a figure crouched on the balcony outside the French windows.

She stiffened – it had to be Daniel. Her pulse quickened – if he saw the two women making love, would he assume one of them was her? She had left the window open so that he could climb up but now it was shut tight. She imagined him soaked to the bone, watching, wondering if this was some terrible, cruel, teasing joke. Quickly, forgetting Petra and Anthea she turned away and hurried downstairs.

From the hall cupboard she pulled out an oilskin jacket and then threw open the front door. The wind outside hit her like a body blow, stealing her breath away. It was sheer madness to be out on a night like this.

As she stepped into the garden the rain and the cold seemed to seep into her skin. Wild gusts tore at her hair and clothes like talons. She looked around frantically and called Daniel's name. The roar of the storm mocked her, whipping her voice away like flotsam.

'Daniel!' she called again, peering into the gloom. Beyond the garden wall, amongst the dunes she thought she saw someone moving – it was hard to tell. Why would Daniel be down there when he knew he could come up to the studio? On the edge of the jetty was the old boat house, barely more than a shack. If he had seen Anthea and Petra together and assumed one of the women was her had he decided to go to the boat house to get out of the rain? She paused for a second and tried to focus on the windswept dunes. She was certain there was someone out there.

Grabbing the coat tighter around her throat she hurried down through he wind torn trees, towards the ruined jetty. 'Daniel?' she called again. Every step was a struggle against the storm. She battled to open the garden gate. Further out, the sea was a bubbling boiling cauldron, God help any sailors caught out in it tonight.

Rachel scurried for the shelter of the dunes, eyes fixed on the make-shift boat house. Out of the wind the air was strangely still. She struggled to catch her breath before continuing on. She bent over, rubbing her face with her hands to dry it, and as she straightened up she sensed she wasn't alone. She spun round, expecting to see Daniel.

Ted Grey his wet clothes moulded to his body, grinned maniacally.

'Foul night, Mrs Ingram,' he said with a leer. 'Not the sort of weather you want to be out in.'

Every fraction of Rachel's body prickled with fear. She took a step back.

'What are you doing here?' she hissed.

Ted grinned. 'I came over to see the show.' He nodded back towards the house. 'I didn't think it would be this wild,' he snorted. 'Worth the effort though – your friend and that little bitch Morton certainly know how to entertain themselves.'

Rachel stared at him in horror, realising that the figure she had seen on the balcony had been Ted Grey not Daniel.

'Where's Daniel?' she said.

'Your little bit of rough? Expecting him tonight, were you? Shame he's not coming,' he said laughing. 'I always thought it was a mistake to ask a boy to do a man's job. He won't be coming over here again. I told him you and Julian were getting married – I think he thought you were mucking him about, using him. He looked real hurt when I told him.'

Rachel stared at the man, unable to find her voice.

Ted grinned and pushed back his sleeves. 'So it looks to me like you might be needing a bit of company. It's a rough old night to sleep alone.' He stepped forward, eyes alight with a mixture of lust and amusement. Just as she turned to run he lunged towards her and grabbed her wrists as she lifted her hands to protect herself. He came at her with such force that they both fell backwards onto the sand.

Rachel was winded by Ted crashing down on top of her, dark stars forming and reforming in her mind. Ted's face was so close that she could smell the alcohol on his breath. He pushed her legs apart with his thigh, one hand holding her down, while the other fought with her coat.

'Let me see what it is you have under there, Mrs Ingram,' he snorted. 'What is it keeps that boy of mine so close to your skirts?'

Rachel's mind screamed out in protest. Even if she cried out there was no one to hear her cries. She tried to get away from him, desperately trying to unseat her tormentor. To her horror he grinned and tore furiously at the front of her dress. The wet fabric gave way like tissue. He laughed, one hand catching hold of her naked breasts. She screamed in horror as he pulled her up towards him, teeth closing over her nipples. Her vulnerability seemed to fire his desire. His hands and mouth worked back and forth, then his fingers snaked lower to jerk up her skirt. He pulled up the silk, exposing her belly. A hand ran experimentally over her stomach and down to the mound of her sex. Rachel gasped and tried to wriggle away. Ted's fingers caught in the waist band of her knickers, closing around the elastic in a tight fist. Rachel mewled in terror, renewing her efforts to unseat him.

'Please,' she sobbed, fighting to bang her fists on his chest, 'please let me go.'

'I like a wench with a bit of fight in her,' he gasped, dragging the fabric down. Makes taking her all the sweeter.'

He rubbed his groin against her. She could feel the angry press of his erection.

'I'll give you something better than that boy gave you,' he whispered thickly. He jerked her kickers lower, exposing her sex. Against her pale skin the dark triangle of soft curls looked like an open invitation. She had to do something quickly. She could sense his excitement growing like a dark obsession, a few more seconds and she would be lost.

'I know what it is that you women want,' he whispered, staring down at her nakedness. His lips were wet and slack, all his consciousness focused on the junction of her thighs.

For one moment Rachel wondered if it might be easier to do as he wanted – he was strong as an ox, his strength intensified by drink and desire. She looked up into his eyes and forced herself to smile. Her mind was racing – while he had her pinned down in the sand she hadn't a chance of getting away from him.

'You're right,' she said in a brittle, unnatural voice.

He grinned, eyes showing his confusion.

Rachel lifted her hips to meet his. 'I thought that when you came into my house the other day,' she said unevenly, praying that he would be taken in by her lies. 'But you must understand it's so hard for me to just let go.' She felt his grip on her wrists slacken a little. 'I have to keep up appearances.' She lifted her torso, rubbing her breasts against his sodden shirt. She felt him shiver and knew then that he was almost convinced.

'I want you, you must know that. There's no need for us to fight, is there? Why don't we go to the boat shed? We'll get frozen out here,' she paused, waiting to see how he would react. 'There's some sail cloth in there, we could make somewhere to lie down . . .' her voice trailed off and she looked down, afraid that her eyes might reveal her real intentions.

Ted pushed himself up onto his knees, his expression triumphant.

'I knew I was right about you all along,' he said with a grin.

He leant forward and pressed his lips to hers. Rachel struggled to hold back her revulsion. She kissed him back, letting his tongue slip between her lips. He grunted and his hands lifted to cup her breasts, his work-roughened fingers toying with the cold, wet peaks of her nipples.

Another belt of rain lashed across them. It seemed to convince Ted that Rachel was right. He pulled away, got hold of her hand and jerked her to her feet.

Rachel stood up slowly, straightening her coat, covering her nakedness, trying not to appear reluctant, but all the time preparing herself to take on Ted Grey.

She crouched for a second and then, just as he began to tug more insistently she swung round, raking his face with her nails. He shrieked and clutched his cheek. As he did so, Rachel, still holding tight to his hand, pulled him closer and brought her knee up into his groin with as much force as she could muster. He screamed and then crumpled and fell to the ground as if she had shot him.

For a split second his hand tightened around hers and she thought she had failed and then he let go, both hands clutching his crotch.

Taking a great, sobbing breath Rachel broke into a run, head down, arms flailing, heading back towards the lights of Albion. She had to get inside before Ted recovered. If he caught her she had no doubt he would exact his revenge. It seemed as if the house was miles away and the harder she ran the further away it seemed to get. Above her the storm continued to roar, its wild heartbeat matching her own. She slammed the gate shut, glancing over her shoulder – Ted Grey was nowhere in sight but the dunes offered him shelter, he could still be where she had left him or no more than a few yards behind her.

Every breath felt as if her lungs were on fire. Stumbling through the rough grass she cleared the trees and then staggered up onto the terrace. As her fingers closed on the handle she heard Ted Grey's voice whipping on the wind behind her. She pushed – to her horror the door did not open, Anthea must have locked it when the storm broke. Sobbing she turned and ran round to the front door; she knew that was open. From the corner of her eye she saw Ted Grey staggering across the garden and quickened her step. Finally, she threw open the front door and slammed it shut behind her, sliding the lock into place. Gasping Rachel turned, pressed her back against the cold wood and tried to gather her mind back together.

What seemed like an instant later there was a barrage of furious knocking at the door. Rachel screamed and backed away, staring at the door as if she might be able to see through it.

'Anthea!' she screamed up the stairs in desperation. 'Anthea! Please help me.'

Above her she heard her friend moving and replying, but it was Ted Grey's voice that filled her mind.

'You little cow!' he roared through the door, 'I'll be back, you won't trick me again. I'll fuck you and those two bloody queer whores as well.'

Anthea and Petra's faces appeared over the stairwell. Anthea was hastily pulling on a robe. 'What is it?' she said anxiously.

Rachel couldn't find any words and instead let out a soft whimper. Ted Grey continued to bang furiously against the front door. Anthea, her face tight with concern hurried downstairs, while Rachel collapsed in a sobbing heap against the hatstand.

Petra Morton followed close behind and crossed the hall as if to open the door.

Rachel held out a hand to stop her. 'No,' she gasped finally able to find her voice. 'For God's sake don't let him in.' After a few more seconds the banging stopped.

'Who is it?' said Petra, eyes firmly fixed on the door.

'It's Ted Grey, he tried, he tried—' Rachel closed her eyes struggling over the words, reluctant to say them aloud. 'He tried to rape me—'

'Oh my God,' Anthea whispered, as Rachel felt Anthea's arm close around her.

Petra peered out of the window and sighed. 'It's all right. He seems to have gone now. Stay here, I'll go and ring the police.'

Rachel shook her head. 'No, please don't, just let him go. Please.'

Anthea helped her to her feet. 'Come into the sitting room, I think we could all do with a brandy.'

Shivering violently Rachel let herself be guided into the warm.

Anthea picked up the phone. 'I'll ring Julian.'

Chapter 13

Daniel Grey pressed Molly down into hay. From outside the barn the sounds of the storm seemed to intensify his passion. Beneath him the girl giggled provocatively and slipped her blouse down over her shoulders. Beneath she was naked, her ripe, full breasts jiggling and rolling like playful puppies.

Her eyes darkened. 'I never thought I'd get you alone, Dan Grey. But this is what you want, isn't it? I've seen you looking at me when you've been working over at Albion.' She cradled the heavy orbs in her fingers and lifted them up towards him. He shivered, feeling a split second's reluctance. Closing his eyes he sucked one plump nipple into his mouth. He felt her tremble with delight and let his tongue trace a spiral around its taut outline.

Molly's hand found its way into his lap, boldly seeking out the contours of his cock.

'My, my, what have we got here?' she murmured thickly. 'You are a big boy!'

Her fingers struggled with his flies, and then, when he was finally free, she bent forward brushing his cock with her nipples before taking him deep into her mouth. Her tongue was like quicksilver. For an instant she pulled back and licked her lips hungrily, looking up into his face, her eyes alight with amusement. Her body seemed to swim and Daniel ran his hands over his face, struggling to focus on her bright, eager features.

'You just don't know what you've been missing, Dan,' she said with a grin. 'All that time we could have been together

205

this summer. Seems such a waste – but at least we're here now. Here, come bit closer and let me suck that great thing some more.' Her eyes darkened mischievously and her voice lowered to a husky purr. 'I'll give you better than that other tight-lipped bitch.'

As her hands closed on him he struggled to block out the sound of her insistent, teasing voice.

He really hadn't intended to take Molly into the barn behind the Cutters Arms, and was almost surprised himself in the throes of making love to her. All he had thought of since he left Medsham Hall to collect the wood was Ted's news about Rachel. He couldn't believe she had lied to him, or led him on, when all the time she intended to marry Julian Morton. The thoughts were like arrows, so hurtful that it had taken him all his time not to cry as the horse had meandered back towards Carfax. By the time he got to the Cutter his pain had slowly transformed itself into anger.

Although he had no real desire to go back into town, he hadn't wanted to be alone at the cottage either, and so once he had put the horse in its stable he'd walked down to the quay.

Ted was nowhere in sight. He had bought a pint and set about waiting for his stepfather to return – and then he had bought another and another, trying to dull the unhappy, angry ache in his chest, while outside the weather worsened.

Just as he thought about going home, Molly, Rachel's housemaid, had arrived, all wrapped up in a shawl, windswept, her face pinched pink by the cold. She saw him sitting by the bar and smiled at him.

'Hello, Danny, what are you doing here? I just stopped by on me way home to get some beer for me dad. I didn't think you'd been out on a night like this,' she had said with a sly, knowing grin. She glanced around the half empty public room. 'Not many in tonight. A girl could die of thirst waiting for a fella to buy her a drink.'

Daniel nodded towards the barman and the man poured

Molly a glass of beer. The girl slid onto the stool next to him.

'You look down in the mouth,' she said, resting her hand on his thigh.

Daniel had gulped down the last of his beer and slid the tankard onto the bar alongside her full glass. The barman refilled it without a word.

Molly leant closer. 'Why don't we go in the snug and then we can talk? No point me going home yet, the weather's too bad. I only just missed getting soaked through to the skin. Best to wait for the storm to blow itself out.'

And so they had gone into the room next door to the public bar where it was quiet and warm, and Molly had sat so close to him that all he could see was the pulse in her throat and the curve of her heavy breasts, and she had talked on and on in her little high-pitched voice, and Daniel had found himself listening, and drinking and drinking and listening.

As the night wore on she seemed to get closer and closer, images of her ripe little body filling his mind more effectively than any of the nonsense she spoke. She was so close that he could smell the subtle odours of her skin, and almost taste her lips on his. Every time she moved, some part of her brushed against him, sending tiny tremors through his body. And then, at some point that he couldn't really remember, either he or she had suggested that they go out to the barn that backed onto the Cutter.

Now, with her mouth working up and down his cock like a hungry dog on a bone, he struggled to retain some kind of control. Her head, nestled in his groin, bobbed and swayed from side to side, while her lips brought him closer and closer to the point of no return.

As if she could sense his impending climax she sat up and licked her lips greedily. Her breasts were flushed with excitement, eyes dark with need. Without taking her eyes off his she lay back in the tumble of hay and traced the outline of her nipples lazily with one finger.

One hand snaked down over her thighs and began to tug

207

the hem of her skirt up. She was naked beneath, her sex as plump as a ripe peach, nestling below her white, rounded belly.

'What are you waiting for?' she whispered. 'You know that you want to.'

Daniel hesitated, his head spinning.

Molly licked her lips with the tip of her tongue. 'Oh come on, Danny, don't be so selfish, keeping it all to yourself,' she purred. She opened her legs a little and a sliver of moist, pink flesh glinted between the lips of her sex. He could smell the perfume of her body and felt his mouth water. She dipped a finger into her quim and then trailed it back up over her breasts to her lips. It left a ghostly mark. The gesture made him tremble.

What the hell? Rachel Ingram had betrayed him, what had he got to lose? Here was Molly offering herself to him on a plate – she was sexy-looking in an earthy sort of way. She moaned softly and reached out to caress his aching cock. He shivered, still struggling with the last shreds of his conscience. She leant forward a little and ran her finger across his mouth – the smell of her sex ensnared him like a honeyed trap. Why was he holding back?

Molly stroked her sex again and this time her fingers parted the lips, brushing the little pleasure bud that nestled between them.

'Come on, Danny,' she murmured. 'Don't make me wait or I'll have to do it myself. Would you like that?'

Groaning he bent forward and kissed her finger where it rested, and then pushed it aside so his tongue could lap the moist folds. She gasped with pleasure and opened her legs wider, giving herself up to him.

Her eagerness finally overcame any lingering doubts and he began to lick her sex, hungrily, almost angrily, forcing her down into the hay. His fingers roamed freely over her willing body, nipping and stroking, teasing and caressing her into a frenzy. Gasping and moaning Molly thrashed back and forth, her hands locked in his hair as he brought her to the very edge of oblivion. Her juices trickled out onto his face, like a torrent of passion. Every sense was full of her rich, animal smell and an instinctive need he could almost hear roaring in her belly.

'Oh my God,' she whimpered. 'Oh yes, yes Danny, that's it. I'm nearly there, I'm nearly there.'

She thrust up to meet him again and again, making him sweat, making him roar.

Finally as he sensed her storm was about to break, he sat up and pulled her on to him, driving his cock like a stake into her raging, angry quim. She screamed as he closed on her, driving her hips up to meet his, her fingers frantically seeking out the seed of passion that lay between her thighs, desperate to propel herself that final yard down into the maelstrom of pleasure.

He thrust deeper and pushed her fingers aside, replacing them with his own. Molly bayed with delight, arching and twisting as he began to rub the engorged bud. She urged him on with a wild, animalistic roar of delight and at that instant a great white wave of passion exploded deep inside him, driving him over the edge, and he felt for a split second as if he was plummeting headlong to destruction. Gasping and sobbing he fell forward on to her, sweat dripping from his forehead onto her breasts.

He looked down at Molly, who smiled.

'That was good,' she said, eyes twinkling as she did up the buttons of her blouse. 'I knew it would be, I'm glad I came over here now. Your dad said it would be worth the walk.'

Daniel felt an icy chill trickle down his spine. 'What did you say?' he said, attempting to keep his voice calm and controlled.

Molly wriggled out from under him, pulling her skirt down as she did. 'Your dad told me you'd be here and in need of a bit of fun.'

'Where did you see him?' Daniel said carefully.

Molly, still tidying her clothes, shrugged. 'He came over to Albion tonight, something about seeing Mrs Ingram. It was him that told me it was all over between you two.' Her eyes flashed mischievously. 'He said Mrs Ingram would be too busy tonight to worry about what I was up to. What with them other two over there.' She paused. 'You know who I mean, them two women – something real odd going on there, not natural at all.'

Daniel glanced out at the storm. 'How long ago did Ted go to Albion?'

Molly shrugged again. 'I dunno, you're not jealous are you? He told me she liked a bit of rough, said you wouldn't mind, and her neither.' She sniffed. 'Each to their own.'

Daniel was already on his feet, hastily buttoning his shirt and his flies. He turned and picked up his coat.

Molly stared at him. 'Where the hell are you going?' she snapped. 'Aren't you at least going to buy me another drink? I thought maybe as your dad was out tonight we could go back to your cottage—'

But Daniel was already clambering down the ladder from the hayloft. Molly's high-pitched voice followed him out into the night. The pub yard and the quayside beyond were deserted. Rain was being driven in horizontal sheets off the sea, it cut through Daniel's coat like a knife. He had no idea what he was going to do but he knew he had to get across to Albion. His mind was filled with images of Rachel being confronted by his step-father. And if Ted had lied about where he was going, had he also lied about Rachel and Julian? Had he hoped that by putting Daniel off he would have Rachel to himself?

At the end of the quay was the harbour wall which offered some protection to the duned beach, and beside that the track that led along the coast to Albion. In good weather it was a little more than a brisk fifteen minute walk but tonight it looked like the gateway to hell. Great curling claws of water exploded up over the harbour wall, wind wailing like a banshee. Daniel hesitated. Perhaps the causeway was flooded. Then he imagined for an instant that Rachel might be trapped on Albion with his step-father. Dragging his coat tight around him, he headed towards the track, while around him the elements battled on.

He was grateful to finally climb down onto the track behind the harbour wall – at least the dunes and sea wall offered a little shelter from the buffeting wind. He had barely got half-way along the lane when he saw a figure, hunched over, heading back to Carfax. He recognised his step-father instantly and ran towards him, anger fuelling every step. As they drew level, Ted looked up in surprise. His face was scratched from ear to lip with five great gouges. Daniel, ignoring the thunder rolling above them, squared up to him.

'What the hell did you do to Rachel?'

Ted looked amused. 'What do you think?' he said, ruefully rubbing his jaw. 'I can see why you like her so much.'

Daniel leapt forward and hoisted his step-father up by the neck.

'You bastard,' he snarled, driving the older man back into the dunes. Ted was still grinning. Behind them, in the distance, the light of car headlamps pierced through the stormy night, throwing the two men in to sharp relief. Daniel pushed Ted into the cover of the dunes.

'She was real good,' said Ted, salaciously as they stumbled backwards. 'Lovely tits and so grateful to have a real man to service her for a change.'

Daniel drew back his fist. 'I ought to bloody kill you,' he snarled.

'Try it,' Ted said, shaking himself free of the boy's grasp. 'Of course, I had to persuade her a bit, but I think she liked that too. Hot little thing, isn't she?'

Daniel took a wild swing, catching only air. Along the track the car came closer and closer.

Ted crouched now, beckoning the boy towards him. 'And you should see her friends over there – I disturbed them on the nest. That tart down from London, with her tongue stuck up inside that Morton woman – wouldn't be surprised if your lady friend wasn't on her way up to join them.'

Daniel swung again but Ted was too quick for him.

'You're lying,' the boy said.

Ted shrugged. 'Really? Did you enjoy fucking Molly tonight?' Daniel froze as Ted stepped forward, still grinning. 'I thought you would. She's another hot bitch, if there ever was one. I hope you've left me a good slice of that pie.'

Daniel launched himself full tilt at Ted, the strength of his attack taking the older man by surprise. Ted was bowled over backwards and landed heavily in the sand, gasping for breath. His leg bent sharply under him. Before he could recover from the fall, Daniel reared up over him and hit him hard. Ted grunted and shook his head, blood exploding from his nose.

'You little git,' he hissed, attempting to get up. He grimaced. 'I think you've broken my bloody ankle.'

Shoulders heaving, trembling like a leaf, Daniel clenched his fists and stepped forward to hit his step-father again. The anger was fuelled by the memories of years of countless injustices and cruelties. 'I don't care, and I swear to God, Ted Grey, if you've hurt Rachel, I'll bloody kill you.'

As if Ted finally realised the boy was in earnest, he shook his head and held his hands up in surrender. 'Don't waste your breath boy. I never had her. I tried but she got away from me.'

He struggled to his feet, his face contorted with pain as he tried to put his weight on his right foot.

'It's true,' he protested as Daniel moved nearer.

Daniel didn't know whether to believe him or not, and stood tense and ready to spring forward again. 'What about Julian Morton?' he said in an icy tone. 'Is Rachel really going to marry him?'

Ted snorted. 'I dunno. I overheard them talking at Medsham this morning. There's a woman up there, her name's Izzy, or something, said that Morton wants to marry Rachel to get him out of debt, but whether she will or not I dunno. But one thing's for certain, the bastard is after her money.'

Daniel's shoulders dropped. Ted grimaced. 'See if you can find me a stick or something, my ankle is bloody killing me.

Behind them the car they had seen in the distance crept slowly along the lane, past the dunes where they had been fighting. Daniel turned to look at the occupants – Julian Morton was at the wheel. He pulled his coat straight and turned away from Ted.

'I'm going to Albion, I'll be back in a little while,' he shouted over his shoulder.

'You can't leave me here,' protested Ted, taking two steps forward to try and stop him before dropping down onto the sand in agony. A white-hot needle of pain coursed up his leg, making him dizzy. He grabbed hold of a branch of wood from amongst a pile of flotsam. Still on his hands and knees he called after the disappearing figure of his step-son.

'Don't, boy, you won't get across. The causeway was nearly flooded when I came over it! Daniel! Come back, come back!'

Julian Morton found it hard to concentrate on the uneven roadway ahead of him. Albion's lights glittered ahead in the rain, making the house look more like a boat than ever as it crouched amongst the dunes, bound in on three sides by the raging sea.

He smiled to himself. Petra's phone call had been perfectly timed – Ted Grey's attempted rape of Rachel Ingram was just the excuse he needed. The attack ought to make her more than receptive to his suggestion of marriage – after all, look how vulnerable she was alone at Albion. If Anthea and Petra hadn't been there, Ted might well have broken in and brutalised her. He ran the ideas over in his head – he didn't want it to appear that he was too eager, he had to look supportive and understanding, whilst subtly emphasising the dangerous isolation of Albion. Then, in a day or two, when Rachel had had a chance to reflect on how gentle and kind he had been, it would be an ideal time to suggest that they changed the nature of their relationship. He had to play it carefully though. He drummed his fingers on the steering wheel and peered out into the darkness. To his left the waves were thundering up over the breakwaters. It really was a foul night – which would make his trip seem even more selfless. He grinned and shifted the car down a gear.

Picked out in his headlights, he could see that the stone causeway was awash in places, and particularly strong waves broke over its shiny wet flags. He would have to be careful getting across – but surely the tide should be on the turn? If he got across now it would be far lower by the time he had to leave. He grinned again – always assuming Rachel *wanted* him to leave. Perhaps he might suggest he stayed the night to ensure that she was safe if Ted Grey decided to return.

Waiting for a lull in the wind, he crept out slowly onto the causeway, holding his breath as the waves crashed over the stones around the car. The lull was imaginary for as he edged his way towards Albion the storm seemed to gather in around him. Overhead there was a razor of lightning and then another tumultuous roar of thunder. Julian gasped, feeling his bowels turn to water. Perhaps coming to Rachel's rescue hadn't been such a bright idea after all. Out in the middle of the causeway all he could see for miles in any direction was the sea, as grey and angry as an invading army. His fingers tightened instinctively on the steering wheel.

'Not too far now,' he murmured under his breath and braked gently. Slowly he continued on, heart in his mouth, bracing himself as the spray hit his windscreen. Finally, he rounded the last slow bend and saw Albion rising up like a schooner amongst the dunes, just yards ahead of him. With a huge sense of relief he accelerated gently up the slope and drew onto the firm gravel. As he switched off the headlights he looked back towards the sea. His fear, he decided was really an illusion – a trick of the light. The causeway had to be higher out of the water than it looked or else the house would be at risk of flooding – and looking around that patently wasn't so. Here they were maybe twelve feet above the water line. He picked up his coat from the passenger seat and pulled it on. After all, Rachel was waiting.

Petra let him in – and very delightful she looked too in a sheer silk robe that barely covered her breasts. She was cradling a brandy balloon. Her eyes glittered as she saw him and then she smiled. 'The cavalry, I assume?' she said with a grin. He wondered how many drinks she had had.

Julian pulled off his coat. On the short walk from car to house it was drenched.

'You've been drinking,' he said in an undertone.

Petra snorted. 'So would you, stuck out here on this bloody rock with a hurricane blowing and a rapist outside. I'll go and get you one.'

In the sitting room Anthea Leven and Rachel were also dressed in their night clothes, Anthea in a pale green *peignoir* and Rachel in a grey silk negligee, a thick blanket wrapped tightly around her shoulders. Anthea and Rachel were sitting side by side on the footstool by the hearth, Anthea busily stoking a roaring driftwood fire. The firelight shone through their clothes picking out the curve of their up-turned breasts in perfect detail. Julian hastily looked away and hung up his coat. The image created a perfect erotic tableau, and he couldn't help wondering what had been going on when Ted Grey had arrived.

Petra indicated a bottle of brandy on one of the side tables.

'There we are, Jules, let me find another glass,' she said. As she crossed the room it was obvious she was already several glasses ahead of him.

Rachel looked up. Her eyes were dark and slightly unfocused, her lips looked bruised and swollen. Julian composed his face into a sympathetic mask.

'I came as soon as I could. How are you?'

Rachel, pulled the blanket back over her shoulders and shivered violently. 'It was good of you to come so quickly,

Julian, but I don't really know what you can do.'

Julian smiled and knelt beside her. 'Oh my love, don't be silly. I just wanted to be here with you. I couldn't bear the thought of you out here on your own with that man Grey wandering about. Lord only knows what might happen.'

Rachel's eyes flickered into focus. 'You think he might come back?'

Julian's attention was caught by the dark little peaks of her nipples showing through the silk, above the rough material of the blanket.

'Who knows?' he said, insinuating himself closer to the hearth. 'I didn't see him on the way over here but he could easily be hiding out in the dunes.'

Anthea moved wordlessly from the footstool onto the chair facing them. Julian slipped his arm around Rachel, and was delighted to discover that she was still trembling almost imperceptibly. He looked up at Anthea.

'Why don't you go and organise some coffee? I think Petra could do with some.'

She nodded and then beckoned to Petra. 'Come on, I'll show you where everything is.'

When they were alone Julian gently guided Rachel into his arms and lay her head against his chest. She smelt all freshly scrubbed, of soap and warm water. As one hand accidentally grazed her breasts he felt his mouth water.

'There, there, my sweet,' he purred, fingers gently stroking her hair. 'I was so worried about you.' He slipped his thumb and forefinger under her chin and tipped her face up towards him. At first she resisted him, eyes dark with a mixture of fear and surprise. He could smell the brandy on her breath and hoped it would work to his advantage.

'It's all right,' he murmured. 'Why don't you let me kiss all the hurt away,' and he brushed her lips with his. She shivered. His hand moved to her shoulders, pushing the blanket back off her body and then let it drop to her breasts, teasing at her pert nipples through the thin silk. She moaned, pressing herself

216

against his touch for a few moments and then she stiffened and pulled away.

'Julian? What are you doing?' There was a hint of astonishment in her voice.

He smiled lazily. 'Gently, my lamb, this is the best cure I know.' His finger retraced the dark pattern of her areolae in a featherlight arc. 'You look so beautiful. I really couldn't bear the idea of that brute Grey touching you. Did he hurt you? If you'd accepted my invitation to dinner tonight none of this would have happened. Perhaps you'd feel better if you told me what he had done to you?'

Her cheeks reddened furiously. Before she could speak, Julian leant forward and drew one nipple and its sheer covering of silk into his mouth. Rachel gasped and mewled softly as his lips closed around it. Julian couldn't help but wonder how far Ted Grey had got with his advances – the idea of his great filthy paws crawling over Rachel's slim, fragile frame was extremely exciting.

He could sense Rachel's body responding to his caresses in spite of her reluctance. How many glasses of brandy had she had before he arrived?

'Julian,' she whispered again. 'This is really not the time I . . .'

He looked up at her. His eyes holding hers seemed to lock the words in her throat.

'Sssh, don't say anything. Let me touch you, this is the perfect antidote to Ted Grey. Let me claim you back. Let me help you forget all those awful things he did to you.

Rachel moaned and closed her eyes.

'No,' she whispered. 'I can't, this isn't what I want.'

Julian suppressed a grin and cupped her breasts gently. She might say she didn't want to be touched but her body told him something different. This peculiar well-spring desire was the last thing he expected. He had imagined Rachel weeping inconsolably against his shoulder for most of the evening and then perhaps falling asleep in his arms, exhausted.

Instead he could sense a tension and need for release in her, and once again wondered what the three women had been doing before Ted Grey's arrival. He smiled, his imagination taking hold as his fingers worked their spell on her nipples.

Rachel struggled to keep some sense of control. Waiting for Daniel, watching Anthea and Petra in bed together, had whipped her up into a state of intense excitement. Even though Ted Grey's brutal touch had left her cold, the earlier sense of arousal seemed to bubble up, unbidden, to the surface. She could hardly believe the things she was feeling and wondered whether the combination of adrenaline and brandy had somehow unleashed the raw need that glowed in her belly. Fighting to catch her breath she pulled away from Julian and rose unsteadily to her feet. She was aware of how vulnerable she was in the nightdress. It was so sheer it barely covered her nakedness. She snatched up the blanket from the stool and pulled it tight around her shoulders.

'No,' she said with more certainty than she felt. 'No, please, Julian. I can't.'

Julian smiled. 'It's all right, Rachel,' he whispered. 'There's no hurry. I can wait. I just wanted to comfort you and I thought . . .' his voice faded, his eyes alight with something that disturbed her. 'I just thought perhaps I could help you forget Ted Grey.' He got to his feet and stepped towards her. 'I would be so gentle.'

Rachel took a step back, praying that Anthea and Petra would hurry back from the kitchen. From the hallway she heard the sound of knocking and raised voices, and like quicksilver, she side-stepped Julian's determined advance.

In the hall the front door was open, and Anthea, wrapped in an overcoat was looking outside. The wind ripped at her body – and then quite suddenly Daniel stepped inside. He was drenched, his clothes and hair clung to him like seaweed. He looked around wildly, eyes ablaze, like some stormy elemental wraith until finally his gaze settled on Rachel.

'I had to come over and see you,' he said unsteadily. 'Are you all right?'

Without thinking Rachel threw herself into his arms. 'Oh, my God, Daniel,' she whispered. 'I'm so glad you're here. I was waiting for you – and then Ted – Ted . . .' she stopped. White hot tears of relief and shock tumbled down over her face as she pressed herself up against his chest.

Julian Morton stepped into the hallway and looked them up and down.

'What a very touching little scene,' he said in a low, even voice.

Daniel, with Rachel still cradled tight in the crook of his arm, swung round to face him.

'I'm glad you're here,' said Daniel in a menacing voice.

Rachel looked up at him, surprised by the venom in his tone.

'Have you asked Rachel to marry you yet?' Daniel continued.

Julian took a sip from the brandy balloon he was holding.

'No, old chap, not yet. Actually I was just getting round to it. Your rather untimely arrival has trumped my ace.

Chapter 14

There was a tense silence in the hall. Rachel looked up at Daniel and then at Julian.

'What are you talking about?' she said in an undertone.

Julian smiled. 'Apparently your young friend here has been eavesdropping.' He coloured a little. 'But he is right. I had intended to ask you to marry me, Rachel, though I had hoped it would be under considerably more romantic circumstances than this.' He looked Daniel up and down with barely veiled disgust. 'Your boy here has rather forced my hand.' He looked back at Rachel with a warm, tender smile. 'But perhaps it's not such a bad thing after all.' His tone became serious. 'Rachel, I would be very honoured if you would consider my offer of marriage. I want you to be my wife – I am even willing to overlook your indiscretion with the hired help.'

Rachel experienced a strange, uneasy rush in her stomach and felt Daniel's muscles tense under his coat.

'Marry you?' she said in a whisper. 'Julian, I hardly know you. I can't believe this is happening.' She looked first at one man and then the other. Both men's eyes were locked on each other, like two fighting cocks.

Daniel tightened his grip on her but didn't break the stare. 'My step-father overheard him talking at Medsham today. Ask him why he wants to marry you. Ted said—'

'Your step-father?' Julian said with sneer, cutting Daniel's words short. 'And you believed him? The man who attempted to rape Rachel this evening.? I would be very careful what you say, young man.'

But Daniel continued. 'Oh, I will, Mr Morton. Why don't you tell Rachel why you want to marry her so badly?'

Julian's colour flared. 'You impertinent little . . .' He stopped and swung round to face Rachel. 'I've already said I intended to ask you to be my wife. What more can I say? In the short time I've known you, I've become very fond of you. You must know that. I was certain, given time, you could feel the same. Let's face it, Rachel, neither of us are young. We would be perfect for each other—' He glanced fleetingly at Daniel and something about the boy's demeanour seemed to silence him.

Daniel gave a low, throaty growl. 'So you're not just interested in her money then?'

Julian lifted his hands in a gesture that aped amazement. 'I really don't know what you're talking about. If any one could be considered a gold digger here, young man, I would have thought you were a more obvious candidate.' He stared levelly at Daniel, hoping perhaps to unnerve him, but the boy did not hesitate to meet his gaze.

Every eye in the room was on Julian. Daniel's confidence appeared to shake him and he blustered. 'Why the hell should I want to marry Rachel for her money, for God's sake? It's completely ridiculous, I have Medsham, the estate, a sizeable trust fund, an enormous house in London—'

Petra, much the worse for drink swung unsteadily round the door to the kitchen.

'And no ready cash whatsoever, Julian. You might as well tell them the truth.' She hiccupped and grinned at Rachel. 'What he hasn't mentioned is that all our family's money is tied up so tight in a trust fund that we haven't got a brass farthing of disposable income. And as you know, dear Julian has very expensive tastes.' She smiled at her brother, whose mouth had dropped open with astonishment and horror at her candour.

'Oh come on, Jules,' she said with lop-sided grin. 'He's caught you out. You might as well come clean. I've seen all those bills on your desk, darling. Another month and the bailiffs will come knocking at Medsham's door, They're bound to take your new Roadster back, and probably half the contents of the house as well.' She paused and swayed forward. 'But I'm sure Rachel wouldn't want to see that happen, would you, my dear?' She giggled and hiccupped at the same time, trying to suppress the sound with her hand.

Rachel felt the knot tightening in her stomach and stared at Julian.

'Is this true?' she whispered. 'How long have you been planning this?'

Julian's attention was not on her, but on Petra who was slowly sliding down towards the floor. 'Petra,' he snapped furiously. 'How dare you discuss our financial situation in public?'

Petra glared at him. 'It's your fault. You shouldn't be so damned mean, you practically make me beg for every penny – while you're out buying cars and wasting money on that damned boat of yours.'

Julian shook his head and then looked at Rachel, fixing on an uneven smile.

'Please, take no notice of her. This is just a misunderstanding, Rachel, nothing more. It's true that at the moment our finances are a little . . . tight, but it will all be resolved once I've spoken to the trustees. Nothing to worry about.'

He stared at her and then took a step towards her. She knew her face mirrored her shock and disbelief. She tightened her grip on Daniel's arm.

Julian snorted angrily. 'Oh, for goodness sake, how could you ever think I'd treat you so callously? What sort of man do you take me for?'

Petra snorted. 'A complete and utter bastard' she said with another giggle.

Julian couldn't control himself any more. He leapt forward and grabbed hold of Petra, hauling her, under protest, to her feet.

'That's enough, you drunken bitch,' he hissed furiously. 'Get dressed, we're going home.'

But Petra didn't think it was enough. She shook herself free of Julian's hands. 'No, I won't. I'm sick and tired of you telling me what to do,' she growled murderously. 'You expect me to run Medsham on a pittance, you use Izzy as an unpaid whore and housekeeper, yet when I ask you for money—' before she could finish the sentence, Julian grabbed Petra's coat from the hallstand and bundled it around her shoulders.

Rachel stared at them, feeling a strange, abstract sense of regret and hurt.

Julian forced another smile. 'Too much to drink, she really doesn't know what she's saying. She'll feel better in the morning and be so embarrassed by all this – best if I get her home to Medsham.'

Rachel slipped away from Daniel and caught hold of Julian's arm.

'I can't believe you'd treat me like this – but it's a filthy night out there. Why don't you stay until the storm blows itself out?' She was almost as surprised by her invitation as Julian appeared to be.

He coloured slightly. 'No. No, I think we have imposed on your hospitality enough for one evening – I don't want to outstay our welcome.' He paused. Rachel wondered if he realised how ridiculous his words sounded.

Petra slumped in his arms. Julian's face formed itself into an expression of appeal.

'I only came to see if you were all right.' His tone was conciliatory.

Rachel looked up into his eyes. She saw no glimmer of affection, no remorse, just a flicker of pain and a sense that he regretted an opportunity lost. She realised with a start that Julian was annoyed that he had been found out. She pulled her hand away as if his flesh was molten.

'Petra's right, isn't she?' she gasped. 'You only want me because of my money.'

Julian smiled wolfishly. 'Oh, Rachel, you are so delightfully naive. There are so many reasons for getting married. I thought, given time, you might grow to love me.'

'While you lived off my inheritance and introduced me to your dissolute friends?'

Julian grinned, struggling to regain some shred of dignity. 'Oh, come on, Rachel. Don't be so coy. I'm certain you would have enjoyed it. I know I would.'

He struggled towards the door with Petra under one arm. 'No need to see us out. I'll send someone over in the morning to collect the other car. I'm taking the Roadster home.'

As he opened the front door a flash of lightning caught him and his sister in a glittering spotlight. 'Perhaps I should have taken your suggestion, Rachel. If we had begun again, perhaps none of this would have happened. Though to be honest, I've always preferred a more nubile bed partner. You're really a little long in the tooth for my tastes. Even so, you would have done.'

Rachel flushed scarlet – his words were like a body blow. She could hardly bear to look at him.

'Get out, Julian,' she said in an undertone. 'Get out now.'

Julian grinned, nodding towards Daniel. 'How long do you think he'll last? He'll break your heart, Rachel. You'll regret not marrying me – I could have taught you so much.'

Anthea, who had remained silent until that moment, stepped forward with her fist clenched.

'Get out!' she hissed and slammed the door in Julian's face.

Rachel slumped down onto the bottom of the stairs, struggling to get her breath. Daniel, water pooling around his feet, stood staring at the door. Only Anthea seemed to be able to think rationally.

'Come on,' she said to Daniel as she helped Rachel to her feet. 'You had better get that coat off, you look frozen, there's a fire in the sitting room. I've just made a pot of coffee. I think we could all do with some.'

Outside, the storm appeared to be abating, but Rachel

suspected it was because her mind was raging with other thoughts. She was grateful to feel Anthea's arms around her and then Daniel's as they helped her to a chair in front of the fire. She sat for a few seconds staring into the flames. As Daniel stroked Rachel's hair, Anthea discreetly retired to the kitchen.

He threw a tangle of driftwood onto the glowing embers in the grate and then crouched down in front of her. Catching hold of her hands, eyes dark with emotion, he said. 'He's wrong. I'll never grow tired of you.'

She looked up at his face, wishing she could be so certain.

As if he could read her mind, Daniel's hands closed around her shoulders, pulling her closer. His lips brushed hers, stirring the embers in her stomach into life. He smelt of the sea, of the wild storm wind, and she did not resist as he held her close against him. It gave her such a sense of comfort to feel his warmth and the soft beat of his heart as his arms enveloped her.

'How did you find out about Julian?' she said in a thick, strangled voice.

Daniel's hands slipped under her blanket, stroking her skin. 'Ted overheard him and Izzy talking this morning. I think he must have been planning it since he first met you.'

Rachel shuddered. 'I feel such a fool.'

Daniel shook his head.

Under the blanket his fingers grazed the soft peaks of her breasts, and instantly she felt them harden. It astonished her that this boy had the key to unlock such intense desire in her. She realised that, amongst the passion which grew like a hunger in her belly, was a need for reassurance, as if Daniel's touch could undo her pain and the sense of betrayal.

'I want you now,' he whispered. 'And I will always want you.'

His hands cupped her breasts, thumbs teasing back and forth against the sensitive rise of her areolae. She could feel the flutter of desire building inside her, spiralling out from under his fingertips like a helix of stardust. She moaned softly and lay back, letting him push aside the blanket. Her nightdress – the one she changed into after Ted Grey had assaulted her amongst the dunes – was as thin as gossamer. Made from silk as delicate as a bridal veil, far from covering her body, it gift-wrapped it for Daniel's pleasure. He leant forward, murmuring words of love and endearment and pressed a kiss to each nipple in turn. His breath warmed her skin as he drew each flushed peak deep into his mouth. She shivered.

This was love, uncomplicated and pure as the storm wind. She opened her legs, relishing the sensation of his body weight on hers. Despite everything that had happened he had a way of making her forget everything except his physical presence. He kissed her neck, her shoulders, her throat. Between her thighs, her sex seemed to have turned to molten gold, wet and hot, longing to feel him deep inside her. He moaned as his fingers slid up over her thighs, tracing the moist outer lips of her quim. She gasped, moving up to encourage his caress, almost overwhelmed by the delight of feeling him slip a finger inside her. Her body closed around him, drawing him deeper.

She wanted him more than anything, and as if he sensed the urgency that bubbled and rolled like a furnace inside her, he sat up onto his knees and gently, oh so gently, she felt him undo his flies and guide his cock into the folds of her quim. She gasped and threw back her head as her sex contracted, holding him fast, welcoming him home. She looked up into his eyes and found herself being drawn down into his soul. They began to move, gently at first, his fingers working their magic on the soft hood that covered her pleasure bud.

She lifted her legs to encircle his waist, aware in some distant corner of her mind that his clothes were soaking wet and clung to his strong muscular frame like kelp. In her imagination it seemed as if he had come up from the sea to claim her. A merman, a water spirit . . she smiled. No fantasy was as

227

compelling as the reality. Their eyes were still locked, unashamedly, eagerly drinking in the flickers of pleasure on the other's face. He bit his lip as an eddy of delight rippled through him and then smiled and then leant forward to kiss her again.

As their lips met he began to circle her clitoris. She surged up towards him, meeting his lips, opening her mouth, matching his desire with something of her own that was as hungry and excited as anything she had ever experienced. As she felt the first wave of the pleasure that would carry her out into an ocean of ecstasy, she closed her eyes, fixing his face in the dark, still places of her mind.

At that moment there was no past, no present, no future, only the sensation of Daniel's cock pumping deep inside her and the call of an ancient tide that propelled them both on towards release. It seemed as if they were caught up in the storm, carried up towards the stars by the rhythm of their desire. The sensation was breathtaking.

His fingers and body moved on and on, growing more intense, blurring the boundaries between them until it seemed they were one being, linked body and mind. Finally she felt him reach the pinnacle of pleasure and as he tumbled over the edge he carried her with him.

In the seconds afterwards when she lay in his arms, Rachel's mind was blissfully still. Julian Morton's betrayal seemed as if it had happened in another lifetime. Daniel pushed himself up onto his elbows, eyes alight with tenderness.

'I love you,' he whispered and then kissed her so tenderly that she thought she might cry. In a distant corner of her mind she heard raised voices, but struggled to exclude them for a little longer, afraid of losing the sense of oneness that filled her heart.

'Rachel! Daniel!' Anthea, her face ashen, threw open the door to the sitting room, ignoring the fact that Daniel was still laying on top of Rachel. 'You have to get dressed. Petra and Julian's car has just been washed off the causeway.'

Oblivious to her nakedness Rachel leapt to her feet, with Daniel fast behind. 'What?'

Anthea waved them out towards the hall, where Petra, drenched to the skin, and now stone-cold sober stood, bent double, in a pool of water.

'You have to come,' she said breathlessly. Her eyes were bright with terror. 'The car – the car has gone over the edge into the sea. I managed to get out, but Julian is still in there. Please hurry.'

Anthea wrapped a blanket around her shoulders while Daniel, hair flying, snatched up his coat from the bottom of the stairs.

'Show me,' he said, grabbing hold of Petra's arm. He looked back at Anthea and Rachel. 'Get on the phone and call the local police – and the Cutter – they'll send help. I'll need a rope—'

The next few seconds were a blur. Anthea grabbed the phone, Rachel hurried upstairs and pulled on the first clothes that came to hand. From the pantry she picked up two storm lanterns and lit them. It seemed only a matter of a few seconds before she was out in the storm, with Anthea close behind her.

'I can't get through, the lines must have come down since I rang Julian. Have you got a rope?' said Anthea, buttoning her coat.

Rachel waved towards the garden and handed her one of the lanterns. 'There's one in the garden shed, behind the door.' She turned to look back towards the shore line. The wind whipped her breath away. In the gloom she could see two figures on the edge of what should have been the causeway – it was now part of the channel, water lashing and boiling up against the island Albion had become.

As she set out towards them, Anthea grabbed her arm. 'Be careful,' she gasped.

Rachel nodded and then, head bowed against the wind, hurried towards Daniel and Petra.

Petra was clinging to Daniel as they both peered into the boiling tide.

'I can't see the car,' she sobbed, 'I can't see it—'

As if in a cruel mockery of her words the wind suddenly whipped the sea up into a frothing peak. In the seconds when the sea parted, Rachel lifted her lantern and, to her horror, she saw the back bumper of Julian's Roadster in the watery trough. Daniel began to pull off his coat. Rachel caught hold of his arm.

'You can't go in there,' she shouted as he brushed her hand away. 'Daniel, please listen to me. You can't, you'll drown. You can't go in – it's madness.'

Daniel, slipping off his boots, nodded grimly towards the far shore.

'It seems my dad did. Petra said Ted was over on the far side. He must have seen the car go on. That's how Petra got out – he was coming back here after me and dived in to save the two of them. Petra said she saw him go back in to try and pull Julian out.'

Rachel stared into the storm-torn darkness. She could see no one on the far shore, but the beach was almost obscured now by mountainous plumes of spray. Perhaps Ted Grey had already hauled Julian and himself up out of the water and they were crouched now, exhausted, amongst the dunes. Anthea hurried up behind them with a length of stout rope. Without looking at Rachel, Daniel took it from her and tied it tight around his waist before passing the other end back to Anthea.

He nodded towards one of the fence posts that marked the boundary of Albion's garden. 'Tie it on tight. The current will try and drag me under. I'll need you to help me get back.'

He turned and grinned at Rachel, pressing his lips to hers for a second and then before she could stop him he leapt into the thunderous waves. She screamed out in protest but it was too late. She lifted the lamp up high, almost too terrified to look, afraid of what she might see. A lightning flash illuminated the ocean – and amongst the tumult of surf and foam she saw Daniel's head, as sleek as a seal's, ploughing doggedly through the waves. Anthea shouted to her.

'Tell Petra to go and get one of the other cars, we need some more light.'

Rachel nodded, but on the water's edge Petra was rooted to the spot, her eyes bright with fear and madness, fixed on the stormy water.

Anthea handed Rachel the rope. 'I'll go.'

Rachel nodded but her concentration was on Daniel and the life-line she cradled in her fingers. As he reached the spot where they had seen the car she saw him turn and then dive. Heart in her mouth, she waited. A few seconds later she let out a long, gasping breath as his head reappeared above the inky water. The sound of the car behind her momentarily broke her concentration and when she looked back at the water Daniel was nowhere in sight. She peered into the inky gloom. Anthea parked the car alongside her and its lights cut across the water like a beacon. Rachel jumped as Anthea caught hold of her arm.

'Look, over there,' she said pointing towards the far shore, well away from where they had seen the car. To her relief, Rachel could just see Daniel's head bobbing amongst the waves.

Without thinking, Rachel's hands tightened on the rope and then with a strength she didn't know she had she began to pull on it. For an instant it resisted her and then she saw Daniel explode up from the waves, his face as pale as the full moon amongst the darkness. Without waiting to see if he would dive again she pulled the rope harder and it seemed to her as if he lay back on the water and allowed himself to be pulled back to shore. Anthea grabbed the rope as well and Petra, as if she had suddenly woken up, hurried over to join them. Rachel's super-human burst of strength was short-lived – it took the three women all their strength to pull Daniel through the waves towards the shore.

It seemed as if the sea wanted him for her own and clung tightly to him, dragging him out towards the main channel. Finally, after what seemed like a life-time he was within a yard or two of the shore. Rachel and Anthea waded into the water, oblivious to the cold, and hauled him up onto dry land. A wave crashed over them and it felt as if only then did the sea decide to relinquish him. Daniel clung to them, coughing and retching, and then finally crawled up onto his hands and knees.

Rachel pulled off her coat and wrapped it round his shoulders as he struggled to get his breath. When Daniel finally looked up at her his eyes were bright and glassy, as if he had a fever.

'The car's empty,' he spluttered. 'There's no one in there.'

Petra let out a thin mewl that was neither pain nor relief.

'They could have swum ashore on the other side' she whimpered, 'they could have. Julian was a good swimmer.'

Anthea put an arm round her. 'You're right, but we've got no way of knowing until the storm blows itself out. Let's get you back to the house.'

Rachel looked up into Daniel's eyes. For the briefest of moments he looked out at the sea and Rachel knew he believed with an ice cold certainty that neither of the other two men had reached the far shore. It was impossible to see the other beach clearly and she wondered fleetingly if Daniel might be mistaken.

Rachel, suddenly feeling lost and totally impotent, crouched down on the water's edge and did not resist as Daniel pulled her into his arms. A few minutes later Anthea reappeared behind them.

'You have got to get back inside,' she said in a tone that brooked no contradiction. 'Daniel, you need to get out of those wet clothes. Now! You'll catch your death out here.'

Clinging to each other they made their way back to Albion, a pall of silence dropping over them that even the sounds of the storm could not breach.

Chapter 15

For a moment, on waking, Rachel was filled with a sense of stillness and calm. Out of the bedroom window the sky was blue and the glow of the new day eased in between the curtains, its soft light pooling on the floorboards. She rolled over slowly and was surprised to find Daniel curled up beside her. The sheets barely covered him. Naked to the waist, the sunlight picked out the hairs on his chest suffusing his skin with a golden glow. Seeing him there, her first thoughts were wordless, almost without form, an amalgam of desire and tenderness – he looked like an angel.

The events of the night before gradually seeped into her consciousness but had an abstract dreamlike quality, and for a few seconds Rachel wondered if she had imagined it all.

She ran a hand over Daniel's belly, feeling the pulse and the heat of him beneath her fingertips. He stirred, rolling over towards her, still unconscious but instinctively responding to her caress. As his arms enfolded her she struggled to hold back the thoughts of Julian Morton, Petra, and the storm.

Surely, no one would begrudge them a few more minutes of this bliss, it wouldn't make any difference. As Daniel pulled her closer, belly to belly, she felt the hard contours of his cock brush against her skin. She closed her fingers around it and was rewarded by a sleepy groan of pleasure. Rachel could sense Daniel rising up toward wakefulness. She kissed his shoulders and his throat, guiding his hand down between her thighs. Whatever her mind demanded it was her body, in that warm space so close to sleep, that cried out to have its needs met. As his fingers brushed the outer lips of her quim, she shivered. Daniel's eyes slowly opened.

'Rachel?' he whispered, as if he could hardly believe she was there.

She smiled. If he had said they had to get up, if he had pulled away from her, leapt from the bed and got dressed, she would have followed his example without a trace of offence or hurt. As he lay in her arms, looking up into her eyes, she guessed that, hot on the heels of sleep leaving, images of the storm and the tumultuous water would fill his head as it had hers.

But he didn't move, instead he pulled her closer, his body cemented to hers by desire – and something else that she recognised as a sense of relief. They were alive, the touch of their warm bodies was a confirmation of the fact that they had survived the storm.

His fingers grazed the soft lips of her sex, opening her up like a flower in bloom. She knew she was already wet. His fingers eased into her in a single seamless stroke as if all night long her body had been waiting for that moment. She gasped as his thumb stroked down over her clitoris, her own hand tightening on his shaft.

Gently, as her fingers began to work on him, he rolled her over onto her back, looking down at her with his deep blue eyes. She was afraid to speak in case she broke the spell. He leant forward, his body blocking out the sunlight as he kissed her eyes, her nose, her lips – soft, tender kisses of love and reassurance. His lips moved lower, mouth working at her shoulders, the deep hollows of her collarbones, her breasts, her nipples, the soft curve of her ribs – each tiny kiss seemed to light up another gem in a twinkling string of diamonds. She moaned as he ran his tongue over her belly. Reaching down she stroked his face, relishing the roughness of the stubble that clung to his chin. She stroked his hair, fingers tangling in the curls, and then slowly she lifted herself up onto his tongue as his fingers opened the prize they both knew he was seeking. The first brush of his tongue over her clitoris was almost too intense. Like a branding iron on tender flesh it roared through her, igniting every nerve ending. She gasped in surprise.

He kissed her again, more tenderly this time, letting just the very tip of his tongue outline the sensitive bud. The caress was tentative, nearly reluctant. She realised that Daniel was almost seeking permission to continue. This was not how she wanted it, she wanted to share, to give. She opened her legs wider, offering herself up to him, and then as she felt him relax she rolled over, bringing him with her so that her sex was above him, open and alive – an offering to his desire. She turned round, touching and stroking him as she did so until his cock was just inches from her face. It was framed by a bed of glittering golden curls, a single droplet of moisture clinging to its end.

She closed her eyes, consumed by a desire to possess him, and took him in her mouth. His hardness was a startling contrast to her soft lips and moist tongue. He shuddered and then thrust up to meet her. With one hand she cupped his distended balls, her finger working his foreskin back and forth while her lips drew him deeper into her mouth. For a moment he seemed rooted to the spot and then he caught hold of her waist, pulling her sex down onto his lips. His tongue plunged into her, exploring the depths of her quim. She could feel the delicate folds and curls of flesh throbbing and swelling under his tongue and finger tips.

It seemed so cruel that she couldn't feel his cock alongside his tongue, plunging into her at the same time, in some vast, abstract collage of pleasure.

She rolled and bucked, her mouth and hands guiding him further and further towards oblivion. His caresses echoed hers, his fingers and tongue seemed to be working in complete harmony with her own.

Even when the first explosive waves of orgasm crashed over her she couldn't bear to let him go – she rode out the climactic storm, out through the intense blasts of pleasure that took her to the shores of pain, on and on and on, clinging onto him like a touchstone, letting surge after surge crash over her. She knew he was close to oblivion, she could sense him fighting to control the tension and the power in his belly. At the last second, when it seemed she might lose consciousness he struggled out from under her. She cried out in frustration and then gasped as he caught hold of her hips, dragging her back onto him, fingers still working the sopping depths of her quim. His lips brushed her spine, his hot kisses making her writhe in anticipation. For an instant she felt the crown of his cock nudging desperately at the outer lips of her sex and then her body opened, and he entered her from behind, driving his cock deep into the throbbing confines of her quim.

She had never felt more ready or more needy in her life. The channel his cock breached was engorged, its walls as soft as gossamer, and yet its hold on him was as tight as a clenched fist. It seemed as if, once he was inside, her body closed around him, holding him inside her.

As he began to move, one hand slipped round to cradle her breasts, fingers teasing at her pert, flushed nipples, and then his other hand locked in her hair, jerking her back towards him like a primed bow. She screamed out in pleasure and surprise. He drove deep inside her and as he did she felt his balls swinging against her thighs – it was enough to catapult them both into the abyss.

Deep inside her she felt his cock throb hungrily, once, twice then on and on and on, a wild, ancient rhythm that echoed and intensified the pulse of her own explosive orgasm.

Finally, after what seemed like an eternity, he collapsed down onto her back, his sweat trickling between her shoulder blades. The hand that had been locked in her hair dropped to her shoulders, holding her tight against him.

There were no words that could describe the state of connectedness she felt at that moment. They were one, a single entity. She couldn't bring herself to speak. Another few seconds and reality would reassert itself: the storm, the causeway – as they lay amongst the tangle of bedclothes Rachel's mind filled with images of the things that would soon have to be faced.

Gently, Daniel slipped from her body and rolled over onto the sheets alongside her.

'We have to get up,' he murmured in an undertone. She knew he had spoken reluctantly.

She nodded and climbed slowly off the bed. On the floor were the clothes – still damp and rimmed with salt – that they had worn the night before. By the bathroom door was the robe she had discarded on her flight to try and help rescue Julian from the sea. She picked up her coat and threw it over the back of a chair; there was no way she wanted to put into words the thoughts her mind was conjuring.

They had walked back to Albion in stunned, painful silence. Anthea had put Petra to bed while Rachel stayed downstairs and poured herself and Daniel another brandy. As she huddled by the fire, wrapped in a blanket, watching Daniel's pale, unhappy face, she was glad that Anthea and Petra were lovers.

She imagined her friend gently taking Petra in her arms, her soft kisses and gentle, murmured words some small comfort in the stormy darkness. Crouched beside her Daniel looked physically and emotionally exhausted. He had turned the brandy balloon in his fingers and stared into the fire.

'There was never any love lost between me and Ted,' he said unsteadily. 'He married my mum when I was a little boy – five, six. I never knew my own father and Ted insisted I took his name.' Rachel could see the tears forming in Daniel's eyes. 'I never loved him. I always thought he had taken my mother away.' He looked up at Rachel, a single tear rolling down over his cheek. 'And then when she died I blamed him – I've always blamed him. But tonight he came back for me – he came to make sure I was safe.'

Rachel knew there was nothing she could say that would ease his pain. Daniel sniffed and brushed the back of his hand across his face. 'When it came down to it, after all the trouble he'd caused, he still felt he had to take care of me.'

Rachel caught hold of his hand. 'He might still be all right.'

Daniel sighed, and folded her into his arms. She felt his tears against her skin, and felt a surge of tenderness that glowed like a beacon.

'I love you,' she whispered against his damp hair.

He pulled away and stared at her. 'You love me?'

Rachel nodded. 'And whatever happened, I would never have married Julian – I couldn't have left you for him.'

He had smiled and slipped the blanket off her shoulders, eyes moving over her body. 'Will you stay with me forever?' he whispered.

She nodded and then said 'Yes, Daniel, yes I will.'

The intense emotional memories of the night before made Rachel shiver. She picked up a dress from the chair by the bed and then finally turned back to Daniel, who had begun to pull on his clothes. 'We have to go down to the causeway.'

He nodded, not meeting her eyes. When he looked up his expression was set, eyes like bottle glass. 'They may not be lost.' he said in an undertone. 'They may have got ashore on the other side, no way to tell.'

Rachel felt a tremor in her belly, tears pressing up close behind.

He smiled as he buckled his belt. 'Do you remember what you said to me last night?'

She nodded. 'How could I ever forget?' she said unsteadily.

Daniel was on his feet, arms around her before the first flood coursed down over her face.

'I'm so afraid,' she whispered. 'What if Julian and Ted are drowned?'

Daniel's arms tightened. 'We did what we could, no one could have done more.'

They stood side by side on the causeway. The car looked vaguely ridiculous, nose down, lying a few feet away from the retaining piles set amongst the tumble of sand and pools of water left by the retreating tide. By the garden gate were the remains of their rescue attempt – a tangle of rope with one end still secured to the fence post. Rachel wrapped her arms around her waist – the sight of the rope gave her an unpleasant chill.

Anthea, who had heard them going out, stood in her dressing gown and looked down at the Roadster. 'I'll get dressed and drive into town,' she said flatly. 'Daniel, will you come with me?'

The boy nodded. 'Aye, I'd better take another look in the car before we go.' He hesitated for a few seconds and then clambered down into the shallow water. 'If Ted is all right he's probably gone home to sleep it off. He'd had a fair bit to drink—' he looked up at the sky '—and it's early yet.' His voice sounded uneven and tight.

Rachel glanced at him, feeling a dark tightness in her chest. She knew he didn't believe what he was saying. She looked away, swallowing back the tears that threatened to resurface. 'What about Petra?'

Anthea sighed. 'She was still asleep when I left her. Try and keep her here until we have some news, will you? She shouldn't be on her own. Come on, Daniel.'

Rachel caught hold of her friend's arm. 'What if they've both drowned, Anthea, what are we going to say?' She glanced at the car again, praying her terrible sense of foreboding was misplaced.

Daniel was peering into the inside of the car. It had seemed so far away the night before, but in daylight they could see that it lay no more than a dozen yards from the garden wall.

Anthea smiled grimly. 'We'll tell them the truth. Daniel came over to see if you were all right. Julian and Petra wanted to get home-' she paused and glanced at Daniel who was still staring at the Roadster. 'Ted must have come over to make sure Daniel got back safely. Whatever happened here, this is not our fault, Rachel. You even asked Julian, after all that bloody nonsense, if he wanted to stay until the storm blew itself out. And besides, we don't know for certain that they're dead. Come on, let's get back to the house so I can get dressed.'

It was as Anthea was about to get into Rachel's car that they saw a vehicle heading along the track towards the causeway. Daniel spotted it first and held up a hand to shade his eyes, trying to pick out who it might be.

'Police,' said Anthea, pulling her jacket tighter. Rachel's stomach contracted sharply as the car slowed to cross the stone causeway. Her first instinct was to grab hold of Daniel but she resisted the temptation and waited in silence as the car crept towards them.

The car drew to a halt in front of the house and a uniformed police sergeant climbed out. He looked up at their expectant faces. 'Mrs Ingram?'

Rachel nodded. 'That's me, officer.'

Before she could continue, Anthea said, 'We were just on our way over to Carfax to see you,' She pointed towards Julian's Roadster. 'There was an accident here last night during the storm. The causeway was flooded, Mr Morton—'

The officer held up a hand to silence her. 'We found Mr Morton this morning,' he began, Rachel felt faint and was infinitely relieved when she felt Daniel's arm on hers.

'A man out walking his dog found him up there by the dunes,' he pointed towards the shore, and then glanced back at Daniel, 'And Mr Grey as well.'

Daniel made a strange little strangled noise and Rachel felt his fingers tighten on her arm.

The police officer sniffed. 'Rough old night last night. There's been an awful lot of damage up and down the coast.'

Rachel took a deep breath and then said in a thin, unsteady voice. 'Were they . . . were they—' the words wouldn't form themselves in her mouth.

The sergeant looked at her and then suddenly grinned. 'What, drowned? Good lord, no, Mrs Ingram. I should have said that right out. No, they're up at the cottage hospital. Mr Morton is a bit bruised and the doctor thinks Ted may have got a busted ankle, but they're fine. No, good lord, they're just fine – and very lucky to be so, if you ask me. I've just seen the car in the channel there, very lucky Mr Morton was to get out of that alive.'

He paused and looked at Daniel. 'Your dad said he knew you'd come over here to check on Mrs Ingram and was worried you might get into trouble, what with the weather an' all. Lucky for Mr Morton he was so concerned, eh boy?' He pulled his jacket straight with an air of finality. 'Well, if everything is all right here I think I'd better be getting on. Morning.'

Rachel stared at him in astonishment. 'Would you like some tea, sergeant?' she heard herself splutter.

The man shook his head. 'No, very kind of you to ask, ma'am but I'd better be getting back. We've got a lot of work to get through after last night's storm. You were lucky out here.'

They watched him leave. No one moved or spoke until the car was almost out of sight, then Anthea said, 'I'd better go and wake Petra and tell her the news.'

The sound of her voice broke the spell.

Rachel looked up at Daniel. 'They're alive,' she whispered, almost unable to believe what she was saying. Daniel turned and pulled her into his arms. He grinned.

'I always knew that the old bugger was tough as old boots,' he said, and then stopped, the grin freezing on his face. 'This puts us back exactly where we were. For a second, when I thought Ted and Julian Morton were dead I was relieved. Without them around I thought you and I might be able to have a proper life together.'

Rachel blushed furiously, she had had similar thoughts but had been afraid to voice them. She lifted his fingers to his lips. 'It doesn't matter. We can have a life together with or without Julian and Ted. We can find a way.'

* * *

Anthea Leven brushed her hair back off her face and stood back to look at the shutters. Outside, the chill autumn wind nipped and whistled in the casements. Behind her Rachel shook the last of the dust sheets out over the sofa.

'I really thought you'd stay here in Albion forever,' said Anthea. 'I thought you had found a little slice of heaven here.'

Rachel smiled. 'Me too, but then again, heaven can be whatever you want it to be.'

Anthea snorted. 'Oh, Rachel, you are such a romantic.'

Rachel laughed. 'Really? By the way, I've had a letter from Julian. He's decided to rent Medsham out to his friend Tippy, and go back to London. He says he's not cut out for life as a country squire – and that only a fool would get himself drowned in the Serpentine.'

'He'd better be careful then,' Anthea said with a mischievous grin.

Rachel puffed thoughtfully and stood back to admire their handiwork. The shutters, which had been fixed to every window cut out the last of the summer sunlight, and the furniture was now all hidden away under dust sheets and covers.

'Has Julian found a rich heiress to help him out of trouble?'

Rachel pulled off her apron. 'No, in fact I have a sneaking suspicion he may end up marrying Izzy. She was very good to him after the accident and at least she knows exactly what sort of man he is.'

A familiar figure stepped in from the hall. Petra Morton, dressed in a new autumn suit caught hold of Anthea and kissed her full on the lips.

'Not gossiping about my damned brother again are you?' she said.

Rachel smiled. 'You look wonderful.'

Petra did a slow, languorous turn. 'Do you like it? At Julian's suggestion the trustees have finally agreed to pay me a reasonable allowance, which means I can finally get myself a decent wardrobe, amongst other things.' She turned again, eyes firmly on Anthea this time. 'So, your darling friend, Anthea, won't be taking on a charity case after all. And I'm almost tempted to suggest you reconsider Julian's offer of marriage – you'll find him much improved. Actually since he stared death in the face he's a completely changed man.'

Daniel, carrying a large tea chest, struggled in from the hall and snorted. 'That wasn't death he saw, it was my step-father. Where do you want me to put this, Rachel?'

She waved him towards the sideboard. 'Over there, I've just got one or two more things I want to pack.' She smiled at Anthea. 'You really ought to be going, I know Petra's eager to be off – it doesn't do to keep a lady waiting. Thank you for all your help.'

Anthea kissed her gently. 'Don't mention it. You will keep in touch, won't you? Petra and I will be staying at my old address.'

Rachel felt a lump in her throat. 'Of course. Take care. Look after yourself, won't you?'

Anthea pulled Rachel into her arms and held her tight. 'Of course I will. Besides, I've got Petra to keep an eye on me now. No more wild weekends with unsuitable men.'

Petra snorted. 'At least not unless we're both invited.'

Albion seemed unnaturally quiet after they had gone. With the windows shuttered and barred it looked as if the house had closed its eyes. Rachel pulled her cardigan tighter and looked out towards the shore line. Without Daniel to tend the garden it would soon return to the wilderness of marram grass and wind-contorted shrubs. Daniel put his arm around her as they watched Petra's car creep over the causeway.

'I've given my housekeeper, Mrs Weirs, the key,' said Rachel. 'She said she'd look after the place while we're away.'

Daniel grinned, lifted her face up toward his and kissed her gently. 'No regrets?'

Rachel shook her head. 'No, no regrets.'

He picked up the picnic basket that stood on the front

door step. 'Shall we eat now or do you want to save this for the journey?'

Rachel shook her head. 'I thought we could eat it down in the dunes. I just want to have one more look around before we leave. It might be years before we come back again.'

He nodded and took her hand. Dumbly Rachel followed him across the garden towards the dunes. They would travel for a few years away from the village gossip and, when they felt the time was right, come back to Carfax-Staithe. There were so many places in the world they could go: across Europe to Africa and then perhaps America, Canada or Australia. There was so much to see and experience. She glanced across at Daniel and smiled; travel would broaden his mind and give him the maturity and depth he feared he lacked.

She still hoped that one day Daniel would teach. She knew that wherever they went she would paint. As long as he was with her everything else would fall into place.

As they reached the sand dunes the sun broke through the clouds and the wind, as if on cue, faded and died. Daniel turned towards her and kissed her again. This time his kiss was fervent, a hungry request for more.

'I love you,' he murmured, his fingers lifting to the buttons of her blouse. She stood very still, relishing the tenderness and desire in his expression. She was naked beneath the soft fabric. The first chill of autumn made her nipples stiffen into tight, pink buds. Daniel moaned softly and then leant forward to kiss first one and then the other. His tongue lit a little beacon of delight in her belly. Gently he unbuttoned her skirt, letting it fall into the sand. His hands felt cool and strong against her skin. He knelt down and pressed a moist kiss to her navel, while his fingers gently pulled down her knickers.

'I can't believe this is real,' he said, looking up at her, eyes misted with emotion. 'I keep thinking I'll wake up and discover that I'm dreaming. How long can something this special last?'

She smiled, running her fingers through his tousled blond hair. 'Forever,' she whispered. 'Forever.'

He made a soft noise of delight which echoed against her skin. His lips meandered over the curve of her belly down towards the corona of hair that surrounded her sex. She shivered and arched her back, thrusting forward onto his tongue. The first tentative stroking caress of her clitoris was like a lightning flash, making her head swim. Smiling, he pulled away, lips already wet with her juices and lifted a hand in invitation.

She sank down into the sand beside him, revelling in his touch, shivering as his mouth moved without hesitation over her neck, her breasts, her stomach. There was no part of her that she held back from his eager tongue and fingers. Crouched over her, with the sun behind him, his hair spun into a sunlit halo, Daniel looked more like the spirit of the pagan god in her portrait than she had ever seen him look before.

As he gently guided his cock into the soft folds of her body, her heart tightened with love and a wild hungry need.

'My God, I love you, Mrs Grey,' he whispered.

The new wedding ring on her finger glittered in the sunlight as Rachel pulled him into her. Her mind filled with the sound of his breathing, the heat of his body moving in time with hers and the soft wash of the sea as it rose in the channel beside them.

On the rising tide a fishing boat made its way back to harbour after a starlit night on the eastern fishing grounds. Sailing slowly through the maze of salt marshes, the little boat passed under the shadow of Albion House, a sure sign that they were no more than a mile or so from home.

A Message from the Publisher

Headline Liaison is a new concept in erotic fiction: a list of books designed for the reading pleasure of both men and women, to be read alone – or together with your lover. As such, we would be most interested to hear from our readers.

Did you read the book with your partner? Did it fire your imagination? Did it turn you on – or off? Did you like the story, the characters, the setting? What did you think of the cover presentation? In short, what's your opinion? If you care to offer it, please write to:

> The Editor
> Headline Liaison
> 338 Euston Road
> London NW1 3BH

Or maybe you think you could do better if you wrote an erotic novel yourself. We are always on the look-out for new authors. If you'd like to try your hand at writing a book for possible inclusion in the Liaison list, here are our basic guidelines: We are looking for novels of approximately 80,000 words in which the erotic content should aim to please both men and women and should not describe illegal sexual activity (pedophilia, for example). The novel should contain sympathetic and interesting characters, pace, atmosphere and an intriguing plotline.

If you'd like to have a go, please submit to the Editor a sample of at least 10,000 words, clearly typed on one side of the paper only, together with a short resume of the storyline. Should you wish your material returned to you please include a stamped addressed envelope. If we like it sufficiently, we will offer you a contract for publication.

Adult Fiction for Lovers from Headline LIAISON

PLEASE TEASE ME	Rebecca Ambrose	£5.99
A PRIVATE EDUCATION	Carol Anderson	£5.99
IMPULSE	Kay Cavendish	£5.99
TRUE COLOURS	Lucinda Chester	£5.99
CHANGE PARTNERS	Cathryn Cooper	£5.99
SEDUCTION	Cathryn Cooper	£5.99
THE WAYS OF A WOMAN	J J Duke	£5.99
FORTUNE'S TIDE	Cheryl Mildenhall	£5.99
INTIMATE DISCLOSURES	Cheryl Mildenhall	£5.99
ISLAND IN THE SUN	Susan Sebastian	£5.99

Headline books are available at your local bookshop or newsagent. Alternatively, books can be ordered direct from the publisher. Just tick the titles you want and fill in the form below. Prices and availability subject to change without notice.

Buy four books from the selection above and get free postage and packaging and delivery within 48 hours. Just send a cheque or postal order made payable to Bookpoint Ltd to the value of the total cover price of the four books. Alternatively, if you wish to buy fewer than four books the following postage and packaging applies:

UK and BFPO £4.30 for one book; £6.30 for two books; £8.30 for three books.

Overseas and Eire: £4.80 for one book; £7.10 for 2 or 3 books (surface mail)

Please enclose a cheque or postal order made payable to *Bookpoint Limited*, and send to: Headline Publishing Ltd, 39 Milton Park, Abingdon, OXON OX14 4TD, UK.
Email Address: orders@bookpoint.co.uk

If you would prefer to pay by credit card, our call team would be delighted to take your order by telephone. Our direct line 01235 400 414 (lines open 9.00 am–6.00 pm Monday to Saturday 24 hour message answering service). Alternatively you can send a fax on 01235 400 454.

Name ....

Address ....

....

....

If you would prefer to pay by credit card, please complete:
Please debit my Visa/Access/Diner's Card/American Express (delete as applicable) card number:

Signature .... Expiry Date ....